No Matter What

By

Beverly A. Morris

Cover design by Larry Norman
Editorial support and interior design by DBePub.com.
ISBN: 978-0-9859722-1-9

DEDICATION

This book is dedicated to all the special people in my life who have believed in me and encouraged me to keep on writing. These include my big brother, Larry, Sara, Janice, and a fan whom I like to call "You Know." And, a forever tribute to big little sister, Carry, and best friends, Beechnut and Tyronda, may they rest in peace knowing that I finished this story NMW.

FROM THE AUTHOR

In this book, I take you on a short journey where you come to relate-not relate, understand-not understand, sympathize-not sympathize... feel, curse, swear, and get really, really, angry at this group of characters that I like to call "no-matter-whats."

Don't be surprised in this novel if you run into someone you might know, or even some characters with similar characteristics to yours. Don't worry... only you will really know that, 'cause, it's fiction and I don't know you, either.

Now, some people have it, and some people don't.

Some people will, and some people won't.

There are no-matter-whats that are good and there are some that are bad, and some, quite frankly, that are really, really, sad. Now, let me ask you... how many no-matter-whats do you know?

Tell me! How many times have you heard people use the phrase "no matter what"? Think about it, not a day goes by that you don't read it or hear somebody you speak to somewhere say it. Stop for a minute and think about the last time. Who did you hear say it? Was it on TV, radio, the evening or morning news? Facebook, Twitter, Instagram, Instant Messenger? At the grocery, gas station, work, church, the mall? Where? When? I bet you heard somebody, somewhere, use that phrase, maybe even today.

In my first novel, called "Secret Tennessee," I say, "In Tennessee, we keep secrets, no matter what." In this story, you'll read about all kinds of different intertwining situations and stories of people that live by, stick by, that phrase "no matter what."

Have you ever seen a friend's relationship and said, "If it were me, I wouldn't take that shit, I don't care what he's got or what she looks like." Or "I know she could do better." Or "why doesn't he just walk away?" Or "why won't he get some help?" Or "they need to go for counseling," "what's love got to do with it," "how much longer is she gonna take that?" Or "he just ain't worth it, if it were me, I'd give up and walk away." Some people even say, "she needs to kick his ass and move on." Or maybe you think they ought to be happy with what they got, "She needs to stop all that praying, whining, or crying, and be happy with that man; at least he helps pay the bills." "What! That big beautiful house, that bad ass car, all that money, they've got it made." "A good woman is hard to find these days, he ought to be happy." "Ain't nothing out there in these streets now days, it could be way worse." "They should trade places with me, then they'd be grateful for what they have."

But you know, until you've walked in a no-matter-whats shoes; you just can't, won't, don't understand. Now kick back, relax, and let me tell you all about it.

GEORGE HENDERSON

Henderson and Henderson Psychological Services has been operating for twenty years now. We met in college and realized we shared a passion for trying to help others. We started the practice straight out of grad school. The first place we started was a cute little duplex in midtown. We lived on one side as roommates and the other side was office space. We only counsel adults and our specialty is marriage counseling. We've worked with clients before, during, and after marriage and even counseled some people ending long-term relationships who were never married, but the majority of our clients are married couples.

Ana and I come from different ethnic backgrounds, but similar life experiences. One of the main things we share in common is our relationship with our parents. We both grew up watching our parents fuss, fight, laugh, cry, lie, cheat, give each other the silent treatment but never, ever leave. They'd fight one another, but would never let anyone else talk bad about or harm the other. They'd never let others get in their business. Coincidentally, another thing we have in common, our surnames, yes, we have the same last name. Until I met Ana, I'd never had a woman friend like her, especially a female friend that I wasn't sleeping with. She didn't try to control me, she wasn't insecure, she gave me my space, let me be creative, and she always gave me her honest opinion, and I always felt comfortable giving her mine. If we disagreed on something, we'd air it out and get it resolved at our weekly meetings. We always had weekly meetings. We'd talk about our concerns, whether they were about the business, our clients, or personal stuff. Yes, Ana Henderson and I were best friends.

Ana dated several guys, and I had my share of girls. It even seemed like all my female clients wanted to date me. I never fell for it, I always kept it strictly professional, but it wasn't always easy. Ana never had that problem at all, she's a no-nonsense kind of person and her clients seemed to know it. Me, I'm on the softer side, and I guess they could sense that.

At one of our weekly meetings, out of the blue, Ana said, "George, you're gonna be my husband one day." I chuckled, as I thought to myself, here I go again and I thought naw, not Ana, too. We've been business partners for so long, why would she start this now? I said, "Ana, girl, you've had a little too much wine." But, she said, it's not the wine, I love you, and I know you love me, I feel it. We've been great business partners for two years now, and friends since day one of college. Let's really become partners. Hell, we already have the same last name. We have a lot of a-likes, George, let me name a few for you. We both say we never want kids, we both swear we'll never be and treat the person we're with the way our parents treated each other. We like the same crazy cars, mini coopers and hummers, and even our damn dogs are best friends. Roscoe and Roxy have been great companions for each other, and so have we, when you stop and take a look at it.

At that point, all I could do was stand up, walk over to her and kiss her, and that was it. Two weeks later we were married. We went right downtown to the courthouse on a Monday and Tuesday we were right back to work as usual. It was the craziest thing, and now, fifteen years later, we're still married, still best friends, still business partners. We truly love and respect each other, and we accept each other just as we are.

Now that's how Henderson and Henderson Psychological Services started. Me and my Ana have never looked back or had any regrets. We've come a long way from the two-room office in midtown to our spacious downtown office now. We're on the 27th floor overlooking the mighty Mississippi River. It's a beautiful office and all of our clients seem to really love it. When you get off the elevator, the first thing you see is the circular waterfall filled with beige and sage colored stones with a few fish floating around the bottom. The office is very serene. We have the jazz station, "Watercolors," playing from XM Radio. If I must say, the place is very peaceful. I've heard some of my clients say it's so relaxing they feel as if they could fall asleep in the waiting area.

Loretta, our receptionist is really good with people. When we hired Loretta Ann Franklin it took a while for me and Ana to adjust. We were so used to running crazy as our client list grew, trying to handle everything ourselves. This young lady was practically training us. She was receptionist/secretary/billing and friend. She's the first person our troubled clients would see. Her smile along with her dimples would soften all. She could calm even our most agitated client. She was definitely a people person.

She was dependable, always on time, and kept it strictly business. She never spoke much about her personal life except that she loved jazz. The three of us have become a great team.

We accept all forms of payments and arrangements. We've acquired quite a few contracts with some of the large companies around town. We have FedEx, MLGW, Smith and Nephew, Coco-Cola and the biggest is Kellogg's. Now, we're trying to get a contract with Nike. I'm glad we chose the Peggy Knight Interior Design Company to do our interior decorating, because she's done an excellent job. All of the sofas in the waiting area are sage green. The seats are leather and the backs of the sofa and chairs are sage, gold, and grey print and all the chairs and benches are trimmed in cherry. The entire office smells of sage and citrus and in the area where we meet our clients we have some very unique furniture. My office area is brown and sage green, Ana's side blue-grey and brown. Loretta is not only good with people, she's good with plants, too. We have the largest and most beautiful plants in the entire building. People often ask if they're real.

Ana has mostly quiet, calm clients. Me, I seem to get all the lively, emotional ones. We work with people from all walks of life and we've seen and heard just about everything. Our goal is to help people stay alive and be the happiest they can be, no matter what their situation is. Our mission is "acceptance." We try to help people learn how to be happy, love, and accept themselves and others as they are. And, if something, some person, place, or situation becomes too much, we help them accept it and move on with their lives as healthily and happily as they possibly can. We get them through their transition, our motto: "The Courage to Change." We have it posted all over the place, in the waiting area, in the bathroom, in the office, at the counter. Yeah, me and Ana have a pretty good life. We wouldn't have it any other way. We don't look the way we did fifteen years ago, but we're still here, we've grown in strength and also ha, ha… in... but, anyway, we're still together and still love each other. Once a year, we shut down the office for a month and go away to spend time together, and, of course, we take our four legged kids, Roscoe and Roxy.

PARKER IVY

When I met Chad, he was working at the neighborhood tire shop. It was when I was still driving that damn '90 Pontiac Grand Am. Got it from one of those Tote-the-Note places and I called her Cora. Every time I turned around, Cora had a problem. She was always running hot or leaking oil, and she was constantly getting flat tires.

This particular time, my girlfriend, Natashia, was with me. She looked at the flat tire, then looked at the others that didn't look much better. "Girl, you need new tires. You can't make it like this much longer. Let me take you to Real Deals. They sell new and used tires, and they can fix this one."

I took the flat off. She threw it in her trunk and off we went to the tire shop.

When we got to Real Deals Wheels, Natashia warned me, "Girl, watch out for Chad. He's the ugly one who flirts with every single woman who comes in this damn place. You'll see, watch what I tell ya."

"Hello ladies, who can I do today, ha ha? I mean, what can I do for you ladies, today?"

Natashia rolled her eyes. "It's my friend, Parker, here. She's got a tire problem and she's really low on funds. She probably needs four new tires, but one's flat, and we need that one fixed now. I told her you guys have some pretty great deals on used, though."

"Let me have a look at the flat first. Where is it?"

Natashia opened her trunk.

As he lifted out the wheels and started running his hands over the tread, I said, "It doesn't have to be a new tire, but I'll take your best used one."

"It's not that bad. Let me see what I can do." As he rolled it into the garage, he was grinning all the way.

6

Natashia muttered, under her breath, "His short, ugly ass better hurry up! He's always so dirty, finger nails dirty, always has on some kind of nasty, dirty old cap and ragged t-shirt."

The t-shirt he had on that day said, "It's a great day for me to whoop somebody's ass."

Natashia scowled. "Ugh... what a toad! He's been looking and drooling over me for years. I wouldn't give his dirty, tire changing, country ass the time of day."

I shrugged. He just looked like he worked in a garage to me. Garages are dirty. "He seems like a nice brother to me, just needs cleaning up a bit! Don't be so mean."

"Ugh, not by me. All he can do for me is fix my car or give me some damn tires."

"Ms. Parker, if you ain't ready, you don't have to replace this tire today. You just ran over a nail. I can patch it or... it's small enough, I can plug it for you for ten bucks."

"I don't need a new one?"

"You've got a little more life left in this one if you want to wait, but if the others look like this, you do need tires pretty soon."

"Ok, I'll take the plug, thanks."

"Will do. Listen, I got some now that are about $160, not bad at all, but I get better deals in here all the time. If you wanna leave your number, I can let you know if I get something that'll work for your car." He gestured toward the list pinned to the wall under a dirty pencil hanging from a string.

"Sure, thanks." I added my number to the list.

In a moment, he lifted the plugged, filled tire off the rack and bounced it on the ground at my feet. "Can you put the tire on yourself? Or you got someone at home to help you? If you bring the car here for me to do it, it's another

$7.50." Then, he winked. "'Course, if you want, I could come by your place and do it for you. Soon as I get off work."

Natashia came up behind me and I heard her mutter. "I just bet you could."

"No," I said. "I can change it myself at home."

He rolled the tire out to the car. "Listen, I wasn't trying to hit on you, I just like helping a beautiful sista whenever I can. Here, take my card, and if you change your mind or you have any trouble, hit me up." He held out a smudged business card between fingers creased with dirt from the tire.

"Sure, thanks." I took his card, gave him the $10, and thanked him again. He lifted the tire back into Natashia's trunk, and she took me back to my place.

In front of my house, I got my tire out of her trunk while she sat with her engine running. "Are you gonna be okay? I'm sorry, I gotta go."

"No, no, I'm fine, go ahead, thanks for the help. I'll call you later."

I grabbed the lug wrench. I could wait for one of the boys to get home, but changing a tire is no big deal for me. My Dad and my brother were both mechanics. They taught me quite a few things about cars before they left this earth. I got down on my knees in the driveway, a rock stabbed my knee – damn! Yeah, I could do it, but that didn't mean I liked it.

I struggled a little with one of the bolts.

Sometimes, I do get tired, frustrated, even disgusted, with always having to do everything myself. And, for many years, when the boys were young, it was really everything! Not just changing my own tires, but changing my oil, jump starting my battery, cutting my own grass, painting my own house, cutting down trees…. And, yeah, it's my choice, but that shit does get old after a while.

And, it had been a really long while. I hadn't had a really serious relationship since my kids' father, and that meant taking myself out and pleasing myself, too. Me and their father, we started out ok, but two years in, I was barely twenty with two babies, and their father, he was still such a kid, I felt like I had three. Well, we'd never been married, and it wasn't going so great, so I finally said, fuck it, I can do bad all by myself! On my own, I figured I was just as good at taking care of business as any man, and I could do it without the headache of having to look after one at the same time. My friends would all ask me all the time why I didn't settle down with this or that guy that I went out with, but I'd say, I ain't putting up with shit from any man.

I'd go on a few dates, and if the guy wasn't right, I didn't care how good he looked, how much money he had, what kind of car he drove, or even if he was good in bed. If he didn't treat me the way I know I should be treated, I'd move on. The way I figured it, ain't nobody got time for that.

But, yeah, it'd been a long time. My boys were about to graduate high school, and they were both so excited about going to college - one on the east coast and the other on the west. They were also a little excited about being apart for the first time ever. I was just hoping it'd be good for them. To help them along, I'd always given them three rules to live by, and they better remember them, 'cause I asked them all the time... Justin, what is rule number one? Oh Momma, we know the rules. Yeah, yeah, but let me hear it. Okay, Momma, number one - no drugs. Joshua, number two? No grandbabies. And they always both say, "And stay away from the police!"

I couldn't say how I survived taking care of two boys all by myself. I used to tell them, when they'd ask "Mom, how you do this? How'd you manage that?" I'd say, "It wasn't me, it was Jesus." And, I think it must have been, because somehow we just always made it.

I had no idea what it'd be like without them around. They'd been my everything, and, suddenly, they were almost grown up and hardly needed me. I'd just about worked my way out of a job. Well, except for the usual job most parents never got out of. The job of "drop me off, pick me up, give me money." Old folks used to say kids this age start "smelling themselves." I didn't know about that, but the hormones were raging and they wanted to be men, that was sure. They weren't my baby boys any more. I had to let them spread their wings and fly.

Truth be told, though, I was a little excited about it, too. At 37 years young, I still needed some fun time for myself, and maybe, just maybe, I thought, once they were away, I'd get it. And it all started that summer while the boys were off in California visiting their father and his family. They'd leave right after graduation. And, how lucky was I? I'd finish two for one. Never thought I would feel like it was not a punishment having twins. When I was young, I wished and prayed for twins, but as they say, "careful what you wish for, you just might get it." I had no idea what I was wishing for. But, finally, it was about to pay off. I felt lucky, blessed, really, because they would both graduate at the same time. I smiled to realize, hey, I'm through with school, too.

I finished the tire, stood up, and dusted myself off. Just think, I'd never have to attend another parent/teacher conference as long as I lived. Now, that was something to celebrate. I headed into the house for a much-deserved glass of wine feeling excited and happy.

*

The day they left, I felt so lost.

They had graduated over the weekend, and I'd just put them on a nonstop to LA to stay with their father. The plan was for them to go straight from there to college. I came back from the airport and walked into the quiet house, and, suddenly realized – they were gone.

The house was empty, and I suddenly felt so alone. I think it was the silence more than anything. That whole first day, the phone didn't ring every few minutes like it usually did. The doorbell didn't buzz like crazy. The silence was so loud, I kept thinking I heard this bump, bump, bumping sound on the outer wall. For so long, I'd heard the sound of Justin and Joshua throwing the basketball against the front of the house. Even though I knew they were gone, I'd swear I still heard that sound.

I had to shake it off, so I thought, now what can I get myself into? I didn't have much money left. It had taken most of my mad money to pay for graduation and two plane tickets for California. I've never been one to cry about money, just did my job taking care of the boys the best I could. My Momma always told me, "Children don't ask to come here, we bring them here, so the good Lord holds us responsible for taking care of them." I'd done just that and a few family members had given me pats on the back for being such a good hard-working Mom and raising two fine young men alone.

All that was fine, but once I got time to play, I didn't have much money to play with.

I thought, no problem, I could use a quiet evening hanging with the cat, catching up on reading my magazines. Turns out I'd missed a lot of stuff in about nine months' worth of Essence, Tri-State Defender, Ebony, the Memphis Flyer, the Daily News, Soul, and Oprah. The boys had bought me a glider-swing for the patio and I'd always intended to sit out there, but so far, all I'd done was pile the magazines out there in a crate next to it.

Well, I got me some wine out the box in the fridge, sat down in the swing with Ms. Muffin curled beside me, and took up two issues of Ebony and three of Essence and tried to ignore the bump, bump, bumping in my head….

I was just about to see what Beyoncé was up to six months ago when I thought I heard the phone ring in the house. I thought I have got to stop hearing things! Then it rang again and I realized it was ringing for real. Girl, you going crazy! I jumped up to get it, dumping Ms. Muffin and a couple magazines off the swing. Maybe it'd be Natashia with something we could get into. I hadn't heard a peep from her since she dropped me off with my tire.

"Hello?"

"Ms. Parker, this is Chad Edwards. From Real Deals Wheels?"

"Um… how'd you get my number?"

"You asked me to call if I got in a good set of tires for you. I got a real good set for cheap. They'll run you $180, but they're like new."

Oh, yeah, I did need tires, but this just wasn't the time. "Tell you the truth, my kids just graduated and I'm kinda short right now."

"Listen, if you can give me ten percent down, you can take em today, if that'll help you out. I don't usually do this, but you seem like a cool lady so, I'll trust ya. Plus that'll give me a chance to see you again."

Mama also taught me to take advantage of a good deal when I had a chance. "Ten percent down? That I can do!"

"Great. How soon can you come in?"

"Ok, I'll be there within the hour. Assuming I don't have a flat on the way."

He laughed. "You get a flat. You give me a call. I'll come to you."

*

Well, it makes a pretty funny story now, because I went out to my driveway to get in my car to go down there to buy those tires, and damned if I didn't have two flats! I called Chad laughing, and that's how we started seeing each other. He came to the house with a second spare, got my car to the shop, and got the new tires installed. By the time I signed the paperwork, we were both ready for a break, so when he offered to treat me to a smoothie if I wanted to step across the street with him, well, of course, I did. So, I guess our first date was Smooth Move Smoothies, both of us still a bit grimy from wrestling the tires, but both of us still laughing at the situation.

The next time we went out was decidedly fancier. Chad invited me to dinner and when he picked me up, I almost didn't recognize him. Chad, all cleaned up! He had on a great-fitting pair of light jeans, a buttoned up polo in a rich purple, and nice Gucci loafers. No dirty old cap, no dirty fingernails, no ragged greasy t-shirt. And he had a beard. I'd never noticed it under the dirt, but he wore it well. I was impressed. He looked very handsome and smelled good, too.

Over dinner, I told him about my twin sons and how they'd just left for vacation and were headed to college. I told him a little about how I raised them myself.

Then, I learned he was from Oxford, Mississippi, and moved to Memphis when he was seventeen. Out of high school, he had a construction job with his father, but didn't want to follow in his footsteps, never having a dependable paycheck, always at the mercy of the weather or the housing market, so he joined the Army. He was in the service for fourteen years, stationed all over. He hinted at some trouble, a fight with a Sergeant Major or something. But, ultimately, he got an honorable discharge and came home to start his business. That's when I found out he actually owned Real Deals! While he was talking, I couldn't help but notice a tattoo on his arm, just

"Brooke" in a fancy script. I was curious, but wasn't sure I wanted to ask on a first date.

He brought it up, though, told me it was a girl he married while he was in the military, but it just didn't work out. He'd wanted a housewife, a family, but she never wanted that. Said she was a free spirit. She wanted to make and spend her own money, didn't want any man to ever control her. I could kind of sympathize given my own story, but when he said she had told him she definitely didn't want to be stuck with him or any of his kids, I could see how hurt he must have been.

He said the girl had broken his heart, and, since then, he hadn't really gotten serious with anyone. I told him I was the same, had never been married, and hadn't been serious since my kids' father. I patted his hand for a moment and we were quiet, then he shrugged it off, and ordered us more wine.

After that, we shifted the talk to how he'd put all his energy in the last years into his business. While he told me all about it, I was thinking, I could hardly wait to tell Natashia the "tea," that old greasy Chad didn't just work at the tire shop, he owned it.

*

After that, we just started going out. We went to dinner, a couple movies. We heard R-Kelly at the Orpheum. And, 4th of July weekend, we went to a barbecue at his friend, Shelly's. We started to get close. Chad came over and helped me rearrange furniture in the boys' rooms and paint my bathroom. Honestly, it was nice having someone to help me, and I started to get attached to him, but, I felt ok about that. We really enjoyed our time together. We had just started painting the living room one weekend when he asked me about Natashia.

"What about her?"

"Well, I was wondering if she might be interested in double dating with us? I have this friend, Shelly. He'd like to meet someone new and I thought about your friend, Natashia. If she's not seeing anybody."

"I hadn't heard from her lately so I don't know, but I'll ask."

"Okay, I was thinking we could go to a casino or a comedy club. I heard D.C. Curry is coming to Chuckles."

"I don't think that's Natashia's kind of thing. What about a concert? Earth, Wind, and Fire is coming."

"Really? EWF were the bomb back in my high school days and my boy, Shelly, likes the old school music, too."

"And so does Natashia."

"Okay, EWF it is. If you find out she wants to go, I'll set it up."

*

As soon as Chad, left, I started texting Natashia. She lives on that phone. *Tashia, I need u 2 go on dble date wit me nd G.chad call me 4 more info ASAP.* I barely hit send and she was calling me back.

"Girl, what is a g.chad?"

"That's 'greasy Chad.' From the tire place you turned me on to?"

"What? Are you talking to him?"

"Yeah, for a while now. We've... been on a few dates."

"Ewe, what? You desperate? Let me hook you up--"

"No, listen, he's a nice guy. And, he *owns* that garage! And he cleans up real nice, so... will you come? We're going to Earth, Wind, and Fire. Chad's treat."

"What kind of friend does he have? Is he fat, old, young, skinny, got gold teeth snatch outs, what?"

"I'm sure he's fine, but c'mon, you know you like EWF. And we'll sit on the lawn, have a picnic - you don't like him, you can wander off."

"Probably need to bring my Ray Bans. And keep them on the whole time."

"Good, so you'll come, you can bring water and plates and stuff. I'll get the food."

"Okay, I'll go, but Imma kill you if this turns out to be a disaster."

*

It wasn't quite a disaster, but it was close. At least as far as those two were concerned. Shelly was definitely not a love connection for Natashia. I actually thought he was kinda handsome, beautiful grade of hair, short and skinny, with a little pot gut, but he was obnoxious as hell, and country. What were we thinking? I knew Natashia was pissed, but she actually played it off cool. Acted like she was looking for a bathroom and wandered off. While she was avoiding Shelly, she texted me she'd met someone else, so we ended up being a threesome sitting there listening to the music, the whole time with Shelly rubber-necking the crowd and making comments like maybe she was lost and maybe he ought to stand up so she could find us easier. I was just glad she left us so she wasn't there telling Shelly and me, and probably Chad, too, just exactly what she thought of us all in English and Spanish.

I tried to just enjoy the concert, but it wasn't easy. Chad acted like he didn't notice a thing wrong and just sat there enjoying EWF and sipping on his Heineken and every now and then giving me a little smile or patting my hand or leg. I didn't know if he really thought it was ok or was just making the best of it.

Natashia came back before the last set and sat next to me, absorbed in texting her new friend on her phone. Then EWF sang the song "September." Chad grabbed me and Shelly got Natashia and it seemed as if everyone at the concert was up singing, too. People were dancing everywhere. That was the most time Natashia actually spent with Shelly. As they danced, though, Natashia had her back to him and was looking at me and moving her lips saying I'm gonna kick yo ass, sticking her finger in her mouth as if to throw up…ugh!

Then suddenly, a couple guys dancing started getting a little too close and friendly with me and Natashia. Chad started getting loud saying what's up man, who the fuck y'all looking at, don't start no shit you can't finish, back the fuck up!

Chad was actually ready to fight! Was he drunk or what? Jealous? I felt like I had to step in between him and this other guy. Like they was about to come to blows! I really just thought those guys were enjoying the concert, same as us.

I tried to calm Chad down, but he snatched away from me. I'd never seen him like that before! Thank goodness for Shelly. He got him calmed down saying man don't let them young punks make you lose your cool.

As the concert wound down and we were all packing up Chad's car with the blanket and food and stuff, I thought the usual thing would be to suggest we all go out for a drink, but no one did.

Finally, as we all packed into the car in silence, Chad said he'd drop me and Natashia first, because he and Shelly had to make a run. Before I knew it, I was standing in my driveway alone, Natashia barely giving me a look before she jumped in her car, and nothing but taillights from Chad and Shelly.

Just after I got in the house, though, my phone rang, and it was Chad. Hello, hello, Chad? But he didn't say a word. I could hear him, but he didn't answer. Then I realized he'd butt-dialed me. I tried again, Chad, Chad, hello, hello, but he never heard me. I hung up, but it just dialed me again. In the background, I heard they were playing EWF, and I heard my name. So, that's when I thought, to hell with it and started listening.

"Man, I don't run into girls like Parker every day. She has a good job, seems real, the kind of girl that would have my back. You know what she did last week? Brought me something down to the shop for lunch. She'd made some pasta salad and thought I should try it."

"Any good?"

"Nothing I would have for a Sunday dinner, but healthier than the shit I've been putting in my stomach lately."

Then, I heard Shelly laugh. "Sounds like you're getting serious."

I really wanted to hear what Chad said to that, but it got lost in the chorus of Keep Your Head To The Sky, "surely the clouds are gonna tell you why—"

"...And she doesn't trip about my clothes or me being dirty at the shop all the time. She never asks me for a dime and don't expect me to buy her stuff, so I'm enjoying taking her out and she's smart, real good with computers and organizing. I was even thinking of asking her to help me straighten out some of my business stuff—"

"Yeah, yeah, that's great, but what I want to know, is she any good, she got good pussy?"

"Man, we ain't rolling like that, yet."

"Still not back to your old self?"

"What?"

"Wilson ain't always cooperating? That's what them blue pills is for, man."

"Shut up, man, I'm fine. I just think this woman is a keeper, she just might even make a good ass wife. You know ain't too many out there worthwhile these days."

"Yeah, ok, but you got some pills? Me, I don't leave home without them, keep them in my wallet with the condoms. Never know when the chance might come up, and I wanna be ready. Got some now. Was ready tonight for that girl you set me up with."

"How'd that work out for you?"

"Not my type. You know I'm a leg man."

"Right, that was the problem."

"Hey, she was your idea. In fact, I think you owe me. Let's go to the casino. It's early, I could still pick up something tonight. You know I can talk a cat off a fish truck. Man, I can't believe you ain't even tried to hit that yet. Dude, you better at least try it out before you get so serious. Don't want to end up finding out she's as crazy as Brooke."

17

"Don't mention that nightmare to me. I was young, in love, naïve, scared 'cause I was going into the service. I had no idea what I was doing. One reason I'm taking this slow."

"Hey, the casino! Exit's coming up."

"Yeah, all right, we'll do it." I heard the change in the road noise. Chad must have pulled into the parking lot.

Among the sounds of the doors opening and closing, I thought I heard Shelly say, "Now, let's see if I still got it! See if I can win some money and some pussy!"

Whatever Chad said was garbled, then the phone went dead.

I know my mouth was hanging open! I was too through! Couldn't believe what I'd just heard. Those fuckers were talking shit just like two women. I didn't know what to think. And what was that about Wilson and the blue pills? Did he have issues in that area? I thought I'd probably better find out before this went too much farther. But, after hearing the way he talked about us, I thought we were onto something. Made me think I should also find out sooner rather than later if I was dating the kind of man that would bond with my boys or not.

I decided to have a get together Labor Day weekend at my house. It's time I let the boys know what's going on with Momma. Lately, Josh has been calling more than usual, I think he's feeling something. Thought I'd shock them and use three way on my cell phone. Show them that Momma's keeping up to date with new technology, too.

First, I dialed Josh. "Hey, baby, how you doing? It's Momma, are you busy? Got time to talk to me?" But before he could answer I said, hold on. Then I added Justin on the line, too.

"What's up Mom?" Josh said, then Justin said, "Yeah, you using your phone skills and got us both on the line. Man, we know something's wrong."

"Well, I need to talk to y'all. I want you two home for Labor Day to meet someone special to me."

Right away, Josh said, "Oh damn, Momma, I know you ain't finna to tell me you trying to marry some old skeezer…." Then Justin said, "Be quiet man let Momma talk."

My boy, Josh, could go into panic mode at any given time, but he said, "Go 'head Momma tell us, I'm sitting down, and I'm sorry for cursing, Momma."

"Well, y'all know your Momma has worked hard taking care of y'all all these years. I hardly ever do anything for myself and now I've found a man who I think will be a great companion for me. He's good to me and I feel safe with him. I really like him a whole, whole lot."

Josh said, "Momma these men out here in these streets are all full of shit! They got game is all and you don't know nothing about that!"

"Watch your mouth, boy! And, yeah, I do know about that, but this one's different. I think we could have a nice life together with time. You and your brother are starting to build y'all own little lives and it's time for me to do the same."

Josh asked, "Well has he been married before?"

"No, yes, why?"

Justin said, "I just wonder why he ain't married now."

"I don't know, he said he just hasn't found the one for him, no one he could trust."

Josh said, "Hump! I think we should do a little background check on him, Momma," and Justin agreed, "Yeah, get me his info, I'll check him out."

"No, no, you two just stay out of it, I'm a big girl, I can handle it."

Justin said, "Momma, I just want you to be happy."

"Thank you, baby."

"So, what, you planning on getting married soon?"

"No, but we are getting kinda serious. So, I just wanted to let y'all know what's going on."

Josh asked, "Does he have any children?"

"No."

"Well, he might be okay, he ain't got no Momma drama."

Justin said, "Momma why not give it at least a year? Then see, and if he's still okay after that, go for it."

"Okay, babies, that's enough of that. I'm gonna get off this phone, I love you both. I'll be in touch."

Josh said, "And Momma, you ain't doing the nasty with that man are you?"

Justin groaned. "Ugh, I don't even want to think about that, man." Then, they both chuckled.

"You boys are going too far, now. Bye now. Love you."

"Love you, too."

"Bye, Momma. See you soon."

I really liked Chad. At that point, he'd slept over two, three, maybe four times, but no nasty… as the boys said. We'd promised each other that we'd take our time before sex. Once sex comes in shit always change.

Chad and I did a lot of kissy-feely moves and cuddling, but that was it. Just intimate, no sex. It felt nice to have a man to cuddle up in bed with and enjoy just that.

For Labor Day, I invited Natashia and Foy, and Chad invited Shelly and his new wife, yeah, wife, Chad said he didn't tell him nothing about getting married. That Shelly was just too much! I wondered if she knew she got a dog! I invited a few of my neighbors. The boys invited a few of their best buddies. Justin invited his BFF, Morgan, and Josh invited his, Tyler, who I'd never met. That would mix it up a bit and it was all good.

Chad came over and helped me grill the day before. He was acting a little different, but I couldn't put my finger on just what the change was all about. He wasn't his normal talkative, happy self. I asked if he was ok. He said he was cool, but he wasn't, complained about everything: the music was too loud, the grill fire was too high, my cat was in the way, flies were irritating him. And he drank more beers than I'd ever seen him do.

With the boys coming home the next day and everything in place, I was dying to see how they would interact with Chad. I asked him, again, "Are you okay?"

"I'll be honest with you, Parker. I'm nervous as hell about meeting your boys. What will they think of me? You know most boys are very protective of their Momma."

That made me kinda happy and relieved. At least, it showed he cared. "It'll be okay, Chad, you'll see."

*

The get together was in the evening, so the boys flew in, one after the other, early in the day. They were surprised how I'd fixed up the house since they left, but they both said they loved it. And after just about an hour of being home, you know what happened. The walk ins and texts, the phone ringing, doorbell ringing, their friends, constantly, in and out, the whole day. When, it got closer to party time, Josh introduced me to his friend, Tyler. He seemed like a nice young man. Morgan, I knew. She'd been a regular around my house. They would pass by me and say Momma, where this man at? We waiting on him. He coming? He ain't standing us up, is he?

"Y'all be nice now. He'll be here."

But, everyone started showing up, one right behind the other, and he still wasn't there. We had the patio set up, long picnic table with chairs in the back yard. The boys hooked up speakers. We had the citronella candles all over the yard to keep the mosquitoes away for the evening and everything was all good. Finally, Chad drove up in his canary yellow Corvette truck, the last one to arrive. My boys immediately stopped laughing and talking and watched him pulling into our driveway.

Shelly was first to say, loudly, "Man, what took you so damn long? Everybody is waiting on your ass!

True, I thought, but still obnoxious! "Chad, come on in, and meet my boys. This is Josh and Justin. They both said, hey, what's up man and did the hand/hug shake.

Then Natashia said, "Let's eat." She rolled her eyes as she passed Shelly and his wife, but, otherwise, everyone seemed to be having a good time. The food and fellowship were great. Everyone sat around talking or joined in with the rise and fly spade game going on. All seemed well.

At first, Josh was kinda defensive. He's always been overprotective of me. But Justin warmed up to Chad right away. They started talking sports, and found they both liked the same NBA and NFL teams. That was enough for Justin to make a connection.

Then, Josh asked. "Are you too old to play basketball, or do you know how?"

Chad said, "Boy, you looking at the baddest defense around."

"Then let's see what you working with, dude, let's take it outside." They played outside for two hours. Chad and the boys seemed to get along great. Talking shit and laughing the entire game. It was as if they've known each other all along.

Everyone seemed to have a good time. I noticed that Josh and Justin had a little spat, something to do with Morgan teasing Josh. Even though Morgan had been around them forever, like most people, every once in a while, she'd still get them mixed up. I stay out of their spats, though. They've always been able to work out their differences themselves. After everyone was gone, Chad stayed to help and we talked as we cleaned.

"Was Shelly married when we went on that double date with Natashia?"

"Nope! He just got married a month ago and I had no clue. He'd mentioned Stella, but he never said he was planning to get married. That's my crazy pal. I'm just glad someone signed up to put up with his ornery ass."

"Yeah, I wonder what it takes to put up with him. She better be stronger than she looks." She seemed ok, kinda quiet, and she had some issue with her arm and seemed to limp a little.

"She's sweet, has a little handicap, but she's good to him. Hey, who's the gay guy?"

"What gay guy?"

"Tyler, I think his name was."

"He's not gay, that's Josh's friend."

"Ok. I still think I'd have a little trouble telling them apart, but I like them. They're good boys. Though, Josh... well, we'll give it more time."

"Oh, he's always been more reserved, and he's awfully protective."

"Well, that's fine, that's how sons should be."

After the holiday, the boys went their separate ways, back to school. For a few days, again, I thought I could hear the thump, thump outside in my driveway.

A week went by, and Chad and I hadn't seen each other, just talked and texted over the phone. He told me he had been extremely busy at work, seemed as if everyone was having tire problems. Chad said he wanted to make all the money he could 'cause it was getting close to Thanksgiving and Christmas, and he wanted to make the holidays nice for me and the boys. "Are we having Thanksgiving and Christmas at your place?"

I was glad he was thinking of us like that, but I decided it was time to address something that had been bothering me for a while. "It's been months, Chad, when are you gonna have me over to your place?"

"Oh, babe, I'm such a slob. I need to get it cleaned up before I let you see it, and I just haven't had time."

"Chad, we've been kicking it for a while now, and I haven't been to your place. I'm starting to wonder, thinking things like, have you been lying to me about being single? Do you really live where you say you do? Has someone else been living with you all this time and I'm number two, your side piece? Or you just got bodies buried in your basement? Or what? I thought we were starting to get closer, thought we were a steady couple now, but, I don't even know where you live. That's weird, man."

"Baby, I have been telling you the truth. I don't have anyone else, it's just like I said. My place is such a mess that I'm embarrassed."

"So, you're a bachelor. Let me help. I don't mind."

"No, no, you would definitely mind if you saw the place."

"Look, I been thinking we gonna take this to the next level, but how can that be, if I can't even see how you live? You do know that's part of being together, right? You see how each other live?"

I guess that did it, I finally convinced him. He said okay, okay, girl pick a day when you want to come.

So, a week later, I was driving to his place. He lived in Cordova, gave me directions to take 240 to exit 17, get off at Appling Way, turn left, and it'd be the third street from the stop sign. When I pulled up, I said, okay, then! It was a very beautiful home, more than I expected. I rang the doorbell and Chad said hey babe.. come on in. He gave me a quick smack on the cheek as I walked in. There was an oval-shaped pool out back, fireplaces in the living room area as well as the great room, bedroom, and patio. Tall vaulted ceilings, mud room, pecan hardwood floors, granite counter tops, all stainless appliances, and he even has a pot filer. It was all great, just great, except for one thing, one big, big thing. The damn house was filthy. There were two cars in the garage, one antique grand am and his yellow corvette truck. They were clean. The house was a horror. Shit was everywhere: shoes, paper, clothes, old plates with dried up food, old dishes in the sink, and it had this God-awful smell. This place looked like some shit I've seen on TV. I realized that Chad is just shy of being a hoarder! When I looked at him, it was clear he saw the look of shock and horror on my face.

I knew he was embarrassed, he kept pacing side to side and looking down at the floor. Then he chuckled, "I tried to tell you I'm a slob. You sure you want to deal with this, girl?"

"Yes, Chad, somebody's gotta do it."

"Well, ok, I'm gotta go back to the shop, now, so I'll get outta your way. Oh! Let me show you how to set the alarm just in case you leave before I get back."

I didn't think I'd be anywhere near done before he got back, but I watched him work the alarm. "Ok, got it, go on Chad, I'll be fine, and I'll call if I need you."

When he left, I sat my purse down, that is, where I could find a halfway clean spot, and went to work. I found gloves, Lysol cleanser, comet, and bleach. I really needed ammonia. I didn't think this man had cleaned in years. Chad had all of the things you could ever want in a home. He had big screen TVs that were still in their original boxes, a KitchenAid mixer, Blu-ray players, another huge 3D TV upstairs. He had a Bose stereo system piped throughout the entire house. He had cordless phones, Yamaha keyboard, selfie sticks, Apple MacBook Air, two MacBook Pros, fancy coffee makers and all kinds of gadgets, Nintendo, Wii, Xbox 360, he even had two Hoverboards; you name it, he had it. I had to admit the house was beautiful, but he had shit everywhere. I particularly noticed the MacBook Pros, because my boys had been constantly talking about how they needed that for class, and I hadn't ever been able to get them one.

As I was cleaning up Chad's big beautiful unattended house, I ran across a lot of papers. Papers from the VA Medical Center, Brunswick Mental Health Institute, and Lakeside Behavioral Health. Then I ran across prescription bags, some with medication still in them and some without. I didn't want to be nosy, but I ran across one too many and I started reading. I just couldn't help it.

The documents stated that Chad had been under something called (MOT). I thought I better find out what that meant. I read further and found out that he had been under treatment for the last four years. He had prescriptions for Depakote and Haldol, looked like while he was in the hospital they gave him something called Risperdal. Chad had been hospitalized three times: 1998, 2008, and again in 2010. As I read on, I found some VA hospital release papers. It stated that as long as Mr. Chad Edwards takes medication as prescribed and keeps weekly appointments, he may continue as MOT patient. There were a number of appointment cards in the papers from Henderson and Henderson Psychological Services. The most current appointment was November 12 at 11a.m. I thought back, then. I'd never gotten him if I called him on Wednesdays during my 11 a.m. break. He'd told me that was his lunchtime, but he was never available then.

The only person who could help me understand all this was my girl, Foy. She worked at the VA hospital. Maybe she could find out something for me or at least tell me about some of these medications. I noted all the names from the medication bags and paperwork in my phone. Could this really be true? I wondered if he was taking medicine every day, wonder how he'd act if he didn't. I wonder if I've met him with or without medication. It was all pretty scary, and it was right there in black and white, right in front of my face, and I didn't know what to do.

So, I decided for the moment to just keep my mouth shut and see if Chad mentioned anything to me. I remembered that time he got a little crazy at the EWF concert. And how he also got a little strange before the Labor Day get together, but that was just being a man, right? He was just jealous at the concert, just nervous before the party? That wasn't enough for me to jump to any conclusions that he was like crazy or something. He'd certainly been the best thing I'd run across in a long while.

As I continued to clean the house, I thought maybe that's the other reason why he hadn't invited me over. Afraid I might see something that he would have to explain. Those appointment cards were all over the house. I ran across two or three downstairs, upstairs in the bedroom, even found one in the bathroom.

Whew, I finally got the entire downstairs in order, took me four hours. I wanted a break, but I kept on cleaning. After I finished upstairs, which took another three hours, I had the entire house looking brand new. It smelled good, everything was in its proper place, at least according to me, and I was whipped.

In seven hours, I'd done almost the whole house. There was another room upstairs that looked like he tried to make into a business office. I just couldn't tackle that room. It was overwhelming: receipts, books, pictures everything to do with his tire shop, maybe next time. I'd bagged up a lot of trash, but didn't put it out. Chad told me trash pickup was a couple days away. I didn't want boxes outside on the curb looking like he'd just bought a bunch of stuff (I'd heard thieves look for stuff like that) so I stacked those and the bags in the garage. He could take them to the curb himself. I was a little surprised he wasn't home, yet, but I wanted to get home. I took a last look around, set the alarm, and left.

As I was driving home I thought of Foy, again. Shit, I forgot she was on vacation, went on one of those all-inclusive trips to Jamaica, some place called Secrets. I'll just hafta wait until she gets back. I was gonna go crazy waiting a whole week to talk to her. I could call and leave a message anyway, thought I just might get lucky and she'd check her voicemail. Soon as I got back home, I called. "Hey Foy, this is Parker, call me, girl, asap!"

As soon as I hung up, Chad called. "Hey babe, thought you were gonna stay here until I got home. I would, at least, take you out someplace nice."

"Another time, I didn't know when you'd be back, and I had a few errands to run on my own."

"Well, girl, I, owe you a hell of a dinner! Soon as you want it. My house never looked this good, but once. When it was still a model home. You're the best, baby, how much do I owe you?"

"Chad, you know you don't owe me anything, I was glad to be of help. I'm just happy that you finally let me come over to see your place, I was beginning to wonder if you were a serial killer or something. Now, this weekend, I'm going to this Christmas Bizarre I go to every year. I'd like to buy some Christmas decorations for the place, so if you want to cover that, then that'll be my pay."

"Sure, baby, do your thang, just let me know how much you need."

Chad came by the house the next morning and left an envelope with $500. It was under my side porch mat. It had a note inside that said, "Thank you, babe, for helping clean up my pigsty. I hope this is enough for you to get whatever you need to make (in all caps) OUR house beautiful for Christmas."

The bizarre was Saturday afternoon. I got there on time and, as usual, it was fun. Ms. Marry always serves all kind of exotic food, and I got to see some of the women I haven't seen since this same time last year. I planned on spending about $200, but my basket totaled $400. Got a little carried away, but I found some beautiful decorations, just perfect for Chad's/our house.

My birthday was coming up and Chad also wanted me and the boys to spend Christmas at his place, now that it was clean. Everything except that one room. We'd have to tackle that one together. But, before I brought my boys to his place for Christmas, I really needed to figure out a few things.

I still hadn't heard from Foy, so I just started "rewinding," playing the tape back in my head, as I call it. I thought about the things he'd told me over the past months. He'd told me about first cousins that he was very close to, but other than that he hadn't really talked much about family or friends, except for that crazy ass Shelly. If I thought about it, I really didn't know that much about his past. I thought I better start being more observant, watching what he does and listening to everything he says, even closer than before. I had so many unanswered questions, and, if I was considering keeping this man as my regular boo, I'd better start asking them soon.

Finally, Foy called me back. "Hey girl… sorry it took me so long to call you back. I just got back, had a ball. So what's up?"

"Thanks for getting back to me. How was Jamaica?"

"Loved it. You gotta go. But, your message sounded kinda urgent… what'd you need?"

"Yeah, you remember Chad from Labor Day. Well, it's gotten kinda serious, and I need your help. I was about on the verge of thinking he was my match, you know, but I ran across some pretty heavy information about some of his past and present circumstances that's stopped me dead in my tracks! I know you can check him out since he's a vet, and I hate to ask, but you gotta check him out for me."

"Whoa, girl, you know I could get fired for shit like that."

"I hate to ask, but I'm really falling for him. Can you? Please, just look up some information on him? Check his file, let me know what you find out. I gotta know. He's starting to think marriage."

"Okay I'll see what I can do, but I ain't making any promises. I need his full name, birthdate, address, social security number, you got that? If you get me that info, I can go from there. It's gonna take me a minute so don't be freaking out or bugging me every day."

"Okay, okay, I won't." I felt bad about it, but I gave her his details. "He's also…" I hesitated to ask her for more. "Do you know anything about Henderson and Henderson Psychological Services?"

"I've heard of them. A lot of our patients go there after being treated by the VA. They have a contract with us. I don't know, girl, sounds like he's got some serious shit going on. You sure you want to go there?"

"That's why I'm asking."

"Ok. I'll let you know what I find out."

"Well anytime is fine. Like yesterday! But Imma wait! Patiently. I'll try."

I waited all the next week, and no call from Foy. I was getting worried, but I'd promised to be patient. Two weeks went by, still nothing. I thought if I didn't hear from her by the weekend, I'd have to call. The weekend came and went, and I barely managed to hang on. I decided if I hadn't heard from her in three weeks, I'd just hafta call. I hated to be a pest, but I had to find out something or else I'd hafta bring it up with Chad. It was killing me and it was getting harder and harder to look Chad in the eye and act like nothing was going on. By now, though, I was worried, 'cause, I'd waited so long, that when we did talk, he'd feel like I'd been snooping all that time.

But I had to know. I couldn't go planning on making this a permanent thing until I find out who I was really dealing with.

Foy called me on Friday night, three weeks later. I'd just gotten home from dinner with Chad.

"Girl, I found Chad's file and, let me tell you, the boy's got issues. The first time he was brought in to the VA for observation. In the file, it states he was driving the wrong direction on Poplar. The doctor's statement read, 'patient delusional with psycho-affective disorder, refused medication, stated he was going to Texas to pick up his daughter and granddaughter,' but his records state he has no children."

"Wow."

"Yeah. The second time he was brought in was for threatening to do bodily harm to one of his customers. According to the complaint, the customer brought in his van for tires and Chad threatened to kill him, said he was driving a rapist van he'd seen on America's Most Wanted. Said it was his duty as a soldier to protect and serve his country."

"That's… I don't know what to say."

"Yeah, the records also show the medicines he's been given, both as emergency injections and prescriptions. Depakote, Haldol, Risperdal, Cogen Trileptol…."

"Is that bad?"

"It ain't good."

"I know you didn't ask, but given all that, I ran a criminal background on him, too, and his record is just as bad. All due to his mental behavior. I counted six arrests, all landed him in jail first, then straight from there to one of the hospitals. Nothing recent, though. The last time was two years ago. So, I don't know if that's good or bad."

"What do you mean?"

"Well, that could mean he's better or that he's due for a break."

"Girl, I'm scared now! This is some heavy shit, maybe TMI, or… well, I guess I'm better off knowing, but… I kinda wish I didn't. Know what I mean? I'm gonna take it slow, for sure."

"I don't know, girl, I'd be getting myself free, but either way, you really need to know a lot more about him."

"Thanks, Foy, good looking out."

"No problem, but you owe me one! If anyone found out I did this— just, you owe me!"

"Absolutely, girl, thanks, again."

Thanksgiving was quiet. The boys decided to spend it with their father in California, and plan to spend Christmas with me and Chad. We had a quiet dinner, just us two at his place. It was nice. I was a little nervous, but he was calm and sweet. We had a good time. Then, the day after Thanksgiving, we put up all the decorations I got from the Christmas Bazaar. It felt right, and kept almost forgetting that I was worried about anything. I ended up staying over his place for the next two days and we decorated everything, mailbox, trees and all, then we tackled that crazy office room together. It was fun and he even made a comment that maybe I could help him out with his business. He sure seemed like he was thinking we had a future.

Before Christmas came my birthday. That's when, Chad started hinting that it might be more about an engagement. He also kept asking what the boys thought of him.

Then, for my birthday, Chad gave me a car! It wasn't brand new, but it beat the hell out of my old clunker, and guess what, it had all brand new tires. I'm not sure I ever had brand new tires, before, much less a silver drop top! A convertible! Me! I loved it. It was a Camaro with a Bose stereo system, a remote that started the car right from the comfort of the house, and the killing part, he'd already titled it in my name.

"Happy birthday, baby. I really hope one day soon, you're gonna be my wife, and they say, happy wife, happy life, I figure I better get started. Besides, I can't have my woman driving a car with problems when I own a shop. How's that gonna look?"

I brought Chad lunch every day for the next week, with a smile, in my new car. I'd been trying to get him to eat something more nutritious than all that fried chicken and shit he was always after. So, every day, I took him something home cooked, with some vegetables, at least. That is, every day except Wednesday. On the next Wednesday, after my birthday, I knew he'd have an appointment, so I just said I was busy that day, too. He didn't ask any questions, just told me have a good day, but, all evening, I didn't feel right about it.

So, finally, on Thursday, I called him instead of bringing him lunch.

"Hey, Chad, how's your day going?"

"Okay, baby, how about yours? You coming by today?"

"Listen… we need to talk."

"Uh oh."

"No, it's fine, but how about dinner tonight?

"Umm… Sure, baby, where do you want to go?"

I'd thought it might be fun to go where we first met, Smooth Move, but this was a serious conversation. I didn't want to spoil "our place," and I didn't think alcohol was such a bad idea either. "Downtown Grille?"

"Sounds good to me. Meet you after work?"

"You bet. See you there."

Chad and I pulled up just about the same time. He looked so handsome. I just loved his beard, he wears it so well. There were so many things going through my head, so many questions. I was nervous, but I just had to get it all out. There was no wait in the restaurant. We chose a table in the back where it was pretty quiet. The waiter took our drink order. I ordered a glass Chardonnay, and Chad asked for a Yuengling. We both knew what we wanted so went ahead and placed our food orders.

We had some small talk till the food came. He was telling me he'd had a rough day. It made me hesitate, but I couldn't wait anymore.

Once he started eating, I put down my fork and started. "Chad I've really grown to dig you a lot, in such a short time, and it's growing more and more each day, but—"

"Uh oh." He put his fork down and took a swig from his beer.

"No, it's fine, I just… I have a lot of unanswered questions. I've kinda been waiting for you to open up and tell me more about you, your family and friends, but you… you don't seem comfortable doing that."

"I'm sorry, baby, I guess I'm not. I mean… I have some trust issues, from my past. I'm working on them, and I trust you… I just… yeah, I trust you, so if you want to ask me something, go for it, ask whatever you want. I want you to be with me, forever, and I don't want there to be any question."

"Well…" Here was the part where I wasn't going to come off so good. "When I was cleaning your house, I couldn't help it, but I ran across some paperwork. I mean… if, like you say, you want to be together someday, maybe even as husband and wife, you gotta be straight up with me, no secrets."

"What… what did you find, Parker? Oh, my God, see that's why I don't have nobody at my damn house. So, what? What'd you find?"

"Paperwork from the VA and MMHI, and appointment cards from some psychological place…" I thought about saying I'd found police reports to keep my girl, Foy, out of it, in case that came up, but, thought better of it. "I wasn't really snooping around. I mean, you had papers lying all over. I kinda had to look to see what I was keeping or throwing out…" Chad looked a little agitated. "Don't… I mean… I just want to know you better."

As I watched, Chad's expression closed down, his whole demeanor changed. He started mumbling, but looking away from me, then he stared out the window.

I didn't know if I should shut up or get out, but it'd been so hard to get started, I was just determined to go on. "I also found all kind of prescription bottles, some full that look as if they have never been opened, some empty. I'm sorry, I just gotta know, Chad, is this medicine mandatory? What happens if you don't take it? I saw some pretty heavy names and I've looked up a few…"

Then the server came over to see if we needed anything. Chad snapped. "No! If I wanted something, I'd ask." It was the same sharp tone and sudden anger I'd seen at EWF.

I wanted another drink, but wasn't so sure Chad should have another, so I just waved the waiter away.

"Chad, boo, please. Don't shut down on me. I… I really want us to work."

Chad took a deep sigh. "All right. I'll try to answer your questions as calmly as I can. A lot of shit has happened in my life that I try real hard not to think about, so I sure as hell don't want to talk about it. Probably why I been alone so long. But, now I got you, and, Parker, I want to keep you, so I'm trying."

I patted his hand. "I appreciate that, Chad. I really do."

"I wish the shit never happened and that I could just erase it, but I can't. That's why I see a therapist. And, I'll be honest with you, I gotta go, to keep myself centered. The tattoo, that girl. It started with her. We got married much too fast and I got all tangled up with her not wanting me and I started to get crazy. Always trying to figure out where did I go wrong. I had to have talks with my CO, several times, 'cause I was losing it, couldn't get it together. I got very irritable, then hostile, I got into a fight with MPs. You do not want to fight those guys."

"I thought it was just her, but I got divorced and it didn't stop. I got sent to Iraq, and that sure is not a place for crazy to get better. I started to have thoughts I couldn't stop, crazy things…. I got discharged. Just barely. Instead of thrown out. I got arrested. A few times. Finally, I started listening to the doctors."

"The meds."

"Yeah. I tried to be okay without them. Everybody thinks they can. The meds make you feel better, so you think you don't need the meds… you stop the meds…"

"Bad shit happens."

"Yeah."

I didn't want to push him, but I had to know. "Have I seen you without your meds? Like, since we've been together?"

"Not completely, but I got a little out of whack a couple times."

"At the concert?"

"Well, I also didn't like that guy rubbing up on you. That was real." He started peeling the label off the bottle in his fist. "But, yeah, take it late, drink too much… it can happen. So, now you know."

"Chad, first I just want to say, I didn't mean any harm. I just needed to get everything out in the open."

"Yeah, well, it's out now. And, I guess you'll do what you gonna do. Seems like every time I let my guard down, tell someone this shit…"

"Oh Chad…" I took his hand. "I'm with you, and I do love you. Let me help."

"Yeah, yeah, that's what they all say, but then the results are always the same."

"Ok, but… look, when's the next time you go to those therapists?"

He squinted at me, still a little angry or, maybe, just suspicious. "Why?"

"I was just wondering if maybe I could go with you, sometime. Maybe, I could get a better understanding of what's going on, what you need."

"You'd do that?"

When I looked at Chad, his eyes were watering and, it made me love him even more, because he'd struggled to tell me the truth. Even though it hurt him to do it.

"I could… help you unscramble your medication. I just thought it would help us deal with this if you and I both know what you need." I started eating again, letting him think about that for a minute.

When I looked up, he was just looking at me with so much love and so much hope. "I love you, Parker. I need a good woman like you in my life. I need you. baby, yeah, please work with me. If you see me… getting strange, or…, you'll know what to do, who to call. And I'll listen to you, because I never want to do anything to hurt you, I love you."

I was scared, not sure what I was taking on, but I was taking it on, anyway.

We finished our dinner. Chad paid and walked me to my car. Before he left me, we planned for me to go with him at his next Wednesday appointment.

*

I did ok all week, managing not to think about what I'd gotten into, but the night before the appointment, oh my God, I was a wreck! I couldn't sleep. I tossed and turned and couldn't turn my head off. What da hell! This man has some serious issues! This is fucked up! Will I be able to live with this? Can it really be maintained? Will he snap on me? My sons? In front of people? What am I doing?

When I arrived at Henderson and Henderson, Chad was already there sitting in the waiting area. There he sat, all cleaned up, looking like a man with no underlying issues at all. You know what they say, you can't judge a book by its cover.

The place was nice, really lovely, serene.

He greeted me with a quick kiss on the jaw. "Hey, babe." His voice was a little jittery. "Thanks for coming."

As I sat down next to him, I noticed the receptionist, very pleasant. She smiled and said good morning, introduced herself, Loretta Franklin. What a nice smile, cute dimples.

"Can I get you anything to drink, coffee, tea or water?"

"No thank you, I'm fine."

One of the doors off the waiting area opened, and a well-dressed woman came in. "Good morning, Chad, how have you been? I see you brought your friend with you today." She shook my hand. "I'm Ana Henderson."

"Parker Ivy."

"Yes, this is my girl. We've been dating for a while, and I want to keep her in my life. And for that to happen, as you told me before, I've gotta let her in, let her know exactly what's going on with me. So here I am, to let her know about the good, bad, and the ugly!"

"Well I commend you, Chad, that's a big step for you. Come on in and sit down, and we'll get started."

In the office, Ana Henderson settled into a chair, and I sat stiffly next to Chad. "So, Chad, tell me what's been going on."

He told her some of what we'd been doing, how we been getting closer, then some problems at work that I hadn't heard about that had been stressing him out.

"Taking your meds?"

"Well, yes and no. I've been such a slob and so disorganized at my house… I got mixed up on which meds was which, and… I've been drinking a bit, so… I hadn't been taking them all."

"For how long?"

Chad looked guilty. "Not long, it's just… I just remember what happened when I mixed too much alcohol with some of the meds, made me crazy! I didn't want to end up back at the hospital. But, now, Parker came over to help me straighten up my place and… I'm ready to get it figured out, get on my meds, and stay on them."

"Chad, is it okay to speak freely with Ms. Parker here?"

"Yes, I want her to understand, and she wants to help."

"Ms. Parker, have you had any experience with a person with a serious chemical imbalance? Have you ever seen someone becoming overly agitated, paranoid, aggressive... even delusional?"

"No, but, if we're talking honestly..." I glanced at Chad, not sure how much I should say. "There have been a few episodes where Chad...seemed different."

"Well, that's what Chad has. A chemical imbalance. It's not going to go away, but he can function just as well as any other person with the help of his prescribed medications. You guys can have a nice healthy life as long as you and he remember that he does and always will need his medication."

I nodded soberly. I could feel Chad, tense beside me, almost holding his breath.

"If he doesn't take it, that could cause some serious problems. And, unfortunately, it's not an exact science. The meds can get out of balance, especially if he doesn't sleep or eat or he drinks too much... So, you have to pay attention to the signs, and, if things seem off, come back here or get to a doctor to adjust the medication."

It sounded like a lot. I swallowed hard before I spoke. "I can do that. I can help with that."

She nodded and looked down at the file on her desk. "Ok, for now, let me look over what meds we have listed, and we can go from there. Chad, you seem to have met someone that loves you and honestly wants to help. May I suggest, give this relationship some time? Let Parker help you with your meds, while you continue to be open and honest with her. Tell her what triggers you, and, please, please, continue your weekly visits with me. How does that sound, Chad?"

"That sounds good."

"Ms. Loretta will give you a print out of your medications, with detailed instructions. And set up your next appointment." She smiled at me. "Feel free to come back, again, whenever Chad wants you to. Or, if you need support on your own." She stood. "It was nice to meet you. And, Chad, I think you've found a keeper. Just remember, for every problem there's a solution! You guys take care now and have a great day."

We walked out of the office arm in arm, then Chad stopped. Right there in the lobby, he got down on one knee. "Parker, I don't ever want to lose you." His hands shook as he pulled out a small box and opened it. "Will you marry me? Please say yes, please marry me, Parker, I need you so much."

I almost laughed because Ana had said give it some time, and I think it had been about a minute. But I knew I was in. "How about we just call it a promise ring for now?"

He smiled and slipped it on my finger. It was a lovely white gold pear-cut diamond. "I can go for that, I love you, Ms. Almost-Edwards!"

*

That night was the first night we made love. He had to use his Viagra, and afterwards I told him about the butt dial conversation I'd overheard, and we were able to laugh about it. Our love making was worth the wait, though, and since then, I've learned a lot more about Chad and what he needs.

He still doesn't do crowds well, gets a little irritable sitting in traffic but who doesn't, needs a little Viagra here and there, has poor eating habits which I'm working on, gets paranoid when it rains, is a terrible book keeper, but a hardworking man who loves me a lot. I'm planning to move into "our" home soon, and he says there's plenty of room for the boys to visit or even move in if they ever need to. I didn't tell him, yet, how that might really happen 'cause Josh had been having a little trouble getting settled. I just smiled at my Chad and thanked him for the generous offer.

So far, we've been on schedule with his meds. We may have missed a day or so here or there. He even reminded me one time! But, we're figuring it out, and, for the most, he doesn't miss. So what, my Chad's got issues, don't we all? It could be worse. I'm hanging with my man. The way I feel, love equals… no matter what!

VINCENT MALONE

Camille's a beautiful, pretty, big boned girl, at least that's what she likes to call herself. But really, she's actually, just fucking fat. Each year it seems as if she gets bigger and bigger and bigger. When we first started going out she wore a size 10 now she's up to a size 18. She finally started shopping at the big girl stores where she belongs. She faked it, procrastinated, stayed in denial for as long as she could. She got mad as hell when I finally said, baby, quit playing, gone and go to Lane Bryant, and that new store you know, called Chico's that's the only place that's gonna have shit to fit you right! Aww, damn, that shit cost me two weeks' worth of silence, she didn't fucking talk to me for two weeks. I thought to myself, what the fuck will happen if she gets pregnant? OMG.

I thought for sure last Christmas was gonna be it. See, what happened was I promised to take vacation with her to Hawaii. Man, she went to AAA, got brochures, put in her time off from work, she was ready. Every night, she asked me, baby, did you block off time on your calendar, yet?

And every night I'd say, I'm gonna do that tomorrow, baby. The more I thought about it, in my head I said, I can't do it, I can't take that ride! I love her and all but using up my vacation on a girl just ain't something I'm use to or want to do. That shit makes me feel like an old henpecked ass husband. And where I come from, man ain't a man, unless he rules! No bowing down to a woman.

There's this fight coming up with Mayweather v. Martinez in Las Vegas and I'd rather go there with my dawgs! Camille has a way of making me feel guilty, though. Damn, I just want things to remain the same. Sometimes, she can be such a damn nag. And, I wish she'd stop talking so damn much to her girlfriends. Most of those lonely heart club bitches ain't got a man. Well, shit, the damn boxing match is the same time as when she wants to travel to Hawaii. Now how in the hell am I gonna get outta this shit?

I think I'll let her go ahead and plan the whole damn trip all the way up until almost time to go and then bam! Give her the bad news that I can't make it. By then she would've paid for the trip and she'll hafta go on without me. She can take one of them whining heffas, but not me! I can always tell her it's got to do with me getting my CLE credits in before the year's up. She knows all lawyers like doing shit at the last minute, it gives them a rush. She'll believe that!

When I broke the news to her, damn, Camille was so mad! She cried, screamed, cursed, and promised me that this was it! That this was the last time she would allow me to disappoint her. She swore she was through with my sorry ass and was gonna move out. I let her vent, even let her give me a few love punches. Then I apologized, I'm sorry, baby, as I lied. I tried to massage her fat ass neck in hopes of calming her down. After a few soft kisses I said, calm down, baby I'm really sorry I didn't know how to tell you but the boys had already purchased tickets to the big fight in Las Vegas. I explained, plus I will get in a few CLE hours while there, they have a conference going on. Practicing law has given me a way with words, if I must say so myself. I did know, and I also knew that after one, two, three weeks tops Camille would be over it and would forgive me, as usual, and that's why I'm marrying her. I can get away with anything!

Well part of that is true. She never says a word, never questions me, even when I come home smelling like Peggy, not one single word. When I come home late night, my dinner is always waiting in the microwave, clothes washed and folded, and she always leaves my Crown Black, my favorite crystal glass and a coke sitting on the wet bar. She knows I like to have a little nightcap before coming to bed. She even leaves my pajamas lying on the ottoman at the end of our bed. If I bring paperwork home, she's my at home secretary and she keeps all of my papers in order. Yeah, Camille has spoiled me from day one. That girl knows what I want, when I want it, how I want it, and even when to leave me the hell alone.

Now here I am getting ready to marry her fat ass; what the hell kinda wedding dress is she gonna fit in? Ugh, somebody, somewhere has gotta custom make one for her. There is no way in hell she'll find anything on a rack. I got a card from Ms. Lucy over at the cleaners, some of my other Attorney friends use her. I hear she's a bad ass seamstress.

One thing I know for sure, she loves my no good ass to death, and that's what a guy need these days. A girl who worships the ground he walks on.

Camille takes care of me, I mean she really, really loves a brother. Now, why she puts up with me, I'll never know, but if the shoe was on the other foot, as the saying goes, I wouldn't put up with me. I would've kicked me to the curb a long, long time ago.

As I sit here and reflect back, it makes me laugh out loud, she was so damn excited.

Now let me explain how I got into this mess. Peggy and I went out looking for Camille a Valentine's day present. We went to the Wolfchase mall and everything I thought of just honestly wouldn't work for her. First place was Victoria's Secret and thought, be honest man, come on, you know they don't' have a damn thing in here to fit her big ass. Then I thought about shoes, I saw some sexy red sling back slippers at Off Broadway shoes, I pictured how fat her feet were and said, nope! that shit won't get it either, out of the question. Hell those shoes would've jumped up and kicked my ass for bringing them home to ride her fat ass around.

Then I thought See's Candies comes to this mall twice a year, Valentine's and Christmas. Then a light bulb came on in my head, oh hell to the naw, that's the last thing she needs, more candy to swell her fat ass up. Then my girl, Peggy said, why not just give her some beautiful roses. I said nope, they'd probably just wither and at this point I was frustrated as hell and just wanted to hurry up and find something! There would be no peace at my house if I didn't find something.

My last and final stop was the Jewelry store, Jarred's. I started looking at all kinds of jewelry and decided on a pair of diamond stud earrings and before I knew it that damn jeweler had talked me into purchasing a ring, too. He assumed that Peggy was my girl and had her looking and trying on all kinds of rings. She played along and me, foolish me, went ahead and bought the damn ring as well and the earrings to match. I thought, okay cool. That should get me some big, no, mega points. And I needed mega points because I had plans to really celebrate Valentine's Day with Peggy on Saturday night. I had the jewelry store wrap each item separately.

Valentine's Day fell on Thursday and I would spend it at home with Camille. But Saturday was planned, all day and night, just me and Ms. Peggy Knight.

I'd made reservations at Ruth Chris Steak House and box seat tickets for the concert at the FedEx Forum - they called it the Love Concert. What a great line up Will Downing, Jill Scott, Anita Baker and Kem. They all sang about romance and I loved to show off Peggy, I couldn't wait. She looked good, knew how to represent. I didn't hafta worry about walking too fast, or turning on extra air conditioning, or letting the windows down, due to her sweating so much while she tried to keep up with me, carrying all that weight around. I had everything in place, I just needed to figure out how to tell Camille about Saturday night. I had Peggy in place cause we never spent time together on Thursdays that was her time to herself, she called it her me-time. So with my fabulous gifts for Camille and Peggy, Valentine's should work out great for everybody, especially me!

Valentines night came and what a trip! I got home around 6pm and Camille was waiting, all smiles. She said happy Valentine's Day, baby. I got you a present and I hope you like it, as she smiled at me. All the lights were out and she had candles lit everywhere. The table was set beautifully and all the table accessories were red, white, and black. She had on a long black one- piece halter jumpsuit; I think they call it a cat-suit, except she looked like a lion, red glitter slip on shoes, red lipstick, red polish on her nails and toes. She even had a red flower on the side of her hair. She looked pretty, pretty fat.

Camille is a great cook, she'd fixed all of my favorites, filet mignon, blackened salmon along with asparagus and speared potatoes. She made a special trip to Ruby Tuesdays and got that cheese bread that I love too, it looked fabulous. She had the new Anita Baker song playing called "Lately," and I knew that soon it would be time to pay up by the end of the evening. We ate and listened to Anita Baker. Oh, baby, this is great, you sure know just how to treat your man. I could see her smiling through the candlelight, and sweating like hell.

Camille, I've got a present for you too, let me get it now sweetie… I got up off the sofa and went to the counter where I'd left my bag and pulled out the small red envelope and a red bag with two little square silver boxes. I said close your eyes and open your hands for a big surprise. She followed my instructions. I gave her the card and the bag. Then I noticed she was starting to sweat again. I thought, oh damn, better cut the damn ceiling fan on now, and as I reached up to pull the string, what box did she open first? The damn box with the ring in it!

Her big green eyes got even bigger and as she opened the box she just screamed, yes, baby, yes, I will, I will, I will. She came running over to hug me just as I was releasing that ceiling fan string and it caught me totally off guard. She knocked the shit outta me. I fell back on the floor, the hardwood floor, hard, dead on my ass. I thought, shit, this girl is getting heavier and heavier by the damn day. That's what I thought to myself. She was on top of me, kissing, rubbing, and crying, and hugging all over me. Ugh… I could hardly breathe, twenty minutes went by before she let up. I said, baby, baby, calm yourself. The night is still young and you haven't opened the other gift I got for you.

She smiled and said, my man, I'll be yours, forever. Okay, Okay, baby, I'm just so excited. I can't wait to tell everybody. Then she started singing, My Ship Has Finally Come. I managed to get up off the floor and she went back to the bag and grabbed the other silver box. The one with the diamond studs, again, she was ecstatic, she said, baby, I love you forever, for always.

I thought, that damn Peggy got me into this shit. Now I'm stuck, like a truck, what the fuck! She's calling it her engagement ring! Now I'm gonna have to walk down the aisle with Ms. Fat Ass-Camille. I don't know how, but somehow I've got to get through this shit, can't back out now. Our wedding is in six months, yes, six months before I hafta take that long walk down the damn aisle.

Now my girl, Peggy; she is fine as hell! Just thinking about her makes my balls hot! I'm sure she knows I really love her, but she's just too damn self-sufficient for me. She's a perfect size 6, she's educated, has a law degree, nursing degree and does interior design. We've partied together, studied together, even took our bar exam together and we passed it at the same time. We worked as law clerk's for the same court with two crazy judges. Yes, Peggy has done well for herself; she has a nice condo downtown with a river view; the place is laid. There were two condos for sale on her floor, she bought them both so she wouldn't have a neighbor, the entire 6th floor corner is all hers. Peggy has all the right everything; she's just not the marrying kind. We've been seeing each other off and on now for the last four years, ever since law school. Just about as long as me and Camille.

We have a routine, we meet the same time every time, all the time, Monday Wednesday and Friday. Peggy knows about Camille and Camille knows about her. I couldn't get a better deal than that Camille and Peggy, I love it. I don't call it cheating, cause they know of each other, right. Well that's what I say.

I told Camille that Peggy and I have been friends since law school and that she confides in me with all of her troubles and issues, especially men trouble. I've told her about some of our old law school stories. Like the fact that Peggy and I shared books and food while struggling through law school. I explained to her that we've been there for each other through thick and thin, and dammit, she believed it.

Thank God they've never met, but the way this town is and with all this social media shit, I really don't know why they haven't. Cause in this town, it's always somebody that knows somebody. If they ever met face to face, it would blow each of them away. Camille would be intimidated by Peggy's looks, size, and shape, and Peggy would just plain old freak out if she knew I was with a woman that big, not to mention Caucasian. Now it is time for me to choose and I'm choosing Camille.

I hafta break the news to Peggy, soon. I haven't had the courage to tell her yet. I don't know why I'm tripping cause me and Ms. Peggy Knight have had a lot of fun days and nights together and she's always known about Camille. But to find out that I've decided to marry Camille for real, well, I don't know how she's gonna handle it. She knows it started out as a joke at Valentine's, hell she was with me and played along with the game, damn, she started it.

My dawg, James, hates it, but he's gonna be my best man. He said, man, if I didn't owe you one, I wouldn't do this shit, cause you're a low down dog and don't deserve to have a wife like Camille or better yet a side-piece like Peggy; some guys have all the luck. Man don't hate the player, hate the game. I asked Marlon, first, to be my best man; he said, hell naw punk! I don't want no part in that bullshit, you just too damn scandalous for me. Hell, he ain't the one to talk!

JAVIER DIAZ

When my phone rang at 2:45 in the morning, I knew that meant trouble. My wife, Aja, had told me that she was going to meet her girl, Natashia, and they were going out to the club for a few drinks. But, I never knew what a late night phone call would bring.

Once it was the Tunica, Mississippi Sheriff's department. She'd been detained for dropping a mickey in some poor Hispanic man's drink. He could hardly speak English, but his friend was able to tell what happened. She was accused of taking all of his money. I had to go all the way to Mississippi to bail her ass out of jail. Thank goodness Attorney Malone is licensed to practice law in Mississippi and Tennessee. Ugh, there's been so many times, but Vincent never says a word - just sends me a fat ass bill and gets her ass out of it every time.

After five years of marriage, nothing had changed. I would've thought all that pill popping, blunt smoking, coke snorting, wild drinking, hanging out late, cursing, and clubbing would've stopped, but, it was always the same shit - just a different day.

I rolled over in bed and picked up the phone. "Hello."

"Javier, it's Natashia."

I thought, damn, what has my wife got herself into this time?

"You gotta come down here and get Aja. She's about to go to jail. She's up here cussing out the security guard, trying to fight him, and they're getting ready to call the police. I pleaded with the security guard not to call the police. I told him I was calling you, her husband, and to please wait. He was cool with it at first, then Aja started yelling.

How soon can you get here?"

I could hear my lovely wife screaming fuck you with your punk ass, call the fucking police and the guard saying, you'd better back it up, back it up, and get out of my face girl.

Natashia said, you better hurry, he's either gonna taze her or the police is gonna haul her off.

"Where y'all at?"

"Bluff City Club, over here on Airways."

Just like I thought, another hole in the wall. If it wasn't Bluff City, then it was AC's, or Memphis Knights, or somewhere else crazy. "I'm on my way."

So, there I was, bailing her ass out of trouble, again. I threw on my jogging pants, t-shirt, and out the door I went. I was glad we have a garage 'cause I'd hate the neighbors to see me looking crazy at three in the morning or seeing Aja when I get her back home. I got there in ten minutes.

Before I could see her, I could hear her. "Fuck you, and kiss my ass, punk."

There was a crowd of people looking on. I heard em saying stuff like man that bitch is crazy, and that's a real THOT there, and skank, hoe! Who let her out the cage?

It was so embarrassing, I hesitated to go up there to get her, to have all those people see me claiming her. My beautiful wife had left home looking like a million dollars, and now she looked like two cents.

You'd think me being a therapist, I'd know better, or could do better, and I'd tried to get Aja to rehab, but any time I mentioned it, she got fighting mad. She didn't think she had a problem. It was everyone else bothering her. That was the problem, not her.

She was always telling me, "You think you can counsel every damn body. Don't try to use that therapy shit on me, Javie!"

I had told her, everybody that goes for counseling ain't crazy. The crazy people are the ones who don't go somewhere and get help. I tried to tell her about one of my patients, nice lady, great job, good husband. She was going through a lot with the death of her mother, but she came in voluntarily and, after a three month stay, she went home much, much better. I told her she should, at least, go talk to a therapist, I could set her up with Henderson and Henderson or we could send her anyplace she wanted.

The last time, I offered to send her to Parkwood, or, even, Palm Springs or Los Angeles, Las Vegas, Colorado, anywhere, somewhere. I said, "Just say the word, baby, and I will set it all up. Our insurance will cover it all."

She screamed at me, "Stop, just fucking stop it! I ain't going to no mental hospital, no rehab, no nothing. Just leave me the fuck alone! If people would stop bothering me, I'd be okay. But you know I don't take no shit from nobody. I never have and never will. Ain't nothing wrong with me!"

My co-workers would be shocked if they knew. They thought I had it all together. They talked all the time about how well I handled even the most difficult patients. But if they knew I had a patient at home, who I damn sure didn't know how to handle, I'd be a laughing stock at work. Even my family keeps hounding me to leave her ass, but I won't, I can't, I love her. When I took my vows and said till death do us part, I really meant it.

I sighed and pushed through the crowd. I grabbed her by the hand. "Come on, baby, it's okay, let's go home."

She just got louder. "Now, motherfucker, my damn husband is here, and he'll kick your punk ass. baby, tell this motherfucker who I am. He don't know who he's fucking with."

She looked terrible: mascara running down her face, sweating, nails chipped, her hair looked a hot mess.

"I know, baby, it's okay, let's just go home."

I told the security guard, "Sorry, man. She really doesn't mean any harm."

"Just get her outta here, bro, before the police get here."

"'Preciate it man!"

Natashia was standing there looking embarrassed as hell. "Sorry I had to call you so late, but I didn't want her to go to jail."

"It's ok, thanks. We'll come back later to pick up her car. Do you need me to drive you home?"

"No, I've got my friend waiting for me."

"Thank you, again. Sorry you had to deal with it."

Natashia waved off, and I poured Aja into the car. She smelled like an ash tray and liquor store combined. We rode home in silence; she didn't say one single word. She was totally wasted! Gone. In a zone.

The next morning, Aja got up and fixed breakfast. She was all put back together as if nothing had happened.

I finally felt she left me no choice. I'd have to start her on some kind of medication to adjust her behavior. Hell, I knew I could lose my license for it, but, I had to take that chance. I love Aja, and I would do whatever it took to make my baby better.

I decided I'd put her on something subtle, because if she changed too drastically, she'd know something was going on. I decided to try Xanax first, it's a mild calming agent. I mixed it in that damn pomegranate juice she drank faithfully every morning. We had cases and cases of that shit. If that doesn't stabilize and mellow her out, then Depakote will. But, first the Xanax, it had worked pretty well on some of my patients with similar behavioral problems.

After two months, the medicine seemed to be working. I'd noticed a change in her behavior after about two weeks. She seemed pretty mellow, as if the medicine had leveled her off. She'd started spending more time with me and less time at the clubs. She had fewer confrontations when she was out in the public, no recent fights at the grocery store or gas station and she hadn't been to any clubs in a while.

She'd been over to the Casino in Arkansas once or twice and made it back with no incidents. A miracle, thank God! She'd even picked back up some of her old hobbies, like her quilting. That used to be one of her favorites. She was really good at it, too. She'd always start out good, but never finish. I had even screened in the porch and fixed it up with everything out there just the way she liked: flat screen TV, Bose surround sound, a Schwinn exercise bike, sewing machine, nice patio furniture with a chaise lounge, a few nice plants, and even the right ceiling fan, fancy ashtrays, and the thing she loved most - a

Jacuzzi. It'd been out there a while, but after a couple months on medication, she was finally putting it to use.

She would sit out there working on a quilt for her niece that was having twins. She wanted to have it ready before the babies are born. I couldn't believe it, she'd made an 180 degree change. What a difference a pill, I mean, a day, makes. We could go to bed together, watch TV, and have dinner together every night. When I got home from work, she'd greet me with a kiss and even a smile. She even asked how my day at work went. I thought that was how it was supposed to be, how it used to be in the beginning. It seemed like forever since I'd had that Aja.

But, just when everything was going great, I had to leave town. I was really worried about how to handle two weeks away when I couldn't be there to give her the meds. I knew if she didn't get her daily dose in her juice things could get bad again. I didn't know what she might do. It's hard to predict how fast meds wear off, and I didn't want to take any chances.

I decided to call Peggy, Aja's sister, and ask if she could stay with Aja while I was away.

"Hi, Peg, how you doing, girl? It's your favorite brother-in-law, what's going on?"

"Nothing, Bro-in-Law. What's going on with you?"

"Look, I need a favor."

"What's up? I know it's gotta be something, for you to be calling me."

"Can you stay over here with Aja for two weeks? I have to go to Atlanta for a conference and I hate leaving her alone. She doesn't like it when I leave and she hates going to these conferences with me. She gets bored out of her mind."

"Sure, no problem, I'll be glad to come over and hang with Aja in y'all big beautiful house.

"Great, next Sunday, then."

"Yeah, sure, I have a few things in my calendar. I have a massage appointment, but I can reschedule that, and there are one or two other things, but I can work around them."

"Okay, thanks, Sis-in-Law, I owe you one."

"No problem. Plus, I need to spend a little quality time with my sister, so we can catch up. I'm past due."

Aja and Peggy were totally different, like night and day. Peggy was very stable, self-sufficient, a lawyer who does very well for herself, a fine ass, pretty, dark chocolate-skinned woman. My wife is also fine, and here's the difference, she never went to college, only worked a few odd jobs here and there, but definitely the marrying kind, the kept kind, a one-man woman.

Peggy wasn't. In fact, I'd never seen Peggy with any man. She never brought anyone around for family holiday dinners or birthday celebrations or nothing. For a while, I thought maybe she was gay, but, then, I overhead her and Aja talking about someone named Vincent, another lawyer. Seemed Peggy been dating this Vincent guy for quite some time. Then, after all the time she'd spent with him, he was marrying someone else. Someone he'd been living with while dating her. I overheard the whole thing, but just went on acting as if I didn't know. I didn't want to stir nothing up.

I thought about telling Peggy about the meds, maybe she could give them to her sister while I was gone, but her being a lawyer… I just decided I couldn't put that on her.

Peggy showed up Sunday afternoon. My flight was Monday morning. Peggy slept in while Aja dropped me off at the airport. As I got out of the car and kissed my wife goodbye, I prayed, Lord please help and protect my wife and let no disasters occur while I'm away, please! She looked so sweet as she drove away.

PEGGY KNIGHT

I woke up to the smell of bacon and coffee. Aja had made breakfast and was sitting on the stool at her kitchen counter sipping coffee and looking through the Memphis Flyer. Her house was fabulous and she looked fabulous too. She was in her silk robe looking like a character from "Memphis Housewives," I guess, instead of Atlanta Housewives. Skylights cast perfect morning light on the kitchen. From the open bay window over the deck, I could smell fresh cut grass, spearmint, eucalyptus, even a bit of her roses. She took pride in taking care of her beautiful red, yellow, orange, and white roses. Whenever I spent time at their place, I'd think, yeah, maybe this is how I should've tried to live my life, but I'm much too independent, selfish, impatient, and too damn picky, to settle down and marry.

As I walked in, she looked up with a smile. "Good morning, Sis, want coffee?"

"Yes, please."

She poured me a cup from her Krups. I found the hazelnut creamer and raw sugar and after two sips, I felt better already. "Mmm, this coffee is great."

"How are things with that guy? Vincent? You still seeing him?"

"Oh, it's okay. Yeah, we still see each other."

"Just okay?"

"Yeah, just okay. We don't see each other like we use to."

"He still going through with it? You know, marrying that damn girl? I thought you guys would end up getting married. You've been seeing each other so long."

"Girl, I don't like him like that."

"Are you sure? Seems obvious to me you love him 'cause you've been seeing him, and only him, for a long time. You ever told Vincent the truth about how you really feel about him?"

"No, A!"

"Ok, sorry, I touched a nerve. Never mind."

"I've always liked our relationship the way it was. I never wanted to change it. I just never expected him to up and marry the heifer."

"Well, there you have it, how would he know how you really feel about him, since you never said anything? When's the wedding?"

"Next week, downtown at the Cadre Building! Ugh! I can't believe it. He knows that is one of my all-time favorite places for weddings, we've talked about it before."

"Well, believe it girl, and you shouldn't have let this shit happen. We need to start planning on how we are gonna show up! and I do mean we. I want to see this shit first-hand, what a bastard."

"Now, don't get me wrong, I'm shocked, but, I like the way Vincent and I hang out. I just wish he would've told me face to face about the wedding instead of me reading about it on his Facebook page. He's been avoiding me for a couple of weeks now. I've called his law office, cell phone, sent text messages, email, Instagram, and I even called his home phone. He's just ignoring me and I'm starting to get a little pissed. I'm gonna give him a few more days and if he doesn't call, I'll just hafta confront him at the damn wedding."

"Girl, what you said?"

"I just don't know what changed or why he feels he has to avoid me, I'm in shock. I thought we were cool like that."

"Hmm, well I do, I know what to say to his jackass, and I'm gonna tell him, just as soon as I see him. And the nerve, him not telling you to your face. It ain't like you didn't know he had another woman. What kinda chicken shit lawyer is he? I wouldn't hire his ass to defend me for shit, he ain't got no balls… He's a weenie!"

"Okay Aja, settle down, we ain't' gonna start no shit, he ain't worth it. You're more worked up than I am."

"Oh, yes, ma'am, I am, and we are gonna start some shit, I can't wait."

"Look, girl, you'd better not get our ass put out! Please, please, don't have me looking like no fool, girl. Don't be bringing too much attention to us! I just want to scare him up a bit."

"Hump! Just wait…."

"Now, A-A, promise me, promise me, that you want go too far, girl."

"Okay, okay, I promise, plus you know Javier is out of town, and he's my savior."

"Yeah. and he left me to look out for you, so, don't go messing up my brother-in-law points."

"Yeah, yeah, okay, okay, enough about that punk ass secret man of yours."

"Let's enjoy your big beautiful house before your man gets back home. Okay what do we get into, first? Does Javier still have those massage chairs upstairs in his cave?"

"Sure does."

"Well, let's take it to the cave, and watch some movies until lunchtime."

"Ooo, and how about chicken wings for lunch?"

"Sounds good!"

"And, after lunch, I can make some Margaritas, or we've got some Buzzballz. We can take them outside and get into the hot tub. Javier added that hot tub on the screened porch and we've hardly used it. This is a perfect time to break it in."

We started watching The View or, rather, The View watched us and we snoozed until lunchtime. When we woke up it was afternoon and the news was going off. We took quick showers, Aja put the chicken in the oven and set the timer, and headed out to the porch. She grabbed us two Buzzballz from the bar and turned the jets on and we slid in.

"Aja, why you didn't tell me Javier put this damn Jacuzzi in for you? This feels so damn good, just what the doctor ordered and these little Buzzballz Ritas are kick ass, girl."

"And you know that."

As I slid down further down in the Jacuzzi. "You gotta invite me over more often."

"Girl you don't need an invite, you can come by any time. But I'll call you, anyway, just to make sure you ain't forgot you're welcome, but, honestly, I haven't used it much before. Okay, okay, check this out, we've got a remote for the surround sound. Let's get some music started. Who do you want to hear?"

"Who you got?"

"We've got everybody. My man loves music. I've got that new R. Kelly, Mary J.Blige, , Beyoncé, Adele, and some new jazz. You still like jazz, right?"

"Yeah, I like everybody, and right now, I could probably relate to this song that R. Kelly sings called "When A Man Lies," I think it's track 6. Play that for me. Have you heard this song called "Stay with Me?" I don't know the guy, but Mary J. Blige is singing with him. It's the bomb."

"Yeah I've heard it, his name is Sam Smith. Funny, I like the whole CD."

"Okay, I'll play that too."

"Girl, I'm already getting tipsy in here. How many CDs can you load in there at one time?"

"Eight. Who else you want to hear? Jazz?"

"Yeah, there's something your husband is always playing… I think Euge Groove, and Boney James, too. Javier always got that jazz grooving in his car."

"Okay, you got it, I'm gonna throw in some blues - some Johnnie Taylor and Al Green, too. You know what? I got all of these on my playlist. Alex… Shuffle my amazon music. Girl, I forget about all this shit my husband has hooked up. Now, this way we get to hear it all."

Whether it was the music or the tequila or the sight of my sister looking so peaceful in her happy home, I started doing something I almost never do. I started crying.

Aja looked at me, surprised, and that just made it worse. "What the hell, girl! I've never seen you crying. Let me take that back, cry about no damn man!"

"I just feel like I've lost so many years playing with Vincent. I got comfortable with the way things were, and I thought we'd stay the same forever. I've been kicking it with this man for years. It's been fun, but, now that I know he's really getting married and it's probably coming to an end, that shit really hurts. I didn't mind messing around with Vincent when he had a live in putting up with all the shit from him that I never would, dumb ass Camille. But who's the dumb ass, now? Camille is real and is about to become a bride and me? I'm the old side piece left high and dry. Once, he becomes her husband, I don't think I can or want to hang anymore. I've had fun being his side piece, but once he marries her, this is where I end."

"Girl, cut your damn crying! Let's start planning how we're gonna show up uninvited to this damn wedding. What are you wearing? You know you gotta look good. I was thinking about wearing my white Donna Karen dress with my white Christian Louboutin pumps. All white, just like the fat ass bride with my Michael Kors accessories. You know my MK watch, and purse. What size are you now, Peg? Eight? Funny, girl, I'm still a six, well, between a six and eight. We'll be two of the baddest, sharp ass bitches at the damn wedding."

"And you know that." We high-fived, and for the next few days, we didn't even leave the house. All we did was chill, watch movies and listen to music, soak in the Jacuzzi, and read all the latest magazines. Aja has them all:

Essence, Ebony, Jet, Oprah, Black Enterprise, Vogue. More magazines than I had time, and every day I would fall asleep reading. What a wonderful life! I thought my sister had to be one of the happiest girls on the planet.

The wedding venue was posted all over Facebook. It would be at the Cadre Building. Now that's a beautiful place. We made it downtown sooner than expected - a little before 4:00 p.m. The Parking garage was next door. It should have been convenient but the shit was stupid crazy. The charge was $10, but you needed exact change or a debit card. You had to put your license plate number in and wait for a ticket, then take that ticket back and put it on your dash. When we got out of the car, there was a long line of people complaining, cursing, and swearing, trying to remember their parking stall and license plate number, pay, and get on to the wedding on time. I saw a guy hop out of his car walking fast, carrying a couple of cameras and a tripod. I heard him say fuck that shit as he went on towards the wedding – the photographer.

Aja and I had to park on the 5th level, and the payment machine was on level 3. We made a deal, she went down the steps to pay and get the ticket, and I would go back and put it in the car dash. Then we went on together. Damn, I was out of breath from the 5th to the 3rd level - I'd better start walking or something.

Good thing we both know how to work our shoes. We learned that from back in our young clubbing days. Stand in line or walk in with your flats, then pull the pretty ones out of your bag once you arrive.

Once inside, I couldn't help but notice how beautiful the place was. I saw a few people I thought I recognized from the law community, but I didn't see a single soul I personally knew. Where did all these people come from? All kinds of people were here: Black, White, Asian, Hispanic, Pakistani, South African. I met a woman from Germany and a really nice guy from Iran, named Masoud.

We found seats at the end of an aisle and set our bags there to save them. So, as the bride came down, we would see her from head to toe as well as get a clear view of the groom. I noticed Aja seemed a little distant today, maybe she was just angry for me. I don't know if bringing her was such a great idea.

She'd been a bit moody the last few days, and she was really adamant that Vincent had wronged me.

But, oh my God, this place was beautiful. The ceilings were made with gold crown molding everywhere. All the doors were black, a shiny black lacquer. We wandered up to the second floor so we could look down and see everyone coming in. We watched people fill up the place as we leaned over the gold leaf banister. All the seats were covered with beige and cream linen chair covers with gold bows. We finally went down and took our seats. The wedding was scheduled to start at 5:00, but 5:00 came, then 5:30, then 5:45 and guests started getting antsy. You could hear muffled conversations all around, but no one left. We all waited patiently. I had no idea what the holdup was about, but the wedding finally began at exactly 6:15 p.m.

The bridesmaids' dresses were beautiful, everything in peach and cream, long with a low back and a cream sash hanging off one shoulder. Damn, there were twelve bridesmaids. Their shoes were silver and they all had their hair up in a bun, ringed in peach and cream flowers, very pretty. The bridesmaids were all of different ethnicities as well. Three of them didn't need to wear the kind of dress they had on, but overall, they all looked beautiful. They walked in on some nice jazz music. I thought, for a guy who said he didn't want to get married, he'd thrown an awfully big wedding. There were a total of twenty-six people in the wedding party, twenty-eight if you counted the bride and groom.

I finally saw one person I knew, Vincent's friend, James. As he walked by, I turned my head so he wouldn't see me. It took thirty minutes for them to all walk in. I thought, look at Vincent. He looked so handsome, with his scandalous ass! I knew every inch of his body, every scar, scrape, his birthmark on his right ankle, the texture of the hairs on his head and chest and butt. I knew how his toes looked, how he smelled, how he snored, and what sound he made when he arrived when we made love. Umh… I can't believe, my Vincent is getting married and not to me.

The wedding director said let's all stand for the entrance of the bride. I looked around, the room was full, not an empty seat anywhere. Then Vincent reached for his saxophone and you could hear a pin drop as he started playing. He played the song "You Are So Beautiful," and my tears started falling. A few others teared up, too. It was so, so, touching. I've heard Vincent play once or twice, not something that he did often with me.

Then, there she was, coming down the aisle and my mouth just flew open.. I was in shock and my sister gave me a punch and said, Really! I'd heard many, many, stories about Camille, but I never, ever, had any idea that she looked like this. I'd pictured her short, fat, black, with buck teeth, hair in some natural style like dread twist, but never in my wildest dreams did I expect what I saw.

She wasn't fat, just thick, what these days they call big sexy. She had the most beautiful, big, green eyes, she had long flowing red hair, perfect white teeth and a beautiful smile, and she was, she was... white. And absolutely gorgeous. Her dress was beautiful, and fit her like a glove.

True, as I thought back, Vincent never mentioned to me if Camille was Black, White, or Green, and I never asked, I just assumed. As she got up to the top of the stairs to meet her groom, the wedding director had us all be seated. Aja leaned over and whispered in my ear, we're gonna get this motherfucker.

Then the minister led us in a brief prayer, and everyone sat down. When the minister started reading the vows, from the corner of my eye, I saw Aja pull something out of her purse. I had no idea what it was. The minister said, Camille, do you take this man to be your lawful wedded husband, for sickness and health, to love and to cherish him until death do you part, for the bad that may darken your days and the good that may lighten your ways? And Camille said yes, I do.

Aja had some kind of pen that had a red light on it, and she started shinning that light right in Vincent's eyes when it came time for him to repeat his vows to Camille. Each time he began to speak, she would shine that damn light right in his eye. People started laughing because it seemed as if he was stumbling on his words which made it seem like he was a fake from the start. No one saw where that light came from or noticed that it was my crazy sister.

I whispered for her to stop it, stop shining that light, put that shit away. I even pinched her a few times. It was as if she couldn't even hear me. It was as if she was in some kind of a trance. I finally grabbed her hands. Her palms were so sweaty and clammy. She finally stopped. The Minister said, I now pronounce you husband and wife! Everyone applauded

As Vincent and Camille turned and walked down the aisle hand in hand, Vincent looked directly at me as if he didn't even know who I was. He never flinched, never even batted an eye.

They made the announcement for everybody to go upstairs to the second level for cocktails while they prepared the area for the reception.

I really needed a drink. "Did you bring money with you, Aja?"

She wasn't even listening to me. "What an ass! I'm gonna get him when that damn reception starts for fucking over my damn sister and marrying that ugly bitch!"

"Hell, no! C'mon. What do you want? I got it. Imma have a glass of Chardonnay."

"Well, I need something stronger, get me Sky vodka and cranberry."

Forty-five minutes and two drinks later, it was time to head downstairs for the reception. The hostess announced, please check your card to see what table you're assigned , too. I thought, oh hell, we ain't assigned to no table at all, we weren't even invited. One of the hostesses seemed to have paid attention to us, came over and asked to help us find our table. "What's your table number?"

I panicked. So I blurted out we're late guests of the groom. I saw Aja getting ready to get crunk, so I said the same last name as Vincent's, Malone.

"Oh, ok, the groom's family is at table number seven and eight."

Thank God, no one else was at that table, yet, and it was in the far back. Each table had a large vase with white lily and lavender flowers. All the cloth napkins were in white and gold. There were servers assisting for each table with our sit down meal. Wow, Vincent and Camille went all out. People were mixing and mingling everywhere. Laughing, talking, taking selfies, the photographer snapping pictures of it all. The band started playing and the announcement was made for the bride and groom's first dance.

Suddenly, I heard Aja on the mic! "Attention, Attention everyone, attention" She beat on the mic with her hand. "I would like to make a toast to Camille, the poor bride, and Vincent, the worst jackass groom this side of Memphis, who is a conniving, lying, cheating, controlling son of a bitch and doesn't deserve to marry anybody. He's been fucking my sister for years right along with his new darr..ling wife. Good luck, Camille, I wish you all the luck in your future misery to Mr. Vincent Malone. You're gonna need it, boo."

Then Aja looked over at me, as she jerked her neck and popped her fingers, "Ain't that right, big sis?"

Everyone in the place turned to see who big sis was and I wanted to run for cover.

Aja dropped the mic and it howled, then the whole damn room got quiet, so quiet, you could hear a mouse take a piss on a cotton ball.

Finally, the DJ grabbed up the mic and said, "Let's get this party started!" He launched into the first song! "Love Power" by Willie Hutch. That song got everyone on the dance floor. Thank God!

He went from there right into Zydeco Bounce. One of the favorite line dance songs. And, that did it! The wedding went on as if nothing happened.

I glanced over at the bride and groom, and Camille was crying and shaking her head and pointing her finger all in her new husband's face. Something was going down. It wasn't over by no means. Aja had stirred up some shit!

A group of girls surrounded the bride, then I saw some guys come over and pull the groom away. It didn't look good.

The music was loud so, I really couldn't hear what was said. People were partying everywhere. I looked for Aja to tell her we needed to get the hell out of here. Then I spotted her, she was across the room talking to some guy and had the craziest look I'd ever seen on her face. Not the sister I knew at all. Suddenly I felt it—it was about to get ugly in here.

Then the best man from the wedding was walking toward me. I didn't know his name, but I vaguely remembered seeing him with Vincent before. "Hey,

Peggy, remember me? James. You know, I know you, and all about you. I know how you might be feeling right now, but do you think you could just get outta here and take that crazy ass sister of yours so we can keep the peace? Vincent wanted me to send his apologies and to tell you that he's sorry and will get back with you as soon as he can. We don't won't any more shit to go down. It's already been way too much. So, please, can you get yo crazy ass sister and get the hell outta here?"

Aja walked up, sweating from the dance floor. "Who da fuck are you?"

I tried to talk in a low calm voice to her, "Let's go!" But, she ran off again and disappeared in the crowd.

"Well, James, Vincent should've thought of that when he ignored all my calls. All he had to do was be a man and talk to me about it. He didn't hafta ignore my calls."

"Yeah, I know, I know, but the fact remains, it's about to get ugly and it just don't hafta be. They've paid a pretty penny to have their wedding at this place, and the way things are steamin up, it's gonna cost way more if it gets tore up. Please, just get your sister and go."

Aja was back on the dance floor with some big guy, twerking, her champagne glass raised high in the air, and I saw a couple bridesmaids headed her way. I thought, oh shit, what am I gonna do? The next thing I saw was Aja kicking off her shoes, one hand on her hip and her other arm swinging. People around her stopped dancing… then I heard a scream. Aja had snatched some big girl, snatched her weave, wig, or whatever, right off her head, and thrown it across the room.

She snatched another girl and knocked her to the floor. The girl's dress came down, spilling padding on the floor and flashing her sagging boobs. Oh, my God! I ran to Aja, pulled her by her arm, let's go, someone is gonna call the police.

She jerked away from me yelling, fuck the police, I'm getting ready to whop this big ugly bitch's ass.

More girls were coming. It took all my strength to grab her again and drag her off the floor while she kept yelling fuck all y'all, and fuck that stupid fat ass bitch whose ass I kicked and fuck that stupid, ugly, fat ass bride and fuck you, Vincent Malone, for fucking over my damn sister.

Thank God James was there to run interference from the bridesmaids and ushers, so I could get her out the door.

I managed to get her to the parking garage, but Aja and I were both panting and sweating. When we got to the stairs, she just stopped and refused to budge. "I ain't going back up all those fucking stupid ass stairs to get to your sorry ass car. You go up and come back down and get me."

I was afraid to leave her, but I knew I couldn't get her up the stairs, and I had to get to my car and us out of there. She sat down on the stairs panting and didn't look like she was going to move in the next few minutes. I had to risk it. As, I hauled myself upstairs, I noticed even more commotion. the photographer from the wedding was cursing a blue streak, his equipment scattered around him, while he kicked at a boot that had been put on his car for not paying. I thought way, way too much going on here!

As I kept climbing those damn stairs, I did wonder, though, if he'd caught a shot of Vincent's face when Aja had the mic. My God, his expression, that look of shock, I'd pay money for that shot. But, damn Aja had gone too far! I had no idea she'd clown like this! I never woulda brought her!

It seemed like the four flights of stairs to my car took me an hour, but I could still hear her down there talking shit and talking shit loudly! But, at least, she hadn't moved.

I reached my car, hopped in, and drove down to the exit as fast as I could. When I got there, she was talking loud and laughing at some man in a red Camaro, reaching out his window to hand her a lighted cigarette. I remembered seeing him checking us out earlier in the wedding. She had her shoes in her hand. He must have brought them from the reception and come looking for her. Oh shit!

I got out of the car and reached for Aja's arm, "Hey, let's go."

She snatched away from me. "Leave me alone, P. You ought to be glad I told their ass."

"A, please."

"Fuck you Peggy, yo ass is pitiful. You're a punk ass, chicken shit ass bitch, and you should've been over there helping me get some of those bitches. That man ain't shit and he ugly, anyway."

"Come on Aja, you just need to get in the damn car. Let's go!"

"My husband ain't home, I can go where I want to. I'm tired of your ass babysitting me any damn way. I don't need no babysitter." She took a drag from her cigarette. "Take your ass on home, P, I don't need you."

She turned and opened that guy's passenger door, tossed in her shoes, and hopped in. The Camaro spun off toward the exit, and she gave me the finger just as they turned the corner.

What the hell! My first thought was what am I gonna tell my brother-in-law? I had to find her before he got back home. My mind was racing, do I call him, call the police, wait and see if she shows up at the house, what? Do I go to her house or mine? I called her cell phone, and it went straight to voice mail.

I drove around for a few minutes trying to find the Camaro. I called her phone over and over. I left about ten messages praying she'd call me back. She didn't.

I finally decided I'd better just go home, but as I drove, my mind was racing. How did this shit happen? What went wrong? All I'd wanted to do was show up and scare Vincent, not disrupt his entire wedding, and for sure not bring attention to myself. I was thinking my sister is crazy as hell. How did I never know this?

I got to my place and everything was just as I left it. It felt so cold inside. Not as in temperature but just still, empty. I couldn't stop reliving everything that just went down, wondering what the fuck I was supposed to do. I poured myself a glass of Chardonnay and went to the bathroom to turn on the shower. Then, I saw my answering machine blinking. Two messages. The first was from a few days ago. I hadn't checked messages while I was at Aja's.

It was Vincent. "Peg, I am sorry I've been avoiding your calls, but I just didn't know how to tell you that I was marrying Camille and the wedding is set for this Saturday. Please forgive me, and I will be in touch soon, I still love you."

So, he did try to tell me. Oh, God!

The second message was Aja. At first I was relieved, then I was scared.

She was near screaming. "Come get me! Please, help me! Dude tried to get with me. I fought him, and he kicked my ass out the car on Union Extd. Police picked me up. I'm at Memphis Mental Hospital. Please hurry, please. They're trying to find Javier. I don't want him to know. Please, please, come get me!"

I had to play the recording twice to understand exactly what she was saying. Her words were slurring, and she was crying all at the same time. Oh my God, I threw the phone down and ran to the bathroom jumped in the shower. I knew enough not to show up trying to look like a lawyer the state I was in. I scrubbed off my make-up, pinned up my hair, grabbed a pair of jeans, top, and flats, brushed my teeth, gargled, and headed to my car. Just as I was pulling out, my cell phone rang.

"Hello?"

"This is Ms. Jacobs from the Memphis Mental Health Institute. We have a lady here who listed you as her primary contact. Do you know an Aja Knight Diaz?"

"Yes, that's my sister."

"She's delirious, belligerent, and combative. Are you aware of her condition? Do you know if she's on any kind of medication for her disorder?"

"Disorder? No, I'm not aware of her disorder or any medications that she might be on, but I'm coming down there now."

"We gave her something to calm her down, but is there someone else we should call who'll know what she's on? A doctor? A spouse?"

"No, no, I'm coming to pick her up. I'm her sister… and an attorney. No more medication. Don't give her anything else till I get there."

"Then Ms. Knight, we will hold her here until you arrive. I hate to tell you this, but if we don't give her anything more, we'll have to restrain her."

"Please, just give me 45 minutes, I'm in my car, on my way. Where can I find you?"

She told me where to find Aja, and I hung up, and knew immediately I had to call Javier. I knew Aja would hate it, but I had to. At least, he'd know if she was on medication or not. It was already midnight, but I had to. I dialed his cell.

I knew he'd been asleep, when he answered with a grunt.

"Javier, it's Peggy."

He immediately sounded awake and alarmed. "What's wrong?"

"It's Aja, she went with me to a wedding, she seemed fine at first, but she got crazy on me, caused a scene, got into a fight. I couldn't control her, couldn't get her to leave with me. She, I've never seen her like this before in my life. Something is seriously wrong. They've got her at the Memphis Mental Hospital and want to give her some more medication. I'm headed there now. Is she on anything? Do you know what's wrong with her?"

He sighed. "Damn, not again. Look, Peggy, listen to me carefully, when you get there ask for Ms. Abbey, she knows me. Tell her you're my sister-in law and that you spoke with me and get Aja outta there. Tell them, if they have any questions, to call me on my cell. Call me when you get there. Hurry."

"Okay, okay, I'm going just as fast as I can. This has happened before? Why didn't I know about it?"

But, the line was dead.

I got to the hospital, and saw her… there was Aja, looking like a wild cat. Her hair was all over her head, her dress dirty, nails chipped, make-up running. She looked dazed, her eyes glazed over. She was wrapped up in a blanket and just rocking against the restraints.

I asked the security guard. "Is Ms. Abbey here?"

"Hold on, I'll get her for you, have a seat." I couldn't sit, though. I stood there looking at my sister like that, starting to tear up.

Then, a short, fat lady with a face full of moles, looked like a chocolate chip cookie, came out from somewhere in the back. "Ms. Knight, right? Your brother-in-law already called." She smiled, and I noticed her two front teeth were gold. She patted my arm. "It's okay, baby, she's gonna be okay. We get people in here all the time in much worse condition than your sister, and they don't have any one to come or care for them. Your sister is blessed to have someone who cares about her. I just need you to sign some papers, releasing her over to you, then you can take her home."

I don't know what Javier did or said, but whatever it was worked. They gave me all of Aja's belongings, her purse, cell phone, ID, and even the little thank-you-for-coming wrapped popcorn bag from the wedding that said Vincent and Camille forever on it.

Aja didn't say one word to me, just followed me to the car. I headed straight for her house and we rode the whole way in silence.

Once we arrived, she got her remote out of her purse, let the garage up, and we went in. She headed straight for the shower. I was thinking, oh my God, what is wrong with my sister? I've never seen her like this.

My phone beeped, text message from Javier. "Cutting my trip short. Home tomorrow. Where is she now?"

I texted back. "We're at your house. She's in the shower."

He texted. "See you early a.m. Will explain. Please stay with her. Don't let her out of your sight. Thanks, sis."

A minute later another text came in. "Look in pantry. Fix her a glass of pomegranate juice. Make sure she drinks it all!"

I just thought. Pomegranate juice? Ok.

JAVIER DIAZ

When I got home, Aja greeted me with a kiss. "Hey, I missed you, baby." She acted as if nothing had happened.

I said, "We need to talk."

Peggy came from her room with her bag packed like she couldn't get out fast enough. "I'm gonna leave you now that your man's home. Okay, girl, call me tomorrow."

Aja, smiled. "Okay, I will. Javier walk your sis-in law to her car."

Peggy and Aja kissed each other on the cheek and hugged as they usually did. I grabbed Peggy's bag.

As we walked to the car, I talked fast, giving her the short version. "Your sister's not well. I've been trying to get her to get some help for quite a while now, but she won't. I believe she's bi-polar, but in denial. You have no idea how many confrontations she's been in. I'm afraid someone is gonna hurt her one day. That's why I asked you to stay with her. I probably shouldn't tell you this, and I definitely shouldn't do it, but I've been giving her some medication to adjust her behavior. It seemed to work, but when I had to leave, I couldn't give it to her, and I didn't know how to tell you. I don't know how much more I can take, but I sure can't keep slipping medicine in her juice. It's unethical and I could lose my license."

"What the hell, Javier? Why didn't you tell me?"

"She would have hated that. Peggy, I love her, and I'll fight to get her better, no matter what it takes, but I don't know what else to do. Pray for her, Peggy?"

"Of course."

I knew Peggy had to be mad at me, and in shock, but she loved Aja more.

"What— who— where were you guys when this happened?"

69

"At a wedding."

"Who's wedding? I don't remember her saying she was invited to any wedding."

"Yeah, we weren't invited. It was this guy I've been secretly seeing for the last... too many years to tell. Ugh, it's a long, dumb story."

I didn't say I had overheard the story. "Damn, though... and he married someone else? That must be rough. You okay?"

"Yeah, just in shock. About that, but, more about how I saw my sister behave. Javier, don't give up on her. I know she loves you, and, without you, I don't know what she'd do. You're her everything, plus I don't think anyone else can handle her!"

"Don't worry, I'm sticking with her, I love her; she's my wife. Now give me a hug and let me get back inside, we'll talk soon."

Peggy got into her car. "Keep me posted."

"Will do." When I walked back into the house, Aja was sitting there with this smirk on her face.

"What now, Javier? I don't want to hear none of that therapist shit again."

"Baby, you've got to get some help. I love you. Please, please go talk to these people. I know they can help you."

"I ain't goin."

I rubbed my face, thinking... feeling... I just didn't know how much more of this I could take. "Baby, I'm sorry. You've gone too far this time, and if you want this marriage to continue, you've got to let me help you. You have to go. I've made you an appointment for Monday, and if you want, I'll go with you. But you've gotta go, baby."

"Peggy told you I got into a little bit of trouble. Ugh! What a punk ass!"

"She had to, baby, but she has no idea of all the times you've acted out. That's between you and me. But you're getting scary, and soon, you're gonna wind up in jail or getting hurt."

"I know, I know, but, Javier, I promise I'm gonna do better."

I shook my head, determined. "You can't do it alone, baby, you just can't. And, I can't. I can't take this much more."

I must have looked serious, because she looked scared. "Look, okay, I'll go to the appointment, it won't do a damn thing, but what da hell!"

I was relieved, but cautious. I figured she'd back out when it came time. But, at least, for the rest of the week, she was her old self, She was drinking her juice again and looking beautiful every day like nothing had ever gone wrong. The house was immaculate, dinner ready as usual when I got home, and she seemed just as happy as could be. Monday came. Her appointment was scheduled for 1:00 pm. She said she'd drive herself, but I knew better than that. I drove her, and she was silent all the way until we arrived.

I offered to go with her, but she said no. "Javier, I know you love me, baby, cause you've put up with my shit for a long, long time. Now it's time for me to get it together."

I didn't really trust her to go by herself. I thought she might just run off, but I knew that people only get better when they want to. For themselves. So, I had to let her try. I let her go in alone.

While she was in the session, I went to a nearby Whole Foods, thought I'd get her some healthy food, some of those special potato chips, some fruit, and some fresh asparagus. She loves asparagus. The store was pretty crowded, but the line moved pretty fast. I got back to Henderson and Henderson just as she walked out.

I could see she'd been crying as she got in the car. "Take me home, but stop me by Buster's, I want to pick up something to drink."

I thought, oh damn, here we go. "Do you really need a drink, baby?"

"Hell, yeah, and don't you dare tell me I can't have one, Javie!"

I stopped at Buster's, and as I was getting ready to get out of the car, she turned to look at me and said, "Javier, I can go in by myself, I'm not a kid."

"Okay, baby, just trying to be helpful."

"Yeah, right."

I let her go, but I started praying, please Lord, don't let her start no shit in the store, please just let her get what she wants and come the fuck back out. Ten, twenty, thirty minutes went by. I watched people come and go, getting more and more nervous. I finally thought what the hell, let me go in and see what's going on.

When I hit the door, there she was arguing with the cashier. "Don't I look like a grown ass woman, I ain't showing you no damn ID. When did this shit start? I've been coming here for years, and nobody ever asked me for ID before."

The cashier answered like she'd already said this a bunch of times. "Sorry, ma'am, that's the new store policy, it's the law."

"Then your store policy sucks, and fuck the law, get me the store manager."

I walked up behind her, my license and money out, "Sorry, ma'am, here's my ID. Let's go, baby."

The cashier just looked happy to ring us up and get us out of her store.

Aja turned and looked at me with contempt. "Why you gotta always act so damn soft? Man up. Stop letting motherfuckers push you around." She snatched the bag out of the cashier's hand and walked out.

I get her in the car, and had to sit there for a minute, getting hold of myself. I was pissed. "I'm not a push over for no one, well, except for you, dammit!"

That got her attention, and she calmed down. "I'm sorry, Javier. But these damn people just keep getting on my nerves."

"What did the therapist say? How did it go, baby?"

"They want me to go and stay at Lakeside for a few weeks. They think they can help me. I don't need no help. I just need these assholes to leave me the fuck alone!"

"Aja, do you want me to leave you? baby, if you don't get your act together, you're gonna leave me no choice. I want to be with you, but this is killing me. I don't know how much more shit I can take. And, Babe, you're getting worse."

She looked at me. I could see the anger and fear warring on her face. She finally turned away. "Hump… I don't need no Lakeside. But… I'll go back to those Henderson people for a few more sessions, see what happens. But, I ain't making no damn promises."

I knew promises didn't make no difference, anyway. "Ok, baby, just try it. For me. For us."

She was still mad, but grumbling, instead of screaming. "I'm gonna kill my sister for opening up her big damn mouth."

I started driving us home. "She's just trying to help Aja, that's all. You scared her."

On the way home, she started to calm down and sound more like herself. "We got that wake tomorrow. I'm thinking what black dress I should wear."

I'd almost forgotten about the wake for Shelly. I didn't really want to take her out in public, again, so soon after getting her back on the meds, but I couldn't leave her home alone, either.

Her voice was all sweet and normal. I should have been used to it, but the quick change was still disorienting. "I think I'll wear the one with the sweetheart neckline. That's real flattering, don't you think?"

"Sure."

She reached over and rubbed my hand while I was driving. "So sorry about Shelly."

"Yeah, me, too."

When we got home, Aja said she just wanted to relax. We watched Netflix movies that we'd already seen and spent some time in the hot tub. I was tired from the last couple days and the travel. I was grateful she was calm.

Since I was supposed to be gone, I stayed home from work. We had a nice couple days, listening to music, giving each other massages, making love everywhere…. It felt like old times. I kept saying how nice it was, isn't this nice, baby, hoping she'd remember how good it could be and decide to get help so it could always be like that.

Dressing for the wake, I was nervous, but she seemed ok. When we arrived, the place was packed. The funeral home could hardly hold all the people. Boy, he knew a lot of folk, it was standing room only. The crowd seemed to agitate Aja, though. She almost got into it with someone before we even went in.

"What is that asshole doing? Can't park worth a damn. How am I supposed to get out when he's so close like that?"

"It's okay, baby, I'll move over so you can get out. Don't go getting yourself all worked up over nothing."

Aja was barely listening to me. "Over nothing? That sonofabitch act like he wanted to do something. He doesn't know who the fuck he's messing with."

"Okay, okay, calm down baby, let's go in. It's okay." I looked at my wife. She was still as beautiful as the day I married her. Crazy as hell, but still beautiful!

As we were entering the Funeral Home, Aja stopped dead in her tracks. "Wait, just a damn minute, isn't that those therapists you sent me to?" She punched me in the side. "Look, there, Javier, by the guest book, signing in."

"I don't know, I've never met them in person, I just referred you there."

"Yes, that is them. I know you don't have them damn shrinks following me, now, do you?"

"Of course not! Now come on, you know me better than that. I wouldn't do no shit like that."

"Well, they're here, and it's giving me the creeps. They must do everything together! Who ever heard of a husband and wife counseling service together, anyway?"

"Baby, they're just here paying their respects to Shelly, just like everyone else. Maybe he was seeing a therapist, too, or just a friend of theirs. There's no telling how they know him. But, I told you, baby, a lot of people go and seek help."

"Hump! Well, I don't want to see them. And I don't want to be here long, Javie. Way too many damn people."

"Okay, baby, look there's Stella. Let's go give her our condolences, then we can go."

We approached Stella, just as she was just saying goodbye to some other couple. She looked sad, but very calm, considering she just lost her husband.

"Sorry for your loss Stella, I know Shelly is in a better place now. If you need anything, just give me or Aja a call and we'll be happy to help."

"Thanks, guys, thanks for coming. Will you be able to make the service tomorrow?"

I was trying to think of a polite excuse, but Aja stepped up and took Stella's hand. "Stella, I haven't been feeling well, and Javier's been looking after me, so we won't be able to make it, but I'm so sorry for your loss."

"I understand, take care of yourself, girl, I hope you feel better. And Javie, you just keep taking good care of your wife. You never know how much you take for granted when you're with someone until they are suddenly gone. Y'all got to take care of each other. Just remember, keep the love. Cause, if there's no love, there's nothing, and somebody might get hurt!" Tears started rolling down her face, but she got control of herself and looked up at us. "Just keep the love."

"We will, ma'am. And, again, you call if you need anything."

She nodded and turned to greet the people behind us. "Chad, so good of you to come—"

I took Aja's hand and led her out.

*

The next morning, I fixed Aja's juice, a couple of boiled eggs, and toast with honey butter. She seemed to be in deep thought as she came strolling into the kitchen slowly. "My Queen" who can turn into a witch at any given moment!

She sat at the counter and along with her breakfast, I gave her a soft, passionate kiss. "How are you feeling this morning, baby?"

"You know. I've been thinking, Javie, about what Stella said. About taking care of each other. You do take care of me. I know that. And, I feel bad about all I put you through, all the times you've come to get me in the middle of the night from some club, all the fights I got into."

"It's been rough."

"I know. Not to mention that it's your job to help people like me, and you can't even relax from that shit at home! It's not right. And I'm sorry. 'Cause you been taking care of me, but I sure ain't done a good job taking care of you!"

"Oh, baby, I love you, and you're a good wife... when things are good. You're, a good woman, Aja."

Her face was soft and her eyes clear. "Baby, do you think you can make it without me for thirty days?"

She was finally ready to make a start. I was so grateful, and, in that moment, I knew... I had to come clean, I had to start, too. "I've got to confess something to you. I... I been putting medication in your juice. I know it was wrong, but—"

"No, you don't have to explain. I... knew you were."

"What?"

"I knew you had to be giving me something, and it did help."

"You knew?"

"Yeah, and when I first figured it out, I was furious, but, then I realized I'd been feeling so much better. And when you left, and I didn't drink my pomegranate juice as usual, that was it, wasn't it?"

"Yeah."

"When I didn't have it… I started feeling… I acted out so bad with Peggy, I couldn't control myself at that wedding. That's when I knew, whatever you were giving me, I needed it. But, now, I want to know, what is it? What have you been giving me?"

Honestly, it was such a relief to talk about it. "I've tried several, Xanax, Seroquel, Haldol, Ativan, Depakote—"

"Lord, have mercy, were you trying to kill me, baby?"

"I was desperate. I just wanted to find something that would work to calm your butt down."

"Well, this one seems right. I've been very calm, things haven't upset me as they usually do. Even if I get annoyed, like in the parking lot at the wake, I don't feel like killing the asshole who annoys me. We need to get a legit prescription. I don't need you swiping samples or losing your job 'cause of my crazy shit."

"Yeah, can't be losing my job the way you shop!" I winked at her and she smiled back. It was such a relief to talk openly about all this. I grabbed her up in my arms. "I'm so glad, Aja, so glad you're working on you and that you've finally stopped fighting me. I'm so glad you're mine, and I'm still proud to be your husband, and we're gonna get thru this, no matter what."

STELLA HAYSLETT

Shelly was a fine man. I couldn't believe he was head over heels in love with me. He did everything in his power to win me over, to catch me. He came over every day, brought gifts for my Mom, my son, and, of course, me. He was a small-built man with a fine grade of hair, the kind Black folks call good hair, very wavy and soft, and, to maintain it, all he did was put water on it and brush it back. He had the biggest, most beautiful hazel eyes, and his complexion was like coffee with creamer.

So, why me? I don't know, he could've had just about any girl he wanted. But he chose me, and every time we'd go out, I'd get the looks. Women looking and flirting with him right in front of my face; it happened all the time. Some of these hungry women now days are bold, so disrespectful. I heard all the comments and the snickering , too. Like why is he with her? I know he can do better than that; how in the hell did she fool him, what kind of hold does she have on him? She must be paying him, ugh, she gotta have money; I can't see him just being with her for love, and look at her arm.

But, my Shelly never asked me for one dime. He never disrespected me, well, that was, at least, in the beginning. He showered me with love, each and every day. From the time we first met and became friends, all those years I made him wait, all the way till we got married.

He was a very observant man, paid close attention to detail. I'd like to say he had a mean eye; he wore a different pair of glasses than most. He always made sure I had money and what a great listener he was. He didn't forget a thing I said. Once, not long after we met, he heard me speak of my love for birds and brought me two peach face love birds, cage and all, for my birthday. That was the first of many gifts from Shelly.

I must admit, I always had a tendency to short change myself. I'd want something and have the money to purchase it, but wouldn't. I think it came from fear of turning up broke just like my Mom's side of the family. Shelly made up for that. Always buying me stuff. I finally had so many gadgets from Shelly, every time I used something, I had to think of him. I had universal remotes for my TV and stereo system, remote for my electric fireplace, the alarm system I could use the cell phone to arm and disarm, the clapper to turn the lights on and off, Dr. Drey headphones, cordless house phone, iPod docking station, wireless speakers, Bluetooth to work with my iPhone 7 plus, and Bluetooth speakers, an attachment for my computer that allows speech-to-text, and my favorite voice-activated alarm clock.

After we'd known each other a while, he started paying for my beauty shop appointments every week. He even bought all kind of kitchen gadgets: the slap top, the new soda maker, egg boiler, Calphalon pot sets, the Krups coffee maker, KitchenAid Artisan mixer, just to name a few. If there was a new gadget out and Shelly knew about it, then it would be coming my way.

He even bought me personal items like the Booty Pop that makes your butt look bigger than it is. I never had much of a butt, but I got boobs, and he loved my 40DDs. Most of the time I hid them, I didn't like to bring too much attention to myself. I had Spanxs, waist cinchers, custom made bras from the fitting place. You name it, Shelly got it for me. He came over to my momma's house all the time, and he never came over empty handed, always had some kind of gift or trinket for me or someone in my family.

Still, after all that, I wasn't so sure about getting married. I'd heard so many horror stories from my friends how everything was fine until they got married and then it went downhill. I'd heard how men change and become totally different, like a Jekyll and Hyde. My girlfriend, Peggy, always said she didn't want to get married, "I like it just the way I have it now," she'd say. "Men try to impress you to keep you around in the beginning. They like the chase and then, once they get you, it's all over. No more of that wining and dining like they do when they're trying to get you."

For another thing, I'd heard about children, from before the marriage, just tearing up the new one, and me and Tyler were real close. I'd had Tyler when I was real young, and since he was a little boy, he'd had always looked out for his momma. He was near grown, but if I married and moved in with Shelly, I wasn't sure how they'd get along. I even told my Mom I wasn't so sure how Tyler would handle Shelly taking first place with me instead of him. And I didn't know how Shelly would be as a husband and stepfather. I wasn't sure I wanted to change things. We'd been friends for years and had gotten along just fine, hell, he was my best friend. Why mess it up?

Momma said she didn't think Shelly would change like that, he seemed like a good man. By then, we'd known him eight years, and sure he could be controlling, but momma said he was just an OG. She really wanted me to take this chance.

"He's been very supportive and seems to genuinely have your best interest at heart. He goes to church and Bible study with you, sometimes, and not too many bad guys will go to church with ya. And he sure has been sweet to me. Yes, that say's a lot about a man; how he treats his family. I think Shelly will make you a fine husband, and a great son-in law. We haven't had a man around this family for a while and Shelly has been the man for us all lately. He's come to the rescue to fix stuff around the house, the yard, our cars. You name it, he's helped us fix it. That boy's a jack of all trades, he can fix just about anything.

"I don't know, Momma, Tyler doesn't trust him, thinks he's sneaky, think he's fake!"

"Well, baby, you know I love my grandson, but now... that boy ain't made for tuff stuff. We kinda spoiled him, he's kinda soft. Of course, he ain't gonna get along too well with a man like Shelly. But he's grown now. You deserve your own life."

"But Momma, I'm still scared."

"Well, baby, life is about chances, you've gotta decide if you want to take a chance."

I asked Shelly about it a few times. "Are you sure you want to marry me Shelly, me, really?"

He always reassured me. "Yes indeed, girl I've been waiting and praying for someone just like you all my life. I know you'd have my back no matter what, and that's the kind of girl a guy like me wants and needs, baby, we've been friends for eight years now, how long are you gonna make me wait? What else can I do to prove that I want you to be my wife, girl?"

"I just don't know... Tyler and you...."

"Now, c'mon, baby. Sure, I don't quite see eye-to-eye on how you raised that boy. But he's a grown-ass man now and seems to be trying to start a life of his own. Would be tougher if I had a hold of him long time ago. But I know that's yo baby, so I just leave that alone."

I'd heard, even then, that Shelly talked a lot of shit when he wasn't around me. My girl, Angela, even told me he said he had me "wrapped up in the palm of his hand," but I just thought that's how men talk. Other people said he could be quite obnoxious, that he had a real ugly side, but I'd never seen it. I even heard he flirted and messed around a time or two, but he always kept coming back to me. Why? I didn't know, but he was always good to me and my family.

I still couldn't decide, though. "Well, give me some time to think about it, Shelly."

"Take as long as you need, baby, but not too, too, long, we ain't getting any younger."

In my head, I was thinking, how many dates have you been on, girl? How many other men friends have you had lately, no, better yet, how many have you had in your whole entire life? I could count them on one hand. My relationships had always ended up the same, they act as if they loved me, then left me. Just like Tyler's dad, who really was my one and only. I never wanted to go through that kinda pain again.

All kind of things were running through my head, like the fact that, I'd been to Shelly's place a million times and he'd been to mine, but we'd never lived together, always just been buddies. Me living with a man that I wasn't married to? No, no matter how old I was, that was a big no-no for me. That was just how my momma raised me.

My head was just spinning. "Is he gonna know how to take care of you in bed, will he be gentle and patient with your disability? You haven't had much experience in that area, even though you got Tyler. Will you be able to please him, keep him satisfied? What if I snore too loud, what if he's got some hidden secrets that I don't know about? What about his hygiene? Does he brush his teeth at night? Cut his toenails? Will he leave the toilet seat up all the time? Pick his nose, not wash his hands after the bathroom? I hear some men can be so nasty. Would he would cheat on me? Or just stop doing sweet things for me?"

I couldn't turn it off. It seemed like I had a whole committee talking inside my head. Telling me all of the negative things that could and or would happen, and finally, I said to myself, Stella take a deep breath and calm down. Shelly had assured me that he loved me, only me, and that he'd never change. And he had always acted the same… always, that is, when he was around me. I'd heard people say "watch for the red flags," but, I still couldn't see any. Yet.

In the end, it was Tyler who helped me decide. I sat down one day and had a long talk with him, and he assured me he was okay with my decision.

"I just want you to be happy, Momma. If he makes you happy, that's all I need to know."

I finally accepted Shelly's proposal. He was so excited. He took me right away to pick out an engagement ring, a real nice one, white gold square cut with baguette diamonds on each side.

We started planning right away. Shelly picked the date, about six months after we got engaged, the same day his parents got married, figuring it was lucky 'cause they were together forever, but it was also my fiftieth birthday. I would be fifty and Shelly fifty-five.

I didn't want to go through the big ordeal of a wedding and have a lot of people whispering behind my back. I was always a little insecure with my disability and all, and it seemed as if it only got worse, once I knew I was getting married. I just didn't want to go through all that, so we decided we'd just do it at the court house, with just a couple of witnesses. No fuss. We decided, instead, we'd put all that planning and money into our new home.

For the next few months, before the wedding, we searched for the perfect house. Shelly had only two requests, a man cave and, at least, a three car garage with a shed out back, large enough to hold all of his toys that he called tools. I made sure there was room for that big 4x4 F-150 truck and Corvette, as well as room for my car. After that, it was up to me. We found a place to live in Midtown, close to work for both of us. Shelly'd worked for the

Sheriff's department thirty years and would retire soon. I'd worked at Swift Trucking service for twenty years. We purchased a very nice duplex on Evelyn Street, ten, maybe fifteen, minutes to work for both of us.

Soon as we bought it, we combined our stuff, had a yard sale to get rid of what we had double, and sold anything Tyler couldn't use in his new place, then moved everything in and planned to fix up the entire place exactly how we wanted it. We wanted it all set up before our wedding day.

We hired Clyde's Home Repair and Remodeling Company, and Shelly let me pick and design everything as I wished. Clyde's really hooked us up, everything just as I wanted. This was a huge old house, made into a duplex, it had so much character, and we were making it even better. It was quite unique, made with three levels. The first level had the entrance, our great room, laundry room, and one bathroom. The kitchen, dining, and wet bar (that we called the boom boom) was on the second level with a half bath, and the third level were bedrooms and our master suite.

Clyde did an awesome job, all the way down to restoring the old original fireplace in two of the bedrooms and bringing back the original hard wood floors. We had a room on the first level that we set up like a bar, nice art on the wall, a long black bar with glass on the front, and a ceiling wine rack. It had all the features that you could ever want and use for a bar.

We installed a five-eye gas burning stove, pot filer, granite counter tops in the kitchen and in all the bathrooms, pendant lighting and recess lights all over the house. We even installed an intercom system with XM radio. Upstairs, we had a walk through shower with spa shower system, double vanity sinks, even a heated toilet seat.

Shelly said I did an excellent job picking all the right colors in the house. The kitchen was a beautiful reddish rust color with honey mustard gold accents, then sage green going on in the bathroom, our master bedroom was a pretty greyish-blue with brown accents.

He even said I made the man cave just right for him. I knew he liked brown and I found the perfect brown leather sofa and matching recliner as well as a chaise lounge for when I come to hang out in the cave with him sometime. I found the perfect place for his precious gun cabinet and that 65 inch 3D TV. I even found a sign to hang above his door, "Welcome to Man Town."

He loved it. "Damn, baby! I didn't know you had interior decorating skills like this! Something else to make me love you!" He gave me a big sloppy wet kiss. We'd spent more money than we budgeted for, but I threw some in, too, and Shelly said it was all worth it.

It took almost three months to get the interior just as we wanted.

Then I started on the outside. I had a swing installed that hung from the porch ceiling and a ceiling fan. Mr. Clyde screened in the side porch which would allow us to enjoy the porch all year long, not just in the summer. The porch wrapped around all the way from the front down the entire left side of the house. It was perfect, and it ended up being one of our favorite places.

After all that renovation, we were just anxious to move in and get started on our life together. I was glad we hadn't planned a big wedding. In fact, it was short and sweet. Afterwards, Tyler hugged me and shook Shelly's hand, saying, "Take care of my Momma." Shelly said he sure would, and I thought everything was just perfect.

They were. For a while.

That first winter, we had a routine of lighting the fireplace every Friday evening and having a few drinks, for Shelly, Crown Black, and for me, sweet red wine. We played our oldies music, each picking a couple CDs, and make it a party, just us two. When a favorite song of mine or his came on that we both liked, it was nothing for us to break out dancing together right there at the house. Oh, what fun we had together! We didn't hafta have a crowd to have a party, we could party all by ourselves. Shelly didn't like much company at our house, just us two.

We loved going everywhere together. We got season tickets and hardly ever missed a show or a game. I bought the season tickets for GPAC, and he bought season tickets for the Orpheum, and we split the price for season tickets at the FedEx Forum for the Grizzly basketball games. Occasionally, we'd go to a Red Bird Baseball game.

We had no one to take care of but ourselves. Shelly had a grown daughter that he never really have much contact with, Tyler was doing pretty well on his own. I kept that spoiled ass dog of Tyler's named Ruddy for a while, but Shelly really didn't care much for dogs, so I sent him back home with Tyler once he got settled in his own place. Things were so great that, back then, I often wished Shelly had been around when Tyler was young. Maybe we could've had our own children, but you know God puts us where we're supposed to be when we're supposed to be there. Back then, I couldn't imagine it being any better. Every day I spent with Shelly used to feel like Christmas. He was good for me, and never once did he seem to mind my disfigured arm.

It wasn't long, though, before things changed. Shelly retired early. I still had to work. That's when this other Shelly came out! I started to see a different side of him. I learned that Shelly had a bad opinion of women, in general. He hated women that dressed provocative. Called women bitches, sluts, whores. He talked really, really bad about gay guys, not to mention two women being together. Called them, dyke bitches. Said women oughta know their place.

"The man is the head, the boss and women need to be obedient to their husbands. That's why there are so many lonely single women out there, they don't know how to shut the fuck up! That's why so many young men are fucked up and locked up. They ain't got no man around to keep their ass straight, 'cause women always trying to run some shit!"

When he got like that, I never said one mumbling word.

Sometimes, instead of going off like that, he'd just get distant, cold. Sometimes, he'd get too controlling, but for the most part, nothing I couldn't deal with. Just kept my mouth shut! I didn't dare tell a soul, because one thing he said, over and over, was you don't tell our business.

He scared me once when we were first married. I was just telling him about how I was chatting at the salon, telling something funny he did and he got really angry. Got right in my face. "You never tell anyone my business. You hear me? What goes on in my house, stays in my house. And if you ever want to see the ugly side of me, just let me find out you're telling our business."

He reminded me all the time about his "Golden Rule," so I kept quiet. About everything.

But, it got hard. Especially, when Shelly left our home. Even after he retired, he still wanted to do some kinda work. He took a part time job as a security guard for the VA. At first, he just started working more, five days a week instead of three. Then he started doing things like leaving his cell phone in the car instead of bringing it in the house to charge. The sweet text messages and phone calls he used to send me throughout his day stopped, too. He stopped coming home for lunch, and he no longer wanted the packed lunches I made for him.

I asked him, was he ok, but he'd just say he was fine, stop tripping, Lady.

I felt like the guy I married, loved, and cherished, my best friend, was creeping away! Like that song, "There's a Stranger In My House."

Then one day, he just didn't come home. He stayed away for three nights.

I couldn't get any explanation. Shelly had become so irritable, I couldn't even ask a question. He would instantly become defensive. And if I pressed, it'd send him into a screaming fit of rage. He suddenly had to work on Sundays, when, normally, he never worked on Sunday.

Very rarely, he acted like his old self. One Friday, it seemed like old times, we did our old Friday routine, put music on, laughed and danced together, just like old times. I was so glad to have him back, but I thought he seemed like he was getting a little sad. Then, we were slow dancing by the fireplace and he said, "Mmm, baby, I like the way you make me feel. Oh, Foy….Stella, I love you."

I was shocked. Had I heard what I thought I heard? Did he almost call me someone else's name? Then, I remembered, "Foy" was one of his coworkers. I had barely let myself consider it when he had stayed away, but now I knew my suspicions were right, he'd been messing around with someone else.

I knew I should just keep quiet, like always, but I couldn't help it. I couldn't just keep on dancing, like it was nothing. "Oh, Shelly! Why, why?"

He insisted she was just a friend, someone he could talk to. "I love you, Stella, and I'll always love you, and I'd never leave you. But, sometimes, I'd rather talk to someone else, someone who won't judge me or get hurt from whatever comes out of my mouth. It's not what you think, and... I wasn't always with her. Sometimes, I was just hanging out with my boy, Chad... he gets me."

"How could you, Shelly? When you made it so clear that I was to never, ever, tell anyone our business. Do you know how lonely I've been? Having no one to talk to. And you're off— Do you know how much that shit hurts?"

He never could answer that, just told me he wouldn't see her anymore. He didn't for a while, then it started all over again with someone else. I knew he'd come back to himself, eventually, so I tried to go on and live my life as if he never left, acting like I never knew he was cheating.

He'd stay with the girl, then come home, sometime, on the weekend, take care of the yard and whatever I told him that needed attention around the house. He'd check on his cars and tinker around with his tools in his shed out back. Then, he'd be gone again. It was the craziest thing. He could hardly look me in the eye, but he'd call every night to make sure I was home safe and say goodnight.

At one point, I thought it was absolutely crazy. When Shelly came back home next time, I tried to insist that we go for marriage counseling. Someone had told me about a place called Henderson and Henderson. They were supposed to be pretty good.

All I knew is I wanted my Shelly back! This was not the man I fell in love with, not the man I married. I thought maybe he was going through the change of life, just man style, and maybe they could help with that.

But Shelly wouldn't hear of it. There was nothing I could do and, after a while, I just got used to it. And he always came back.

Shelly took me on this rollercoaster for months and, then, suddenly, it just stopped. He came home and never went out alone or stayed out overnight, again. We went back to doing things as usual. I could feel something still wasn't right, but I didn't know what it was. He just seemed as if he was always in deep thought.

One day, out of the blue, he told me the whole story. "Stella, I have to tell you something. First of all, I've been going to counseling. I knew all along it was me who needed counseling not so much you."

Counseling? I could hardly believe it. But, I'd known for a long time, he was going through something. He told me the therapist prescribed some anti-depressants for him and that he's been taking them daily. I couldn't understand it. We used to keep each other informed about health concerns.

"Stella, well… in my therapy sessions, my therapist told me that I need to be honest with you. So, I'm going to tell you."

"Ok." I think I was holding my breath. I just had no idea what he had to say.

"I went for my annual checkup a while ago and… I didn't get such a good report."

My heart was pounding. "What is it?"

"I don't know how to tell you, Stell…." He looked down at the floor, couldn't seem to look at me.

My Shelly had such big beautiful hazel eyes… I missed them. I couldn't take it, anymore. "Shelly will you just tell me! It can't be that damn bad."

Then he blurted it out, with tears and screams all at the same time. And it was that bad.

"Hell, Stella, I have a tumor growing inside my brain. The doctor said they can operate but they will only be able to get about 80% of it. Then after that, chemo…. Stella, I can't live like that! I don't want that, surgery, chemo—"

"But, if there's something—"

"No! I won't do it. But, I gotta tell you, it's gonna be worse. This shit I have, it causes me to forget things. Soon, I won't know you, won't know how to get from my job to my house, how to spell my name or write, talk or walk."

"Oh my God!"

"Stella, I just want to tell you, while I still can. I'm sorry for the pain I've caused you. And.. if you feel that you don't want to put up with me anymore or what's to come…." He hung his head. "You can put me in some facility, some place where they can take care of me. I'd understand, I really would."

"Shelly, no, never, you're my husband, I love you. You're my best friend. I'm here for you, I always will be. No matter what."

But my best friend was gone.

He quit the part-time job. He stayed home and did nothing but drink, smoke cigarettes and weed, as much and as often as he could! It didn't go quite like he'd said. He never forgot who I was, but he changed in other ways.

His anger got worse and worse. He'd scream at me for any little old thing. He got paranoid. He took control of all our money. Monitored our bank account and questioned every single dime I spent. I had to explain when, why, and where!

He never wanted to eat out, anymore, thought people were trying to poison him, so I had to cook every day, but he insisted on going with me every time I went grocery shopping. Said he needed to make sure I didn't get the wrong things. He would only let me buy generic brands of everything. And when I cooked, he would throw a tantrum if it wasn't ready when he wanted it.

He wouldn't let me drive, ever, even though his driving was getting quite bad. Once he almost kept going through one of the busiest intersections at Poplar and Highland. He was making a left turn onto Poplar from Highland street and the light was red, he just lost it. It was almost as if he was in a daze! If I hadn't screamed, stop, Shelly! I think we'd both be dead.

He monitored the mail. He hid liquor all over the house, the pantry, linen closet, and couch pillows, even though we had a wet bar. He would talk about going to work, even though he'd been retired for a while. He'd always been a small man but I watched him decline faster than I ever thought possible, weight just dropping off him.

He kept changing the finances, so after a while, there was no joint bank account, no credit cards in our name, my name on nothing together with his. The phone bill, the cable bill, mortgage, Netflix account, cell phone, everything was in Shelly's name only. I had no idea how much money was in the bank, because he fixed it so I could no longer find out anything about our finances. The only money I had access too was my personal savings where I had part of my check going. I never went without anything I needed and nothing was ever disconnected, no bill collectors ever called, but I didn't know a damn thing about our finances whatsoever. He started forgetting passwords to everything, losing money, and accusing Tyler of taking it.

I avoided Tyler as much as possible, because I didn't want him to see how bad it was. I didn't want him to have to deal with Shelly. I avoided everyone, never told anyone the truth about what my life had become, being married to Shelly. I felt like I disappeared. I became a nobody.

It was a lot to handle on my own. One day, my friend, Angela asked me about it. "Stella, I can tell you've been going through some shit. Let's talk about it. What's going on?"

I just broke down and cried, but I didn't tell her anything. I wanted to tell someone, but… I wouldn't, I couldn't… I'd promised Shelly that I'd never tell our business. Shelly knew I would obey him, and that's why he married me, said he had me trained. He did. He'd always controlled me. I'd never understood why he wanted me, but I knew now.

Some of my friends will think I just felt sorry for him, and I did. Deep down, I could see through all of his insecurities, and I knew he loved me, and, despite everything, I loved him. I prayed each and every night for the old Shelly to come back to me and for his health. I stood by him, though he disrespected me and put me through hell in so, so many ways. I hated that it took me so many years to finally marry and I thought Shelly was the right one and he… he turned into a monster. Maybe, just maybe, it was the tumor eating at his brain that made him so crazy. I hoped so, 'cause I wanted to believe he was a good man, but, well… only the Lord knows.

Now, here I am, sitting here, watching people come and go at Shelly's wake. Some I know and others I've never seen before in my life. Damn, I bet everybody in this place has problems. Nobody knows, but my husband really killed himself, at least, he shortened his time. I never thought it would progress so fast. I begged him to get some kind of treatment, especially when he was being so awful to me.

One day, near the end, he finally looked at me, I mean really, really looked at me with his big beautiful hazel eyes and said, "I'm sick, Stella. I'm so, so sick… and I've been trying to deal with it on my own. I didn't mean to hurt you, I didn't want to upset you, but I can't seem to help it! I'm pissed! I think, why me? Stella, I'm so sorry for the way I've been. I hate what's going on with me, the way I am right now, and I can't, and you can't, do a damn thing about it!"

I sat down next to him. I knew it was probably too late by then, but I still had hope, and faith, maybe the Lord would help us if we helped ourselves. "Shelly, chemo could help, radiation could shrink it, why not at least try?"

"Hell, no, Stella, I don't want no chemo. I'm just dealing with it in my own way. I'm doing the best I can! So, just… give…. me…. a… fucking… break!"

I didn't know what else to do. He'd made his choice and talking about it just made him angrier. I started to go get him some lunch, but he called me back.

"One more thing, I want you to know. I know you thought I was out cheating on you, had me a side piece and all, but I wasn't. I never did. I'd just stay over at the Marriott, crying and cursing this damn tumor. And drinking till I'd blacked out."

I was so sad. I never dreamed it would get that bad, but it did. I just held his hand, so thin and frail. "I love you, Shelly, and we'll get through this… And, if that's your final decision, you don't want to fight, then I accept that. I won't leave you, I've got your back, baby."

And now he's gone.

Now, I'll have to deal with all the bills, the bank, the mortgage company, everything. I don't know where to start. I'm gonna hafta get someone to help me sort through the mess Shelly left. I've never told anyone our business, but I have got to confide in someone, now. I think I'll ask my brother, Vincent.

He's been practicing law for a long time, and I know he does a lot of work with Probate Court. He'll know what to do. Shelly never wanted me to tell our business, but Shelly's gone, and it's time to tell somebody my business now.

MS. LORETTA A. FRANKLIN

I'm tired of men, such assholes they are. Nothing but momma's boys. Where are the real men at? I'm so fed up. I think I'll just focus on myself for now. I know one day soon my ship will finally come in. While I'm waiting, I have to get my taxes filed. I've only got about two weeks left. I've been so wrapped up in trying to figure out how to buy new furniture to replace and fix up this damn place since Marlon moved out. Damn man took everything he ever bought, even took the damn towels.

I hope Spencer can fit me in. At least, Marlon didn't take the phone--

"Spencer's Tax Services."

"Hi, Mr. Spencer, it's Loretta Franklin. It's that time of year again. Do you have time for me to come by this week? I know you're probably busy, but when's your next opening?"

"Hold on little lady, let me get my appointment book. Let's see, next opening I have is Friday, April 10th. All I have left is an opening at 2:00 p.m."

"Two works for me. The Henderson's don't mind if I take off a bit early."

"Okay, Loretta, I've got you down. Do you have the address to our new location?"

"No, I didn't know you'd moved."

"Yeah, not far from my old place, 7647 Bellevue, more accessible, you know? And you won't have a problem parking anymore. There's plenty of space now."

"Great. I'll see you then, thanks."

Good old Mr. Spencer, he's been preparing my taxes for the last eight years, about time he got a bigger place with ample parking. At the old place, it was always a bitch parking, and there was never enough seating in the office either. He always had more customers than seats or parking spaces. Such a nice man and I like how he takes care of business. I call him "the black business man from Memphis." He stays on top of all the new tax laws, rules, and regulations, and he'll let you know that up front. He has a sign on the wall that says, "I don't lie, beg, borrow, or steal, and I DON'T CHEAT THE IRS." He always says never play with them, they are the real gangsters. But, he'll get you everything you're entitled to.

But, me, I don't seem to be entitled to anything. I thought about going to someone else, because I never get any damn money back. I never owe, but I don't get a damn dime back either. Some of my friends go to Sho Money Taxes and they always get big refunds, even though they have the same status as me. But, I think somebody's stretching the truth a little bit. Hmm!

On the other hand, how can I expect a refund? I don't have any dependents, I don't own any property, nothing to write off at all, what can I expect? Every year, Spencer tells me the same thing, "You just need one dependent or you need to buy some property." And, I tell him that's okay, because that refund would cost more than I want, it ain't worth it. That dependent would cost me more than a yearly tax refund, for at least the next eighteen years, and that property would cost me for a good thirty. I always say, that's okay, I'll pass.

I got to Spencer's Tax Service fifteen minutes early, brought all my papers, receipts from my church donations, Goodwill, and two for casino jackpot winnings. Don't get them too often these days. I hardly ever hear of any of my friends winning jackpots like they used to. Parking was a breeze. The new place had a longer wheelchair ramp and wider doors than the old one. Oh, that's what he meant, "accessible."

Mr. Spencer has always been thorough and accurate, but a little slow. It usually takes him about two hours to prepare my taxes, but he was always chatty while he looked over my receipts. He started out commenting on the winter we'd had, some news story he'd read…. He told me about his horses and a trip he'd been on at Christmas…. "But what about you, Ms. Loretta Ann Franklin." He said it kinda joking, like he was reading it off the form. "What have you been up to since last year? Still with that fellow you were with? Tell me how you been?"

"Good, great..." I said, great, but it was a lie. Those forms may look like I'd made some money, but once I replaced the stuff Marlon took, I'd hardly have enough money to pay Spencer for my tax return. Still, I hesitated to say anything more personal. I've always liked Spencer, he's always so pleasant, and I do always remember to send him a card at Christmas, but once a year at tax time is the only time I ever really speak to him. We know almost nothing about each other. I knew he'd been in some kind of accident when he was young and, I guess, he knew I'm a (SBF) single black female and a hard worker, or, anyway, he knew my salary. It had never occurred to me to talk about my personal life with him, but something about the way he was asking was so warm and comfortable and we'd been sitting here in his cozy little office talking already for nearly an hour... for some reason, I answered him for real. "Thing is, no, we're not together. The relationship, two years, is just breaking up."

He stopped writing and looked up from my return. "I'm sorry to hear that. Are you okay?"

"I am, just okay. But, that's one of the reasons I'm hoping I'll get that refund you promised me last year. I'm trying to replace the things he took when he moved out."

That raised an eyebrow. "That bad, huh? That kind of stuff always seems awfully petty to me."

"I know, right?" I meant it to sound angry, but it came out sounding a little weak.

Spencer changed the subject back to taxes, "Looks like you followed my instructions and paid more than you had to, so, yes, you should have a refund."

"Good, 'cause, if I'd had that money in my paycheck, I just woulda spent it by now."

Finally, he printed out my completed tax forms and had me sign. Just as I started to gather my stuff to leave, he said, "Would you like to go out with me for dinner sometime?"

He caught me totally off-guard. I'd never thought of him in any way other than the tax man, a nice man, but nothing more. Hell, I didn't even know his first name, thought the initial was "A," but had no idea what it stood for, never really cared. "You know, that's a really nice offer and maybe, one day, I'll take you up on it, but, right now, I'm in that don't-like-the-male-species-much mode."

"I understand, take your time." He looked a little disappointed and, it occurred to me, he might think I was putting him off for other reasons. Really, though, it had nothing to do with anything except I wasn't ready to date and, maybe, that I just didn't feel like I knew him well at all.

"I'm really just not ready to date, yet."

"I do understand." He nodded and smiled, and it seemed genuine. "You know, Ms. Loretta Ann Franklin, I've admired you for about... what...? How long have you been coming here now? Seven? No, eight years now." He tapped his pencil on his mahogany desk. "I just never had the nerve to say one word about it to you, but somehow, when you told me you were not in a relationship, today...." He shrugged. "I guess I finally got enough nerve to ask." He smiled and leaned over the table to hand me copies of my completed forms, "You know if it took me this long to ask you out," then his voice dropped lower and deeper, "I can wait a while for you to say yes."

I felt my face grow hot and I didn't know what to say. I stood up to take the forms and shake his hand, then felt awkward when he stayed seated. I just turned and grabbed my purse and jacket. On the way out the door, I stammered something like, "I'll give you a call. Thanks again for fitting me in, and I'm glad I listened to your advice for getting that refund."

My heart was beating a little fast and I felt a little sweat in my armpits as I walked to my car, I definitely felt the heat back there. By the time I got in my car, though, I was wondering if I'd embarrassed myself. Should I have shaken his hand while I was still sitting? Was that insensitive? Did he think I'd turned him down because he was in a wheelchair? Had I? No, definitely not. That had been the last thing on my mind. What I'd really been thinking was, oh damn, here you go again. The first thing that flirts with you, and bam. ..you go for it, forget about how much you hurt the last time, yeah, yeah, one half-decent man pays attention and I get CRS (Can't Remember Shit)!

Ok, so I really wasn't ready, but maybe a bit later…? I mean he's pretty stable, and he's not half bad looking, and he's not married. But, would we have anything in common? Then I thought, no, shut up, head! Don't even go there. Don't even consider starting up that shit. You're just tired, frustrated, lonely, and that's what has gotten you into trouble so many, many times before. I decided to put the whole thing out of my head for… I don't know… a month. Let me be single for a while. Yeah, a month, then I'd think about dating someone. I just needed a little distraction and shopping is great for that.

Now that I knew the amount of my refund, plus the two thousand I'd saved in the bank I was gonna do a little shopping. I left Spencer's and headed straight for the places I had on my list: HHGreg, Best Buy, TJ Maxx, Ashley Furniture and Haverty's, and this new store I heard about called Home Goods.

I shopped around for the best prices on flat screen TVs, a Blu-ray player, as well as new living room and bedroom furniture. I even needed sheets, I can't believe that fucker. He even wanted his sheets back. What a punk ass. I lay-a-wayed my linen and towels at TJ Maxx. I timed it just right. My layaway should be due out just after I got my refund. Mr. Spencer had told me when to expect it in my checking account. I remember my friends use to get frustrated about their tax refund taking so long to get back, but these days, it's quick, maybe ten days or a couple weeks. I kinda like this refund stuff. It's a first for me. All of my girlfriends get so excited whenever tax time comes around. They plan for it. They take trips or buy something special that they've wished for all year long. Valarie said, this year, she was going to get her neck tightened by Dr. Kolh. Faye said she needed to get a new compressor for her car. And me, I'm gonna use mine to replace everything my ex-asshole has taken away.

I put my shopping in the car and started thinking about some more shit I needed done, oil change about due on the car, Marlon usually did that, I should really deal with the library fine that I didn't owe for when Marlon took my card, it wouldn't hurt to weed the yard, but then… I realized, if I did all that stuff, I'd really just be stressing about Marlon and the breakup all weekend. I'd taken off early on Friday to get my taxes out of the way, but did I really want to spend the whole weekend doing boring chores and stressing about Marlon? Then, I realized all I'd done since Marlon left is work and stress, work and stress, work and stress some more. I hadn't done one single fun thing for myself. Okay, Loretta, you are not going to let Marlon ruin another weekend. Time to pick yourself up, dust yourself off, and get it together! Life goes on.

So, in that second, I forgot all about waiting a month and decided to give Mr. Spencer a call after all. Hell, what did I have to lose? He should be wrapping up those last minute tax clients for the evening about now, so I dialed his number. It rang for a minute, then his voicemail answered. I looked at my watch. Oops, it's 5:15, he closes at 5:00, I must've just missed him. I hung up without leaving a message, then, I thought, no, he probably still gets his messages, even on the weekend, so I called back and left one, "Hello, um… this is Loretta A. Franklin. Give me a call at your earliest convenience." As soon as I hung up, I realized, from that message, that he'd probably think there was some problem with the taxes. I didn't want him to think that. I called back. "Um, this is Loretta again, give me a call, when you have time. I… I'd like to take you up on your invitation." I hung up feeling about fifteen. When he didn't call back all evening, I felt pretty silly and wished I hadn't said I'd go out with him at all. I decided if he called, I needed to sound like an adult and not one so desperate.

But, when he called back the next morning and asked if I wanted to go out that night, I thought for a minute that I didn't want to seem so eager, should I say I was busy… but then, what the hell? I wanted to have fun THIS weekend. I accepted and we decided to meet for dinner.

He offered to pick me up, of course, but I declined. On first dates, I always meet up with the person, not have the person pick me up. I've always just been really cautious about other people driving me, you never know. So, I arrived on my own to Houston's, not too fancy, not too plain, just right. When I arrived he was already at the table he'd picked for us. I'd dressed in a simple, but nice, Jones of New York pantsuit with my bronze *Franco Sarto* flats, and I wore my hair pulled back in a bun. Dinner was very nice, and he was quite a charmer. We talked easily. He even made me laugh a few times.

We talked about everything, and I found out we, surprisingly, did have a lot in common. We both liked jazz, not smooth jazz, but that original old school stuff like Miles Davis, Billy Holiday, Etta Fitzgerald, Tony Bennett, Frank Sinatra, and more. He even liked my favorite a cappella group, Take 6. He loved the theater as much as I do, and he'd been to several performances out at GPAC, too. Finally, for once, a man who knew, and liked, Savion Glover, the best tap dancer around these days, the best since Sammy Davis and Gregory Hines. He said he'd been to, and loved, so many of the same places that I've been – a Broadway play in New York, the wineries up in the redwoods of California. He even appreciated a good massage from Gould's. We liked some of the same wines, German wines (Riesling, especially). I thought, can this be true? A male version of me? I found out he even subscribed to *Jazziz* magazine just like me. I had so much fun talking and laughing with him that I forgot the time. I looked at my watch, and it was after ten. The restaurant would be closing at eleven.

I said, we'd better go, it's near closing time. He thanked me for a lovely evening and gave me a gentle kiss on my hand. We waited for the valet to bring his car around. Now one of the things I notice on a man is his shoes. Cheap shoes, cheap man, expensive shoes, better class of a man, well, that is, most of the time. Spencer had on expensive shoes, and I know my shoes – his were nice classic Guccis. Then the car came – a beautiful black Mercedes CLK. I thought to myself, this man is a baller! Lord, knows I have met way too many crawlers! And he drives himself. I watched him interact with the valet getting in his car. I was intrigued, I wanted to know more. His car had to be custom-made.

One week later, we went to see a play, Lion King. I arrived a few minutes late, and Spencer texted me to pick up my ticket at will call. The usher directed me to a great seat in the mezzanine. When Spencer saw me, he gave me a gentle kiss on my hand. I thought, what a sweet man, such a gentleman. I enjoyed the play. The costumes were beautiful and the music amazing. When I was on the edge of my seat during the big fight scene, out of the corner of my eye, I caught him smiling at me. He held my hand and gave it a little squeeze. It was a really nice evening, but as soon as I turned my phone back on, I saw I had a missed call and a voicemail. From you-know-who - Marlon.

I waited till I got home to listen to it. I put it on speaker and listened as I got undressed for bed. "Hey Loretta, I forgot to get my fiesta dishes and my ceiling pot rack. I need to get them as soon as possible. Hit me back and let me know when I can swing by to pick them up, holla."

What, he had some kind of fiesta dish emergency? What a jackass! The whole thing pissed me off, but, then I thought, fine, if that's what it takes to be rid of your ass forever, so be it. I called him back and left a voicemail, as well. "Marlon, Loretta. I got your message. Your stuff will be outside on the porch Monday evening after work. No need to call or knock."

I was a little extra busy at work Monday, catching up from the three-day weekend. It was good to have the distraction so I didn't get too nervous about Marlon coming by. As soon as I got home, I shoved his box of stuff on the porch and went inside locking the door behind me. I heard his car pull up and sit idling on the street within a half hour. I wanted to just ignore him, but I peeked out the window as he loaded his stuff into his trunk. Some girl was in the car waiting for him. I was pissed that he brought her along, but when they drove away with his stupid pot rack sticking up out of his trunk, I didn't feel bad. I was surprised, but it felt pretty good to watch him go. I just felt done.

In the end, Marlon was just one more man like all the others I'd been with. I don't know what it is, but it seems like I always get the same kind. They all start out showering me with gifts and money (I think there must be some kind of sign on my forehead that only they can see) and then bam! Something happens, and I end up holding the short end of the stick and have to start all over a-damn-gain. I am so tired of starting and stopping. Like all of 'em, Marlon was good to me in the beginning. He brought fresh flowers every Thursday. Every Friday night, he faithfully took me out to dinner. He always went to church with me, too, each and every Sunday, and every other Saturday night we'd go out clubbing or to the movies. He was at my house more than his own, so six months in, we decided to move in together. Since my house was larger, he moved in with me.

Marlon kept buying me gifts. He bought all sorts of things for the house. And he fixed things. He replaced wood and remodeled my storage room into a quaint little back house. He bought towels, pictures, linens, lawn furniture, and even flowers to plant outside of the house.

On each of Marlon's paydays, twice a month he gave me $800 toward... whatever. Since I had him splitting the cost, I stopped sticking to my own budget. I started spending more money than I should have on things for myself, things that I wouldn't have ordinarily purchased, things way out of my price range. Like, a new Michael Kors purse, Furula purse, coach shoes, baguette diamond ring and earrings to match, getting my hair done every week, Brazilian weave, my nails done every two weeks.... Never once did I think, Loretta, save some of your money so that you can get yourself ahead. Just about the time my credit card payments got too high to be comfortable, Marlon started to show his true colors and things went south fast.

Now, as I look back, I mean, honestly, look back, at my track record with the men I've had in my life. It's always been the same. The same kind of man seems to find me over and over. Guess that sign on my forehead that says, "give me money and shower me with gifts, and I'll be all yours." But, I just can't seem to pull it off for long. I don't have what it takes to put up with their shit. I want the money and gifts, but the price is too high. I'm thinking now it's a luxury I can't afford. I'm just too stubborn, too spoiled, too single, or just too much of a grown-ass woman to put up with all the shit it takes to be taken care of by a man like that.

Of course, it's not just me. I've got girlfriends that don't do any better with men, some of them a lot worse. Like Beatrice, who will only talk to a man based on what kind of car he drives and where he works, in hopes that he will shell out just as much money on her as he does for his car and clothes. Then there's Charlene who will only talk to older married men. She claims they really know how to treat a lady, yet she has nothing, and they never leave their wives for her. The last guy died after she'd spent five years with him and she didn't get a dime.

And, poor Lillian, who likes to meet men online, met this creep who talked her into transferring from Memphis to Tulsa to live with him. She thought they'd get married. Online, he said he had a great executive position at Tulsa World, the biggest newspaper in town. It turned out, it was true he did work there, only his position was temporary clerk, not executive. Oh, he was as fine as his pictures, but didn't have a pot to piss in. He was six months behind on his rent. He also had a Mercedes like he told her, only it was a 1980 model. But, Lillian goes for those young ones that look good and are built, so that's what it got her. Fucking stuck in Tulsa where she knows no one. Thank God for my big sister Virginia and her family. I called and they were nice enough to let her stay with them for six months until she could get herself together and find her own place. Lillian's still there working day in day out, paycheck to paycheck. She knows if she comes back home with nothing, she'll hear nothing but I-told-you-sos from me and her family. So with her pride and stubbornness, she's still there toughing it out. At this rate, she figures she has to work at least two years before she can transfer back home again.

With all the horror stories from my girlfriends, their friends, and their friend's friends, and my own personal experiences, I plan to take it very slow with anyone new I may come into contact with, including Spencer.

So, we took it slow. After the first few dates I started to get comfortable with him, and even though I'd known him for eight years preparing my taxes, I was just beginning to really know him. For two months, we went to dinner, movies, plays… somewhere every weekend. We were just getting to know one another a little better and better each time. Spencer was always such a gentleman, and he would often say, "I only want the best for you. And when you're with me, I'm with you all the way. That's how I do it, Ms. Loretta Ann Franklin!"

I'd had so much buzzard's luck in the past with men, I just knew that any day the table could turn and the real Amos Spencer (yes, his name is Amos) would come out. I kept expecting all the good times to end and it all to get ugly. I could feel a little hope deep down, that this would work out, but I was afraid. I mean, I always think, maybe, just maybe, this time will be different, never say never, but, hell, how many times have I said that? For a while, before Marlon, I thought Tyler was the one, he said got saved at church and was trying to go straight, but it wasn't working for me, I just didn't trust that. Then, let's see, I thought James was way cool, but he could not let go and stop talking about his ex-wife and was still bitter from their divorce. So, when I met Chad, I thought for sure he was the one, uhm....wrong again, he turned out to have some serious issues. But Marlon, we seemed to gel just right! I thought, two years in, and it was going just great, I was so happy. Marlon just suddenly up and decided it was over, no explanation, no warning, no nothing. Later, I found out he'd been trying to choose between me and some other chick named Brooke. Know how I found out? This heifer gets her taxes done by Spencer, too. As I was leaving, Mr. Spencer's secretary was calling for the next customer to go in and she said, Brooke Boatwright. I remembered seeing the name Brooke B as a missed call on Marlon's phone. Never gave it a second thought. Thought Brooke was a guy, but that's gotta be her. I'll figure out a way to ask Spencer later. She wasn't the only one either, a Natashia, he told me text messages from this girl named Natashia was for a potential car sale. Before that moment, I never imagined he could be cheating on me, just never saw it coming.

So, I kept expecting this thing with Spencer to fall apart, but so far it's been all good. I knew Spencer was looking for something serious, but he didn't mind taking it slow. He'd said, at one point, that he was tired of the dating games. He hadn't complained much about exes, he wasn't that kind, but he did say once that he was tired of dating women who were just looking for a free ride or who were just killing time with him waiting for something better to come along. I knew he'd had a couple of experiences being the "if all else fails, call Spencer" guy. I thought, poor Spencer, he'd been let down just as many times as I have. And he was such a good guy. Really, he seemed almost too good to be true and I was happy, but nervous, too.

Spencer knew all of my financial information from preparing my taxes every year, but he didn't try to get personal with me too soon, if you know what I mean. I had a few questions for Spencer though. I asked him about that customer whose name I heard when I was leaving his office, Brooke Boatwright. He said he used to work with her mother and now he prepared her taxes and… other things. I figured that meant there were some pretty serious money problems, because he'd told me he loaned people money when they were in trouble. All legal, but he did make a lot of money off it. Seemed ok to me. I told him I thought that Brooke woman was married to my ex.

"Umph! Small world." He still didn't tell me anything confidential, but he did smile and say Marlon deserved her.

"Good! I hope she's some kind of horrible hell cat who'll make him go broke! Serves him right!"

For a while, Spencer didn't try to get overly friendly, never asked me about sex. Once we passed the ninety day mark, though, his conversations started to get more personal. One night he started asking questions and ended up asking how I liked to be pleased in bed. I felt a bit shy and asked him to go first, and he just smiled, "I like to please, not tease." Then, he just asked point blank, "Do you like oral?" It was awkward, threw me, really, because I'd never heard him talk like that before. I wasn't used to him talking to me in any manner other than business or about plays or dinner. If I were light complexioned, I would've been red right then. In the end, I just changed the subject.

I knew soon he'd try to take it to another level, and, sure enough, shortly after that, my time ran out. A man gonna be a man no matter what! Valentine's Day is always a little awkward for a new relationship. People are always afraid of doing too much too soon, so I was surprised when Spencer asked me to take off a long weekend for a first class trip to Lake Tahoe and Reno.

I told Spencer I needed to check to see if I could get the days off. Valentine's is kinda busy at a marriage counselor's office. But, I also just wanted a little time to think about it. To be honest, I was nervous in general. With AIDS and all kinds of new STDs, I was never too quick to jump into bed with someone new. And, to be frank, I thought, what could he do, anyway? He's kinda old. He was 62 to my 42. I'd never really had any experience with an older man, and I was nervous about that, too.

But, the Henderson's said I could take a 4-day weekend and, before I could think long enough to get scared, I texted Spencer, *Luv 2 go 2 Tahoe/Reno w/u wknd approved* ☺. He made all the arrangements. The plan was two days in Lake Tahoe and two in Reno. We flew business class which I'd never done before. Getting on the plane was a breeze. He had special privileges for everything. We didn't have to stand in a long line at screening, our bags were checked at the curb, and they rode us in one of those airport carts straight to our gate. We even had special seating on the plane right in front.

When we checked in at the Lake Tahoe Lodge, the room was beautiful with a huge heart-shaped bed. There were red roses lying all over the bed when we got there, and in the bath, a Jacuzzi tub. I thought he must've asked for some special kind of accommodations because our room was exceptionally large. Everything first damn class, just as he'd said.

Spencer said, "When I ask a girl to go with me, she's with me all the way. Once we leave here, we'll head for Reno and do a little gambling there. I'll give you $300 a day, and if you lose it before the next day, you're on your own. How does that sound to you?"

I smiled. "Sounds like fun, I think I can handle that."

We were a little tired from traveling, so we ordered room service our first night there. He said we're going to take our time and enjoy this trip. Room service brought us a bottle of Moët and Chandon champagne, and, for dinner, we had filet mignon, baked potato, tea, salad, and strawberry cheesecake for desert.

"After dinner, he said, Ms. Loretta A. Franklin, what's your pleasure?"

"I'm not sure what you mean."

"Would you like something to go with your champagne? Do you indulge in any mood or mind altering substances? I've also got some nice Djarum."

"Not really, I've tried a line or two of the white stuff around Christmas time and a few times every once in a while when I get with my girlfriend, Aja, and we have a toke or two, but nothing on the regular."

"Come on you're the youngest here, you mean you don't have any vices at all?"

"Not really." I joked. "Guess I have a natural high."

"Well, if you want to, this'll make you feel good, loosen you up a bit." He reached over to the bedside table and got out his shaving bag. He pulled out a plastic bag. It had what looked like joints, and there were about ten of them. "Why don't we get comfortable?" He said, slipping off the onyx ring he always wore on his left pinky and setting it on the bedside table. "Do me a favor and go see if you can figure out how to turn on that Jacuzzi."

I went to the bathroom to do as he asked, but I was a bit nervous. I thought, oh damn. He's coming on fast, I'm not sure…. Then I thought, what the hell, just go for it! The suite was already set with candles. They were placed all around the Jacuzzi. I lit them all and turned on the jets. I'd brought a sexy, short, silk romper in red with black lace trim. I slid into it and came out. He had changed, also. He had on red silk boxer shorts with a black silk smoking jacket. It was very classy and, you know, he had on Bally house shoes. And he smelled so damn good, as usual. I think he was wearing Sean John cologne.

First, I joined him near the bed, and he lit one of those special rolled cigarettes he had. I thought, I can do this, it's just weed. He lit, he pulled, he passed. I pulled, puff, puff, and passed, and no... it wasn't just weed, it was mixed with something else. Something that just mellowed me all the way out after a few pulls, made my lips numb. I thought, what is this shit? But, I didn't say one word, I pulled again and passed it back to him. After we puffed halfway down, he said, let's try the water.

I felt really good. I grabbed the champagne bottle on the way to the tub, he opened it and we made a toast and then kissed. Umm, he kissed good. I honestly couldn't tell if he really was a great kisser or if it was the shit he had me smoking. Didn't matter. We kissed for a while and headed over to the Jacuzzi. He slid out of his clothes and into the water, then held out his hand. I slipped off the romper slid in beside him. We sat for a Moment looking at each other, then he started massaging my neck, then my back, then kissing my ear, neck, lips, arms, and I thought, "Yes! This is how Valentine's Day is supposed to be!"

The room was dark with the exception of the candles, and we didn't do much talking at all after that. Just kisses and groping and whimpers and moans. I lost track of time, Spencer lit that special cigarette again. I inhaled, exhaled, and passed it to him. He did the same and finished it. We got out of the Jacuzzi and it seemed as if I floated to the bed. What a beautiful bed, the ceiling had mirrors, umh... umh... umh... I was just about to move over so he could get in as well but instead he got on his knees, grabbed me and turned me around to face him and pulled me down to the end of the bed to the position just like the OBGYN does when you go for a pap smear. Then he paused and said can I tell you what and how I'd like to do you, Ms. Loretta A. Franklin?

He whispered. I want to lick you all over; and as he spoke he was kissing my hands, my thighs, my legs, my navel, and ooh... I want to find out exactly what you taste like. I want to take my time with you. I'd like to first start with your pretty toes, then move on up and lick, kiss, and massage your long legs. Then I want to taste your belly button. I want to lick you all over on the front then turn you over and massage your back gently and kiss your back side everywhere, too. Then I want to use each of my fingers to see which one fits you best and once I do then I will spread your lips open wide and munch around to find out which munch makes the best lunch. I will enjoy it for as long as you let me or until I get full, whichever comes first.

He was doing all these things along with speaking them and I couldn't say one word! Then he said, however, if I miss a place or turn or munch, please feel free to let me know, I am willing and able to please. And then I will pour some of this delicious champagne down the middle of your breast and drink. Just his words of what and how he wanted to do me made me hot and soaking wet, and not from sweat.

That man did every single thing he said and more. I would have never thought this man could be so damn good, so sensuous. Afterwards we moved to the sofa in the lounge area of our suite. He came close to me, slowly, close enough to where we could hear each other breathing. I could feel his breath on me, and I could smell me on his breath.

Then Spencer lifted his champagne glass, "Let's toast. Here's to us! Happy Valentine's Day, Ms. Loretta Ann Franklin."

I raised my glass, "Here, here."

Then he backed up and gave me the usual soft kiss on my hand, then my arm, then my neck, then my lips. He was so gentle, so sensuous. He then refilled his drink and poured more champagne in my glass as well.

"Would you like to go out and see the town a bit?"

"Only if you want to. I could just stay here and relax until tomorrow. I feel great."

"It has been a long day. Can I do anything else to make you comfortable? Want to just relax by the fireplace and listen to some music?"

I thought the fireplace was about all I can handle, honestly. I was so toasted I could hardly move and I was feeling a bit giddy. I said Spencer I need you to get one more thing for me, it will complete my night. He said what, baby, anything for you. I need some jelly, and he said jelly? I said yes, because I'm TOASTED! That put a big smile on his face. He said, yes, ma'am, I aim to please.

We got comfortable and cuddled by the fireplace. We smoked some of his special treats again, and I tried the Djarum clove cigarettes he'd brought, very nice. About all I remember afterwards was climbing into bed and him rubbing me down with some kind of oil.

When I came to, it was noon, about two in the afternoon back home. He was still sleeping beside me. I went to the closet and found something to wear. Went in the bathroom to shower, then did my make-up and got dressed while he showered. I wore my leggings and the Lake Tahoe shirt with rhinestones that he purchased for me when we first got here at check-in. He came out dressed in his Tommy Bahama shirt, and different shoes, a pair of bad ass Johnston Murphy's. And he still smelled good, but a different fragrance. He picked up his ring off the bedside table and slipped it back on his little finger. The gesture made me blush remembering where his hands had been.

"Are you ready to hit the town, Ms. Loretta Franklin?"

"Ready!" And out the door we went.

We started out with breakfast, more like brunch, at our hotel buffet along with several mimosas, then we headed for the gaming area. He went to the crap table, and me, to the roulette. We set a time and place to meet just in case we got lost from one another. He was heading for his table and quickly turned around and said, "Oh, I almost forgot, here's your gambling money for the day."

I smiled and thanked him. After a few spins with nothing falling on my numbers, I found a two- coin, five dollar machine called triple lucky. I thought since I'm gambling at Spencer's expense I may as well play big and started to put in a $5. Then I heard my big brother's voice, God bless his soul, he passed away seven years ago now, my best buddy, saying to me, "scared money can't win!" So, I put a hundred dollar bill in the machine and… no, nothing. I fed another one into the same machine, and… no. Finally, I had just two coins left, and I hit something! Lights were flashing and the machine was ringing… $5000! Hot damn! Wow, wait till I tell Spencer.

All sorts of people passed by me trying to count my winnings. Some old man passed and said that's $15,000. Then, someone said, no, that's $50,000. Then this little lady that looked just a little crackish said, no that's just $500. Me, I just sat there with this huge smile on my face, smoking my Djarum clove cigarette, waiting patiently for them to come and pay me. It took them forever to come and pay me off. They deducted 25% taxes right away and gave me some tax forms. I thought that was pretty funny given who I was there with, the tax man! Even then, they handed me a bunch of cash and I couldn't stop smiling. I thought to myself, I am loving this…please, Lord, if this is a dream, don't wake me yet!

I saw Spencer over at his table, but he looked like he was rolling the dice. I didn't want to distract him from his game just yet. I took a walk over to the gift shops and boutique area to find myself a little souvenir of my win. I bought some glitzy earrings, then headed back. I was excited to show Spencer my winnings.

He looked up as the dice were passed to the next roller. "Hey, baby, I'm on a roll, help me get up on that stool, these people ain't worth me looking up to! So, I put the brakes on and assisted him as he backed up to the stool, then lifted himself with his arms and hopped up on to it. Then, as he usually did, patted my hand, kissed it and said, sit down and give me some lady luck. How did you do? Are you out of money?"

"No way, I just won a $5000 jackpot!"

"You shitting me?" He grinned.

Nope. I waived my handful of cash. "I got a tax form here for you to prove it!" We both laughed, then I saw his chips were stacked pretty high. He must've had about 30 chips and they were black and white. As I looked closer, I saw that they were $100 chips, then a couple of gold and black chips, worth $500 each. He then reached in his right side jacket pocket and said "oh", this one is for you! It was a pretty multi-colored chip, which was worth one thousand dollars. I said for me, he said, yes, baby! We both were having a great time. Looked like lady luck was on our side.

"Okay, one more round, baby, and then we'll head for dinner? Wow, time flies when you're having fun, right? We left our hotel room at noon and it's already 7pm."

"Hey, Spencer, I have a question. Is this my allowance for the next few days?

"No this is extra. Tomorrow you still get the $300. I promised daily even if you are a jackpot winner!" He paused, then said, I want you to know you're a jackpot winner, baby, every day you're with me!

My mind was racing, I couldn't believe it, I was having the time of my life, but, for once, I was thinking clearly. I was thinking I'm going to the casino cage and transfer $3000 of this straight to my bank account. This time, I don't plan on forgetting who I really am. I need to save some of this money, so it can help me straighten out some of my financial woes back home. Plus, with my lousy track record with relationships... well, I'll just enjoy the ride while it lasts.

We had a wonderful dinner at Friday's Station Steak house on the top floor, the 19th, of Harrah's Casino overlooking the city. We had filet mignon again and the biggest crab legs already split and buttered that I'd ever seen. Then we headed over to the cigar bar at Hotel MontBleu, what an awesome casino and hotel. I ended up buying a few things at the boutique called Something Bleu. We walked around and looked at the different shops. He had a Cuban cigar and I had another clove. They had a store called Romantic Adventures and I was a little bit shy going in because they had every kind of erotic cream, lotion, gadget you could ever imagine. But, Spencer talked me into it. That place made me blush. Spencer picked and I paid for the items we bought. When I checked the time on my cell phone it was 12:45 a.m. I think for our first full day we'd done pretty well. I stopped at the concierge desk before going back to our room and found out where I could send money to my bank.

"That's a smart move, Ms. Loretta Franklin, you amaze me more and more each day. He gave me a soft kiss and we headed back to the room."

When we got there, he went to work on me again. I was lost in passion... bliss... and when he felt like he had taken me to Mt. Everest, he slid in bed. He said I need you to get on top of me... I do my best work with you on top. I was so lost in ecstasy he could've changed into Dracula... I was so ready... He was just as tender at love making as he was with each kiss that I'd gotten from him on my hand all the months prior to this night.

When we finished, we lay there in each other's arms and he said, "Happy Valentine's Day again, Ms. Loretta Franklin, I hope I've made it a happy one for you."

"All I could do was say... yes... indeed, you have." I snuggled up next to him and fell softly asleep. The next day in Tahoe flew by and then it was time to head for Reno. Spencer surprised me with a limo service to take us there. The hour drive was beautiful. There was a light dusting of late snow everywhere and we seemed to be cutting a path through it. It was all so romantic. We stayed at the Atlantic Casino Resort and Spa. They had everything there with a nice adult atmosphere. Not a lot of the young wild kids like I hear are in Vegas these days.

When we first got to the hotel, Spencer tried to give me another $300. But, at the last minute, I turned him down. I was feeling so secure since I'd deposited money in my account and I still had way more than enough. I thanked him. "Spencer, I'm okay now, I can support myself. If I find out I need it, later, I'll tell you, but I'm good now, thank you. It's just... you've done so much, more than enough, you've been so sweet."

"Okay, baby, just say the word, your wish is my command."

The bellman got us checked in up to our room. Another fabulous room, two remote controls that controlled everything, the TV, the curtains, the lights, marvelous. We spent most of our time in the room. We only gambled on our first evening here and it seemed as if we were just losing money. Not winning anything. I lost $500, so quick it made my head swim. I went to the crap table and checked with Spencer and he was down about $800. We made a pact to play for one more hour, then go to dinner.

The restaurant was very romantic, only lit by candlelight. After dinner. we walked around a bit. We bought a bottle of wine from the package store downstairs, then headed back to our room. Once we settled in, it was just as before except this time we used a few of the toys we'd bought at the store in Tahoe. I opened the wine and Spencer again pulled out his little black bag, and we had fun with each other all over again. As we lay in bed listening to the jazz station I found on XM radio, we talked.

Spencer asked, "How far are you willing to take our friendship, Loretta Franklin? I know you just got out of one, are you ready to try again? I don't want to rush you or take you too fast. I'm looking for someone to be real with. It's been a long time since I even had the courage to try again with my condition and all. You've been very patient and kind with me. Pushing me around and all. You even were okay when I ran over your toe that you had to bandage up back at the hotel in Tahoe."

I laughed and tried to stop him thanking me. "It was my pleasure, baby, I've had a great time!"

"Yeah, but you've been really patient, helping me scuffle to get into the Jacuzzi and you definitely figured out how to adjust to the position I must be in to make love. And, how you rode in my lap back to our room after we both had one drink to many, and you didn't care who saw us."

"Of course not. Any woman would be proud to be with you."

"Not always. I know it's a lot to take in. But I feel so good with you. You seem to be real. In the past, all I've run into is women who want me for a season. After they get what they want or someone else comes along, they disappear. I want someone to be in my corner, no matter what, you know? I feel like you could be the girl I've been searching for, I don't want to say too much, but… I think you're the one for me, Ms. Loretta Ann Franklin."

"Well, Mr. Amos Spencer, I've never been with a man quite like you. You've been so kind, and certainly been a gentleman. Am I ready? The answer is, yes, Amos." I paused. "You know, I like Spencer better than Amos. How about I call you Spencer, and you can just call me baby. I'm more than willing to give this a try. Let's go for it. We'll just take it one day at a time."

*

We'd been together about six months and had a lot of fun, and we'd started to get more serious, like I'd made a few adjustments at my house to accommodate him, and he'd done the same for me at his house. We were really starting to be a couple, so when, he told me one of his clients had passed away, and asked if I'd accompany him to the visitation and funeral, I said, of course I would.

Well, I met him at the funeral home, and wow, when I pulled up, JJW and Sons was packed! I thought, they don't have enough room at this place for all of these people. Lord, if this many are here for the wake, I hate to see the funeral tomorrow. So many people I didn't know. It made me a bit nervous realizing I'd probably meet a lot of Spencer's friends here.

When we went in, first thing Spencer did was sign the guest book, then he started talking to me in his deepest baritone voice. To be honest, I felt kinda awkward because I'd never been around him on a sad occasion, never seen him sad at all, even though, he has plenty of reasons to be or to justify sadness if he wanted to.

He was telling me about the man that died. "He was actually a distant cousin, but we weren't close. I've just been doing the old joker's taxes for years, and he was always such a happy-go-lucky kinda guy, though, truth be told, kinda obnoxious, too. I never knew he was sick, or anything. I still don't know what happened."

Then some guy sitting in front of us overheard our conversation and turned around in his seat. "You didn't hear? Old Shelly had cancer, something in the brain, and didn't want anyone to know. He wouldn't take radiation, no chemo, no nothing. They're saying all he did was smoke weed." The man shook his head sadly. "That's my dawg, too! We used to shoot pool together, cool cat, but ornery, and stubborn as hell. Well, he made it a year and a half. If you knew him like I knew him, that's just how he was. His pride and ego wouldn't let him tell or ask anybody for help. I can't imagine what his poor wife, Stella, went through."

I told him I was sorry for his loss. "Seems everyone that has interacted with Shelly says the same thing. He will definitely be missed!"

The man nodded. "Well, may he rest in peace. He was a cool dude."

He turned around and Spencer turned to me, more serious than I'd ever seen him. "You know, this kind of thing… it makes you think…." He sighed, then looked right in my eyes. "Well, Ms. Loretta Franklin, I pray I live a long, long time. At least long enough for us to do and see everything we'd like to while we can, baby."

I squeezed his hand. "Of course, baby, me, too."

"You know, Ms. Loretta Franklin, I can do just about everything to satisfy your every need. I can satisfy your monetary needs, your sexual needs, your entertainment and travel needs. And I can be the best companion you could ever want. The only thing, I can't do is be your dance partner. I've been in this wheelchair most of my adult life. I can't walk, and I never will."

"Spencer, I'm over that, and I'll push you any damn where you want to go. You've been a better man to me than most men walking. I'll be with you right to the end. I've met enough walking losers to last a lifetime. And I certainly never met a man who made me feel the way you've made me feel in bed." I lowered my voice, whispered right in his ear. "Oh! Damn, baby, I shiver just thinking about the last time we made love, umh…umh…umh… Most men I've been with walking can't even do one of the many things you've done right for me." I smiled at him. "I say, yes, I would love for this relationship to go as far as we can take it. Now, I'll need a little more practice learning how to accommodate you with your disability. I still have questions, but I'll learn!"

As we were leaving the funeral home, with me pushing Amos in his wheelchair, I'll be damned who did I see? Sorry, deceitful, disappointing ass, Marlon. I wondered…who did he know, Spencer's cousin, Shelly, or his wife. I watched to see which way he went and he went straight to the deceased's wife. I could barely hear what he was saying, but what I did hear was, "Sorry, cuz, you had a good man, be strong, it takes time to heal, girl. Let me know if

I can help you in anyway." I heard her say, "thanks, cuz, thanks for coming." He said, "Sure, Stella, I'll see you tomorrow."

I tried to hide by turning sideways in an effort that Marlon wouldn't notice me. But he did, I rolled my eyes at him but didn't speak one word! I could feel myself getting hot, my adrenaline was flowing, my heart beating fast! But if you saw me from the outside I looked calm and cool. But my insides were steaming as loud as a tea kettle ready to boil over! How long, how fucking long had he been trying to decide between me and that Bitch… Brooke! I was mad all over again! I watched him stroll out of the Funeral Home with his, now, wife, like he was da shit! Fuck it! Fuck him! I've got Spencer now and he's a good man, screw Marlon's punk ass! And as if he forgot something, he walked back in the door and headed straight to me. Spencer was on the other side of the room chatting with other family and friends of Shelly. There I was standing alone, couldn't move, a large flower arrangement right in my path.

Marlon jerked his head toward Spencer. "Whew! that's what you've got now? Damn, you desperate, huh? Someone to push around, a motherfucker who can't even walk! Damn, I know you don't like being by yourself, but that's kinda pitiful girl!"

"Fuck you, Marlon, and the horse you rode in on! Get outta my face."

"Well, I'm just sayin!"

"Get away from me before I…."

"Before you what? Call yo man? To do what? Run over me?"

"Before I spit on your lying, cheating ass!"

He turned and walked away.

Spencer rolled up and said, "What's wrong, did I leave you too long? I'm sorry, I know you don't know these people. Loretta, you look like you've seen a ghost!"

"Well, kinda… Marlon… my ex… and we had words."

"What was he doing here?"

"I'll be damn if he ain't cousin to Shelly's wife… small world!"

"Don't let that upset you. You with a real man now, baby, you gonna be okay, aren't you?"

"You're right, Spencer, like I said, I'll push your ass around anytime, any day! You're the best man that has rolled up on me yet! Wish I could've met you sooner, let's roll, baby!"

JAMES HOBSON

Until I met Angela, I'd been pretty much down in the dumps. I'd been divorced for three years and I hadn't let go of all the shit, the anger and resentments I had stored up from how that marriage ended. Ugh! My ex took me down through there, she was just evil. She was awarded just about everything in the divorce decree that she wanted: the best car, all the furniture, half of the money that Smucker's paid me to leave and the worse part, I had to sell our big beautiful house that I adored and had worked so hard to acquire, and get myself just a cheap little shack. I'd had everything fixed up just right in that house, and it really hurt my heart! I missed that house more than I missed her. Sometimes, I didn't think I'd ever get married again. But, I was lonely.

So, I tried to get back out there. I'd been through friend hook-ups, church, sisters, blind dates…, nothing. And, I'd almost given up on trying to meet someone nice. All the women I'd dated since my divorce were, always, as they say, wolves in sheep's clothing. Most times I just didn't get anywhere. I think the last time I tried, before I went online, I was checking out this girl at my friend, Vincent's, wedding. Got close to her and tried to make small talk but she wouldn't give me any play. Told me her name was Peggy Knight, but in a cold kinda way, not approachable at all. But when I got a closer look at her, I realized, my bad... she was Vincent's side piece.

Then my friend, Chad, said he heard the way to go these days was online dating. I thought, what have I got to lose, what da hell, couldn't hurt. I went on LastCallMeet.Com. They had a good deal on a sixty day membership. I thought, surely, I'll meet someone within sixty days. OMG, It was overwhelming!

At first, I met so many, many crazy ladies, and some that I don't think were even for real. I got messages from all kinds of women and ones that certainly didn't match my profile. I had women telling me, you don't know what you're missing having a lady with meat on her bones, I can change your mind, bro. Yeah! Mostly, way too much meat. Or questions I got all the time like how much money do you make a month? When was the last time you slept with a real woman? Do you believe in helping a lady pay her bills? Can you cook? Do you know how to give good head? or Do you take Viagra or Cialis? I never knew there were so many bold and obnoxious women out there. It's just like I heard you've got to go through a lot of "crunchies" as the young folk say, or a "lotta frogs" as the old folks say before you find a real match. But, after so many crazy comments and messages, I stopped and really took some time re-wording my profile.

First, I changed my name. At first it was "JustJay50." Then I changed it to ForReal J. This time I was very, very detailed as to exactly what kind of woman I was searching for. I gave details as to exactly what size, age, and nationality that I was searching for. I listed things I did and did not like. I listed that I was looking for someone who was physically fit or at least looked like it. A woman who's self-supporting and can carry their own weight. Someone who likes me for me and doesn't have time to play games, not too clingy, not to controlling, and has a life of her own and wants to share it with someone. A woman who can honestly say what's yours is mine and what's mine is yours, a team player. And at the end of my profile, I said "And by the way a 50-50 love… Not 70-30… Too much to ask? Keep it moving!"

I loaded four pictures of myself. One picture in a casual outfit (head shot), a black tie outfit, a summer outfit, and one taken outdoors at The Music City Jazz Festival, sporting my favorite fedora hat.

The first lady I connected with was ToneTonya. She was from Florissant, MO, called herself big sexy. She was still mad from her last bad break up with a man of 5 years. Every conversation kept coming back to him and how he did her wrong.

Then, there was Brooke, who was definitely a golddigger looking for money. She even asked for some before we physically met.

But after Monique, I was just about done with this stupid site. She went by Half Shell for Paris and she sounded so great on the phone, I decided to meet her. When I arrived at the bar, she was already there. She was just as beautiful as her pictures. Beautiful hair weave, but not too much, she looked gorgeous. She was a little bit taller than I expected, but nice. Nice teeth, hair, nails and casually, but nicely dressed. We had a nice dinner and after three glasses of

Chardonnay, she became more relaxed. She said, "Baby, let me tell you! I can be whoever you want me to be, okay?"

I noticed how she seemed to put emphasis on flinging and turning her hair around her fingers. When she excused herself for the lady's room, I got a really, really good look at her figure. Her hips weren't like most women I've seen. They were kinda square not round. She had shapely legs, but something just didn't seem quite right. I thought to myself, her hands did look kinda big, too. Then it hit me, oh damn! this is a man. When she came back, I asked her, anything else you'd like to tell me about yourself. I would love to know more.

She said, "Yes, I don't believe in hiding who I really am so, yes, James, let me tell you now, I use to be a male, I've been taking hormones for months, and getting prepared for my reconstructive surgery, or should I say, my transition. My old name was Ron, I like to keep it real, so yeah, now, there you go."

I know my mouth was hanging open. But I admired that he/she was honest. Could've saved me some time if I would've Skyped or Faced Timed him… I mean, her. But, it was cool. We finished our drinks and wished each other good luck in finding the perfect match. We didn't even hafta say not interested, he /she and I both felt it. There was no love connection there.

Then, there she was. SunshineA. We started off communicating through the site for about two, maybe three weeks, then we exchanged numbers and gave each other our real names. Her profile name was SunshineA. Her real name was Angela.

She seemed so sweet. She had a great job, and, small world, was from Memphis, living in Florida, but contemplating transferring home. We shared our online horror stories. We had both seen episodes of the show, Catfish, and talked about how that could never happen to either one of us. So, when I asked early on if she was open to Skype or FaceTime, she was a little hesitant about it, but I assured her that I wasn't a pervert, trying to expose myself to her, and I wasn't going to ask her to expose herself to me, she agreed.

She was a very pretty, but a basic kinda girl, and she looked just like her profile. She had natural hair, was built nice, definitely not overweight. She had a nice voice, we had pleasant conversations, and she seemed genuinely real.

We started a routine, where once a week we would Skype each other and have a talk. Usually, on weekends.

Sometimes, she Skyped me and had music playing in the background. The first time she was playing an old school Isley Brothers song called, "I Just Came Here To Chill." Yeah, we liked the same music, we would sometimes both dance as if we were together. Not only did we like to dance, and the same music, but we liked the same food, wine, coffee, tea. We had similar ideas about fitness and similar political and religious beliefs. We both liked nice things and, from what I could see when we Skyped, her place looked very nice, everything was always in place. We seemed to be searching for the same kind of relationship.

I was straight up and honest with Angela from the start, about who I was and my current situation. I told her that I'd been employed with Smucker's for twenty years, but when they decided to relocate the plant to Kansas City, I had to make a choice, and I chose not to go. Memphis was my home and I loved it. I thought for sure by now I would've found another job, but it'd been two years now and no, nothing! So I was still looking for fulltime work. I could've, should've done better, but I got too comfortable, hadn't even tried to learn any other trade. I just thought they'd be in Memphis, forever, at least until I retired after thirty years, but, boy, was I ever wrong! I told her, they say don't put all your eggs in one basket and I get that now, first hand. Nobody was gonna pay me what I was making at Smucker's without a degree.

And, I learned more about her, like how she'd left Memphis right out of high school. How she was raised by her grandmother who use to tell her, child, you were born old. How since her grandmother had passed away, she'd started feeling the need to be close to the few family members that are left, which were mostly in Memphis. She said Tampa's a wonderful place, but after a while you start thinking about family, your life, and getting older. After about three months, she told me that the transfer she'd applied for before she even met me had been approved and she was moving back to Memphis, so it looked like we'd get a chance at a real relationship.

After all I'd been through with my marriage and divorce, I'd sworn never, never, ever again, no more marriages. I swore I wouldn't give my all to anyone else like that ever again. But after three years of loneliness and a few stalkers, and crazy online dates, I was tired of being by myself, and, from what I'd seen of Angela so far, she seemed like an angel from heaven above.

With each text message, Skype call, or phone conversation, we got closer, opening up to each other more and more about all kinds of things. Then, before we'd even met in person, Angela started doing so many kind things for me. The van I managed to buy after my divorce was always giving me some kind of trouble. I told Angela about it once and she sent money to help out, paid to have my van repaired, and later, after I'd been complaining about some repairs on my house, for my birthday, she sent me a card with a check for $2,000. On the check, in the memo section, it just said "To help out, Happy Birthday."

Angela had told me she loved money, and she was very mindful of her money, because growing up she didn't have much. She liked to buy all kinds of things. Said she was a shoe addict, but she also had plenty of gadgets. She had an iPad, iPhone, iPod, digital thermostat, camera doorbell, Kindle Fire, Bose surround sound speakers and stereo system with Alexa, 60 and 65 inch TVs, but she also had gold, sterling silver, diamonds, stocks and bonds, all kind of designer clothes, you name it, she had it. She had money in several banks, two cars, a truck, an electric bicycle. Said she rode it on the beach for exercise. You name any credit card, she had it. I thought to myself, this girl is too much, she's way out of my league. Why in the hell would she want my broke ass?

I didn't keep anything from her, laid my cards all on the table, no secrets. As we got to know more about each other, I always kept it real. And, again, I explained my financial status, the fact that I barely made ends meet from month to month, how I lived on a monthly check. I told her I managed with an unemployment check and a small check from my pension plan. I told her that my credit was shot, and my credit score so low that it's listed as minus.

Her answer to it all was "So what, James, as long as we're together what's mine is yours and what's yours is mine. I believe that for every problem, there's a solution and together we can work through it. I know how to help get your credit back on track, don't worry, we'll be fine."

One time, after we'd had trouble with a Skype call, she surprised me and sent me a new Apple Mac Book Pro computer, said I needed to be upgraded, my system was outdated. All I could say was, thank you. I had to call on my cousin, Chad, to help me set up all that shit. Angela and I missed seeing each other by Skype for the first time that week, just because it took me that long to get everything all together and learn how to work it all.

Our first physical visit finally came six months after we first started talking. Angela was coming home to see her family for Thanksgiving, and she'd be in Memphis for two weeks. Her plan was to spend the first week with family and the second week with me. I was elated.

When I went to pick her up from the airport I was nervous as a chicken in a poultry house, even though we've been communicating for months.

I got to the airport early and parked, then headed for Delta baggage area and waited. She had said not to text or call, just to see if we were, indeed, a match, and could find each other. I spotted her first, she was a tall girl, and even though we've seen each other by photos, FaceTime, and Skype, it wasn't quite like seeing someone in the flesh. She'd always been sitting down when we Skyped, so I could never get the full effect. She was very attractive, though, wearing her natural hair, dread twists, and I must say, she wore it well, no perm, no glued or sewn-in weave like a lot of the girls these days. She did have some color in her hair, though, reddish brown mixed with black. It was the first time I'd really seen her body, and she was a very nice size, my guess, size 10, and shoes…um…size 8/1/2 or 9. I liked what I saw.

I waited to see if she'd notice me, too, and, when she turned around after grabbing her bag from the carousel, our eyes met. She smiled. "James!"

"Angela."

We hugged and she gave me a small kiss on my cheek. I took her bag, and we headed for my car. Kind of lost for words and awkward. I opened the car door, and she slid in.

I put her luggage in my trunk, then got in. "How was your flight?"

"It was fine, James. Hurry and get me over to Avis. I have to pick up my car. I don't want to be late."

"I thought you might want to grab a bite to eat and relax with me a little."

"That's sweet. Thanks, but no, thanks. I've got things to do."

I pulled up to the rental, and she hopped out. "Thanks. Can you pop the trunk so I can get my bag? I'll call you. See you next week."

And she was gone.

I felt weird, I thought that was kinda cold. It seemed as if I'd waited an eternity for this girl, but... I brushed it off, thinking, well, I guess family really comes first for her. But, it was a long week waiting to see her again.

Finally, as promised, during her second week in Memphis, she came over to the house. She seemed very comfortable considering it was really our first date, but me, I was nervous as hell. I cooked something light, pasta salad with chicken, Texas toast, and cranberry juice. I also had wine; I'd splurged a little and bought the Russian River blend of Chardonnay. We decided to just take it easy the first night and watch a movie. I started to put on the movie "The

Perfect Guy," but I was afraid that might scare her off and have her thinking I was that kind of guy. We watched "Good Deeds."

As it got later, I still wasn't sure if she was staying the night or not. Before the movie ended, I kinda wanted to know. "Um… Did you bring more clothes to get comfortable in?"

"Yes, but I left them in the car." She'd insisted on keeping the rental, even though I promised to take her wherever she needed to go while we were together.

I wasn't sure what that meant. I finally just decided to go for it. "Are you staying with me tonight, Angela? Or should I say, will you stay the night with me, Angela?"

"Yes, James, that's exactly what I had planned." She smiled.

What a beautiful smile. "I'll get your bag." I grabbed her keys, went out, and got her suitcase. As I came back in, my heart was pounding, beating so loud, it felt as if it were beating through my ear. I remained cool, and tried not to look too anxious. We had a few more glasses of wine. Then I got a little closer and kissed her.

When we kissed, it was a little awkward at first. She seemed a little stiff. I thought maybe she was more nervous than she looked. "I promise I won't do anything you don't want me to do."

After the second kiss, we were a little more comfortable with each other. I turned the TV off, took her hand, and guided her back to my bedroom. I prided myself on how nice I had my bedroom fixed up. I had my flat screen TV on the wall and a fireplace heater on the wall.

She noticed as soon as she entered the bedroom. "This is a nice, nice bedroom, James. Did you fix this up all by yourself?"

"Sure did, along with a little help from you, HGTV, and Lowes. I've been a bachelor for a while now, and I've learned to take care of myself."

We got into my sleigh bed, and I knew my 800-thread count Egyptian cotton sheets would feel great.

Then she asked, "Which side, James?"

"Right side for you, left for me."

She got in, and I turned on my favorite XM station, Heart and Soul. It was perfect. We'd found out a while back that we liked the same music. Stuff like R. Kelly, Anita Baker, Adele, John Legend, Gregory Porter, Yolanda Hathaway… we both loved ballads.

And, I finally saw Angela's expensive tastes first hand. Her PJs looked expensive, and I'm not up on all women's fashions, but I know expensive when I see it. They were silk, by Ralph Lauren, and so were her house shoes. She was definitely a girl who liked the finer things in life.

In bed, honestly, Angela was pretty basic. Not what I'd anticipated, at all. I didn't think she was nervous. She was just very… quiet. I could tell right away she wouldn't be into any of the wild freaky stuff that I'd fantasized about all that time we were Skyping. She just kinda let me do… whatever.

Now, don't get me wrong, it wasn't bad. I was just expecting a little… more… well, a lot more. For months, I'd fantasized about how she'd be, and "my bad," I hafta say, I got that wrong. No hollering like I'd envisioned, no saying my name, no scratching or clawing my back, no loud moans, no instructions, no harder, slower, faster, more to the right, not yet, now… nothing. But, I decided real quick that I could live with what she was putting out 'cause when you ain't had nothing in a long, long, long, long, time, any sex feels good. Still… it was all very calm, just quiet love making, almost as if it were already routine. It was like we'd been sleeping together for years, like old married-too-long sex. Afterwards, she just went silently to sleep.

I got up to make sure I had secured the house, looked out the window to check on our cars, turned out all the lights up front in the living room area, and headed back to bed. Yeah, it felt just like we were an old married couple already.

But, when I got back under the covers, it did feel kinda nice, for once, not to be sleeping alone. I drifted off to sleep with a smile thinking, finally, someone for me.

The next morning, we got up, and I cooked breakfast.

"What time is it, James?"

"Little after ten."

"Wow! What did you put in that wine? It knocked me out."

As I smiled, I flirted a bit, "You sure it was the wine that did it?" I mean, I knew the sex wasn't really exhausting, but... you know.

She smiled, but didn't flirt back.

I fixed coffee. "I remember, you said you must have your coffee first thing in the morning." Angela had turned me on to hazelnut creamer, and I turned her on to the Almond Joy creamer. We'd both been hooked ever since. We'd had so many conversations before meeting that we already knew a lot about what we both liked.

I handed her the cup, and she smiled. "And, you remembered just like I like it. So, what's there to do around here?"

"Well, we could always go back to bed and get to know each other a little bit more, or we can go over to Auburn Park and have a late morning walk."

"I think I'll take that walk."

"Ok, I've put towels in the bathroom for you if you want to shower, but whenever you get ready we can head out."

She didn't take too long to get dressed, unlike most women I know. When she came out, she had on her Nikes, along with Nike pants, jacket, and cap, all brown and turquoise. And off we went. She seemed to have her shit together, and she seemed to genuinely like me. I thought things were off to a good start.

But, as we walked and talked, she made it clear, she was way past the starting point.

We were still in sight of the house when she said "James, I really like you. We've been kicking it for a while now, and... well, remember the job I told you about here in Memphis? I've accepted it. So, I'll be coming back here to live, and what I want to know from you is... Do you think you could handle us living together? Like, permanently? Shacking? Roommates? Better yet, as a couple, you know... in a committed relationship?"

I didn't know what to say.

She stopped, and looked up at me. "You know that's what I'm really searching for, James."

"Well, sure, that's what I've been searching for, too."

"Good." She started walking, again. "I feel we could have a nice life together someday."

"Well, sure, someday, but don't you think we might need a little more time to get to know each other? I mean, it sounds great, but I feel we'd be moving just a little too fast. We've just met, really."

"We've been talking for months."

"It just seems a little fast."

"Well, I move fast, and when I see an opportunity... or a man... that I like, when I see something I want, I go for it! I've been seriously thinking about it for a while, so I thought, if I take this job, where and who in the heck would I stay with? I have plenty of family here to choose from and a few friends, but I don't think I could make it with any of them for long. I'm so used to having my own space."

Then, as we walked, she started telling me all the people she could stay with.

"I could stay with Stella, but she just lost her husband, and she's just got a mess of stuff to deal with already."

I just kept walking.

"Now my brother, half-brother, Javier. He's half Mexican. You'd think the Black and Mexican would make him extra macho, but, no, he just acts like a fool for his crazy wife. For years, she's been getting drunk, into fights, staying out clubbing all times of the night…. No, I just want to stay out of that shit."

I was just looking at my shoes, taking one step, then another, listening to her.

"Then, there's Camille, God bless her heart, but that girl has got to be the stupidest girl in Memphis! She's beautiful, very sweet, kind, but she just married a man who's been bragging about his side piece for years! Downright fucking stupid! I couldn't be there and not speak my mind."

We'd reached the first mile marker, but she wasn't looking at the scenery.

"Now, my girl, Loretta, she's ok, but she just got into a new relationship with some handicapped dude, so I don't want to bother her."

It was a nice day. The park was green and fresh, starting to fill with families.

"I got a friend, Brooke, great to shop with, but, well… she's just not dependable, and I think her and her man are headed for some serious drama…. Yeah. So, I'm coming back here to live, and I need a place to stay. I don't want to inconvenience my friends, or have them inconvenience me…."

So, that left me?

She stopped. Glanced around at the park for a second, then turned to me. "So, I figure I better try to get a place of my own before I move here. Do you think you could set aside some time tomorrow, for us to go out looking?"

I still wasn't sure how she'd settled on us living together, and, then, so quickly moved on to the practical stuff, but here we were. I wasn't at all sure about it, but I figured I could help her find a place either way. "Sure, I can help you with that."

"Okay, it's a date."

"Do you have a real estate agent in mind, yet?"

"No, I don't have a clue. I got a niece who's an agent out of state. I'll see if she can refer me to someone here, plus that would give her some referral money. She can use every dime she can get. Get this, she's trying to put her daughter through acting school, that kid is, for sure, a damn drama queen but they say she can act her ass off." She shrugged. "Anyway, I try to help her out. When she was a Girl Scout, I must have bought a million cookies. If I don't see another Thin Mint as long as I live, I'll be good."

"Mmm."

"Anyway, tomorrow, I'd just like to look around, see what's out there. I've been gone so long I don't know what the property is like here anymore, plus, you know the city a lot better than I do. It's changed so much since I last lived here."

My head was spinning with all the stories and her switching from friends to family to cookies to real estate…. I tried to sound as no nonsense as she did. "What part of town do you think you'd like to live in?"

"I don't know, what part of town would you like to live in?"

I suddenly realized it was the first time all morning she'd asked me what I thought about anything. Maybe the first time the whole visit. "Well, there are a lot of places around town that I like. It's nice out East, Germantown and Collierville. And Cordova's nice too, but If I had to narrow it down, I guess my favorites are Midtown and Arlington, or downtown. Now, they've really brought downtown back to life. Got some really nice condos, lofts, and townhomes, all overlooking the river."

"Have you been in any of them?"

"A few." I was kinda getting excited about the idea. "They have some awesome floor plans, plus easy access to the expressway and shopping. There's a trolley service that runs right through the middle of downtown. You can ride it to grocery shopping, movies, concerts, Beale Street, the Orpheum, Cannon Center, FedEx Forum, and this new place, Holoran Center, and the Civil Rights Museum. You'd never need to drive your car or worry about parking."

"Except I have to go to work."

"Oh. Sure."

"Well, which area are we closest to, now?"

"Umm…downtown, Midtown."

"Ok, we'll head downtown, first. You've sparked my interest."

We were almost finished with our walk, close to my place. I thought she'd want to go today, but she didn't.

"Let's say tomorrow morning about ten?"

I didn't know what we doing the rest of the day, but ok. "Sure."

We were back at my place.

"Okay, cool. I'll be back tonight."

She was leaving?

"I'm gonna grab a shower, then go hang out with brother. I don't know what time, yet, 'cause, I also left a message for some girlfriends. I'm sure they'll want to hook up, too."

Angela showered again, got dressed, dropped a kiss on my cheek, said "see you later," and left.

I had an empty house and an empty day, no plans. I thought I'd straighten up, but Angela was really neat in a quiet kind of way, I liked her swag. She had cleaned the entire bathroom, folded her towels up neatly, scrubbed down the shower, had it sparkling. She'd rearranged the toiletries along the bathroom sink and even mopped the floor, and never said one word. Hmm… had the mirror even been cleaned? She must have found the cleaning supplies in the bathroom closet.

I was feeling a little overwhelmed, but still didn't see anything wrong with being clean and practical and knowing what you want. Nothing wrong with that, right? I mean… it was impressive, really. Yeah, impressive. I decided Ms.

Angela was quite impressive. And, maybe, just right for me. If she wanted us to move downtown, why not, right? It was a great place. I'd love to live there. She could afford it. I liked her. I could see it....

She got back around nine. She'd had a great time with her brother. They'd ended up meeting for lunch, then spent the afternoon catching up on family news. She said the next time she came to town, she'd introduce us.

Since, I'd had all day, I'd tried to make the place nice, lit a few candles in the living room to set the mood, see if I could bring in a little of that romance I was missing, but the first thing she said when she walked in there was, "Oh, James, please turn on some lights. I can't see a damn thing."

I thought hmm... well... she's the guest. I turned on the lights and snuffed out the candles.

She took a few books and papers out of her purse and spread them out on the coffee table. "I picked these up while I was out. Take a look." She had The Daily News, The Memphis Flyer, and the House Hunter. Straight to business.

I remembered that The Daily News lists foreclosures, divorces, open probate estates, court cases, all kinds of legal stuff going on here in Memphis. My divorce had been listed there. I remembered 'cause all my friends and coworkers saw it before I did. Nice, right? Well, new day! I went to my computer desk, grabbed a highlighter, and we started skimming through the papers together.

There were some really attractive townhomes and condos, and some pretty good prices on foreclosures. Angela had spoken with her niece and decided to go with Keller Williams. So I looked for their number to ask about a property on GE Patterson Parkway, asking $295. I liked the floor plan. There was also a nice one asking $275 on Carolina.

Angela shook her head at those, though. "I don't want to spend any more than $250k, baby."

"Well, you're way outta my price range either way. My little house cost me sixty." I laughed, a little embarrassed. "I surely can't afford any of these."

"Just help me pick one out, James. Something that will fit us two, plus a guest room. I just want to get an idea of what property looks like in town, now."

"Sure, baby, no problem." The next morning, same routine. We got up, got dressed, I fixed breakfast, we took our four-mile walk, came back and showered, but this time together.

She let me wash and massage her back, and she seemed to really like it. I was still hoping she'd warm up as we went on. But, as soon as we got out, she was all business, again.

We got dressed and headed downtown. I insisted on driving. That way, she could look as I drove. Plus, I was more familiar with the city. We'd picked a great day for it. It was beautiful, calm, around 65, sun shining, and the leaves showing off all their beautiful fall colors. It was great. We saw three different places. First thing they asked, "Do y'all have an agent?" Second thing was, "Any kids?" They all automatically assumed we were husband and wife.

I liked one on Carolina Street, right across from the Amtrak Station, but she liked one off Riverside Drive. Then, we saw one with a view of the river and the Arkansas Bridge and a nice entry way which led up a few steps to the main door. It was a nice security feature, 'cause we'd have to buzz our guests into the place. We got more information and prices on them all. I started to get into it. It was fun to imagine us there, starting a new life in a nice place.

When we got hungry, I took Angela to this place called Office At Uptown over on North Second Street, very quaint, with an unusual menu. The food was great. We ate, talked, and enjoyed listening to the jazz they played. A lot of business people, lawyers, and people who work for the city and county hang out here. Nice set up, you can have a nice lunch, and use their computers, printers, and fax machines while eating. I knew she'd like it.

On the way back, she said, kinda formal. "Thank you, James, I really enjoyed my lunch." Then we rode the rest of the way humming and singing songs from 103.5 radio.

When we got back to my place, she came in, kicked off her shoes, and grabbed the remote. She seemed very comfortable with me, as well as my home.

After a while, she turned to me. "James, I want to be your lady, and I want you to be my permanent man, my boo, my one and only. I like you, I'm comfortable with you, and I trust you. Now, I don't have much more time here. I hafta get back to work. Will you keep looking for a place for us? I'll trust your judgment, you know what I like."

"Well, sure… I'll keep looking, but… are you sure, that's a lot of trust you're putting in me, finding a place?"

"The sooner you find something, the sooner I can get you outta this… don't get me wrong James, your place is okay, but I want better for us."

"But I can't afford to buy something now? It's gonna be a while…."

She waved her hand like that was nothing. "I'm not tripping about that. I have the down payment and my credit is excellent. You can live with me as long as you want. If we're together, we're together. We can add your name to the deed later. What's yours is mine and what's mine is mine, ha ha, just kidding. What's mine is yours, too. So, all I need to know is, can I count on you to handle everything for me, just as if you were me?"

I didn't quite know where I was in all this, with me doing things as if I were her. But, she seemed to have it all figured out, so I thought I might as well go with it. "Sure, you can, baby, I'll do my best."

"I know you'll do just fine."

I want to be that sure, but it still seemed awful sudden. "Angela, are you really sure? I'm just… Are you sure this is a good idea?"

"Yes, James I'm sure. Now, what was that you were suggesting yesterday? Hmmm…, something about going back to bed and getting to know each other more? Is that offer still available? 'Cause, I'll take you up on it now."

I smiled. "Sure, baby, let's do it!"

That's how it was when we first started out. She'd tell me to handle things "as if you were me." As long as I let her call the shots on any and everything we did, everything was great. We found a place pretty quickly. I knew her tastes in furniture, so she liked what I bought for her, and, mostly, I liked what she bought. But, once we were in our place and she was working in Memphis, things started to change. Or maybe, once the dust settled on us getting together and moving in, I just started to notice things more.

First, I noticed Angela didn't interact with many people. As long as it was just us two, everything was fine. But if we had to do something with other people, it didn't go well. At first, I just thought she could be a little gruff, and I just brushed it off. I thought, so, she's not a people person like me, that's okay. But, basically, she didn't seem to like very many people at all. I guess she'd always been that way, but after a while, it wasn't so easy to ignore, because everything was "we" and "us" and done together but, after a while, changed for her to "me, myself and I." And her not liking anybody else got to be a big problem. Because I'm not like that. Not even a little.

People say I never meet a stranger, I talk to all kinds of people, young, old, white, black, Hispanics, Christians, thugs, blind, crippled, or crazy. I just have a way. But, not my Angela.

Now, I've always especially enjoyed spending time with my family. We've done the same thing we've always done forever. Me and some of my family members take turns having get-togethers. We rotate around going to each other's houses, and we do it about once a month, at least.

Now, Angela wasn't used to that. I told her she could have her family over, too, but she'd only invited her brother and his wife to our place maybe once or twice in the time we'd been together. They seemed nice enough. Her brother, Javier, was ok, I guess. The one time we'd had them all over, my cousins liked that he could talk shit in English and Spanish. His wife, her sis-in-law, fit right in, liked to party and liked my peeps, seemed like cool people. Only, I really didn't know much, because I rarely saw them. Angela usually went to their place without me. My family was different.

The first time my family came over to our new place, I was so proud, I had my chest stuck out. You could see me smiling from downtown all the way across the Arkansas Bridge. I was so proud of our beautiful new home, and my beautiful new lady. She didn't talk much to them, but I chalked it up to getting use to them all. They can get pretty rowdy. So, she was quiet, but she was able to socialize a bit.

But, after a couple months, she started to complain. She'd say stuff like, "Y'all always want to party, just loud, any old reason to get drunk and loud."

The next time it was my turn to have them over, she made her feelings clear, "Can't they have it at another one of your cousins' houses? What about Sara? Y'all all claim she's a big baller. I'm sick and tired of them coming over here, tearing up shit! They country as hell!"

I told her I couldn't change plans at the last minute, and she finally agreed to have them, but she was curt and a bit of a smartass to everyone, including me. She made all kinds of facial expressions when we were laughing and talking loud. OMG, the looks that she gave them while sitting on the couch could kill a blind man! And when my niece started playing her baby grand piano in the "great room," she almost lost it.

She cornered me in the kitchen when I went in to mix more lemon drops and sex with alligators. "Look, baby, I know it's your family and all… but what damn time are they leaving?"

I tried to smile. "Do you have some place else to go, honey? What is it? Are they too loud?"

She smiled a thin, kinda crazy looking smile. I'd never seen that look on her face before, it was a truly cold look, like she was about to snap. Her voice was ice. "No, I don't James. I'm just sick of their loud country asses, and I don't like any of them. You'd better get them outta here, before I do."

I went back to the living room area with our drinks, smiled, and entertained my family, just as if she never said one foul word to me. Everyone was getting into the music I had playing. This old school song came on, "Baby, I'm Scared of You," by Womack and Womack. That did it!

They all got up! Laughing, hollering… Hey! And me included, I said, damn, that was my song right there. That song, I don't care where you go, to the club, house party, retirement party, wedding reception, driving down the street, it has the kind of beat that makes young and old feel something. Maybe I'd had one to many lemon drops, but I ignored the warning signs and immediately went to Angela and grabbed her hand. "C'mon, baby, dance with me!"

She snatched away from me. "I don't dance, James."

"Oh, come on, baby, this is my song!"

But this time, with a stern quiet coldness in her voice, she growled at me. "I told you I don't fucking dance. Now leave me the hell alone. And, I guess you'll be cleaning this carpet tomorrow, cause it's never gonna be the same now that your crazy ass family been here fucking it up. They need to take their drunk country asses the fuck home!"

And, as she stood there quietly chewing me out, no one paid any attention to us. They were all still laughing, dancing, and having a good time! Next, the song, "Cut It," came on, and you know all the youngsters got up! They were dancing around the room, acting as if they were cutting their neck, singing, and rocking back and forth amongst each other singing, cut it! cut it! Just having a ball.

And, Angela was mad as hell!

My family was laughing and dancing all around me, and she stood there furious. I just couldn't believe it. Who was this woman? Did some other woman named Angela come back from Florida and move in with me. This just can't be the same one I fell for.

From there, things just got steadily worse. She started doing things. Just mean things. Like, she got mad when I came in late one time, and just changed the door locks. She just up and left me, once, at the Levitt Shell during a concert when a Caucasian woman sat next to me and I talked to her. She broke dishes we were eating off of when I said the macaroni needed a little more cheese. She scrolled through my cell phone and would delete any number that had a name other than someone she knew. Once, in a rage, she cut up all the clothes she'd just bought me. Then, the next day apologized and took me shopping for all new ones. A few times, she turned down the hot water heater, so I wouldn't have enough to shower. I asked her about it and she said, "I told you not to shower so long." Then, she started hiding my mail for some damn reason. And, it didn't stop at home. A few times, she embarrassed me in front of her family or her co-workers, talking down to me like I was a kid.

I didn't know what the hell was going on, but after a while, I started thinking, no more! I've taken all I can, it's time to get off this ride. Yea, I liked the picture we painted, but it wasn't authentic, it was fake, and I'd had enough already!

I started believing Angela had only used me to set things all up for her, and how she acted after that was who she really was. She'd only managed to cover it up long enough to win me over and get me as some kind of servant or something, and dammit, I fell for it. I was really mad at myself, 'cause after my divorce, I thought I was being so careful. I thought I'd really found my true match, this time, my partner, my soul mate! I'd trusted her!

I thought because she'd known when we got together that I didn't really have shit, that she must have really, really loved me for me. I thought she'd always have my back. But, it hadn't taken long for the real Angela to come out, and the real Angela was an absolute selfish, controlling, crazy, evil, bitch!

And, I'd already done the evil bitch thing! I finally decided I would not, could not, take this ride, again. I didn't go through all that hell to get divorced the first time just to get into something miserable all over again. I'd promised myself I wouldn't do this again!

Some of my family still thought Angela was a great catch, and, even those that knew she wasn't treating me right thought it could be worse. Everybody said, "Keep her, man, she's your free ride. I'd love to be in your shoes." They said, "Just ignore what she says. All women talk shit, especially when they make the most money, man." They said, "Just let her keep on talking shit and paying."

It was true, she was financially stable; she paid for everything. What more could a guy ask for, right?

But, I couldn't seem to talk myself into it. I started thinking of leaving, and I was so glad I'd kept my cheap little house when Angela bought the new one. The market hadn't been so great for sales, and, with Angela, I hadn't needed the money, so I'd been letting Josh, my cousin Parker's son, use it. We'd even kept it up ok. I'd been tending to the yard and maintenance, and Josh had been doing the rest.

I didn't charge him much for rent. I'd just wanted someone to be in there so the place wouldn't be sitting empty, but, I think the real reason I'd kept it was that something in my heart said, "Don't sell your house, James. You might need that ace in the hole."

Well, thank God for Josh. I finally got a hold of him on the phone. These young folks would rather text than talk. So, after calling him twice with no response for a week, I texted, and that was when I finally got a response from him.

I'd told him when he moved in that he needed to take care of my place as if it was his own, but that if things went wrong, I might need it back, he'd hafta find him another place to live. I told him that I couldn't guarantee how soon or how long that could be or if ever, but I hoped never. Well, never didn't take too long, 'cause there I was giving Josh notice to move.

"I'm sorry, I'd like to give you longer than 30 days, but I don't know how long I can last here."

But Parker raised him right, 'cause he said, "Hey, it's your house, cuz, and if you need to come sooner, come on, I got you! Mom's got a big new house and says I can stay if I need to. No problem. We'll work it out."

I thanked him, surprised that it could be that easy.

But, then he said, "You sure this is what you want to do, man? From what I've seen and heard from others in the family, you've got it pretty good."

It was the first time I'd really talked to anyone about it, and it just came out all at once. "Man, I wish it was as good as it looks. But I need out, the sooner the better. I'm mad as hell and pissed that I've already wasted too much time with her. Man, I give! I don't have time for this bullshit, she's putting down. I'm too old, and life is too short! I tried man, I really, really tried."

"Ok, cuz, just let me know when and if there is anything I can do. Like I said, I got someplace to go, so if you need to get the place back to yourself, I can go hang there."

"Ok, cool." Just knowing I had an out made it better. "I'll try to give you the thirty days, though."

But before the thirty days was even up, I had so much anxiety when I was home that I had to get something from my doctor. I have never, ever in my life needed anything to calm my nerves until Angela. I couldn't stop thinking what happened? Where did I go wrong? How did I not see this coming?

Did I miss the red flags? As I thought back, I realized, hell, yeah, I missed em. The signs were all there. Angela was a very controlling, cold, no-nonsense kinda girl. She had no compassion for her brother, was totally focused on her work, and was very unforgiving of other people, had very low tolerance for excuses if anyone around her made a mistake. Even the first time I met her, when I picked her up at the airport and all she wanted was a ride to her car. I saw it, then. Great big red flag waving in the wind! But, even though I'd known all that, I still never expected her to turn out like this. What a fucking disappointment.

I think I was mostly mad at myself. I mean, what a waste of my time, and I had promised myself after the bitter breakup with my ex that I would have peace as much as possible for the remainder of my life here on earth. I would never fight to stay with a woman when I wasn't happy. But I was right back there again, only this time, it was even worse.

All, I wanted was to be rid of the nightmare I'd fallen into, and needing to go to the doctor finally pushed me over the edge. I hadn't been able to sleep, and once, I thought I was having a heart attack, but it turned out to be some kind of anxiety thing. Angela didn't have a clue, and I didn't bother to tell her, because I really thought she just wouldn't give a fuck.

My doctor prescribed Zoloft and Ambien, and I was in such bad shape, he also recommended counseling, insisted, really, had the nurse make me an appointment with Henderson and Henderson before he'd let me leave the office.

When I talked to them, though, they said, if I wanted to save the relationship, I'd need to communicate all this to Angela, give her a chance to work on it.

Well, honestly, I wasn't sure I wanted to save it, but I guessed it was worth a try. I had to do something, I got myself into this mess, stuck on stupid. So now it was up to me to get out of it!

I decided to confront her. I just caught her when she wasn't busy and told her, this ain't working and it needed to change. Told her I've tried, but I can't do it alone. She needed to compromise on some things.

"I mean… our goal is marriage, right? Isn't that why we're living together. Well, we'll never make it if we don't do something different." I knew it wouldn't work, talking to her like this, if I put it all on her. "We can get some professional help, like therapy… or the church Pastor… some sort of marriage counseling. I've been going to these people, Henderson and Henderson Psychological Services and they said if we want to solve this, we should—"

"You can just stop right there." She looked at me with disgust. "Hell, ain't shit to solve, James. We don't, rather, *I* don't need no damn counseling. Now, I'm gonna tell you this one time and one time only. Make it easy on yourself, brotha, you either take it, or leave it. That's the only option you have with me. If you think you can do better, feel free!"

"But, Angela—"

"No! I'm the best woman you've ever had in your life, and I know you can't find another one like me or better. Hell, I don't know why you're acting like a little bitch, James, you've got it made. I took you out of that little matchbox house in da hood. I make you look good in front of your country ass family. You don't hafta worry about money, and now you even have some nice arm candy, me! to show off! Not to mention I helped you repair your pitiful ass credit score. What more do you want? And I'm betting I paid for your damn counseling, too!"

I swallowed hard. I had to stand up for myself. For us, if there was going to be an us. "I want you to come with me to talk to the Hendersons. I made an appointment—"

Angela laughed in my face. Then, she snatched up her car keys and slammed the door on her way out.

Angela seemed to feel like I should either shut the fuck up and take it, or roll on back to where she got me from, just the way my broke ass was before we met. Well, I could do that! I was perfectly fine all by myself, well… kinda, sorta. I was lonely. But, at least, I was minding my own damn business, but… well I hafta be honest, I wasn't really happy, that's why I went looking for something online. And dammit, I sure got it! I'll be damned if I hadn't hooked up with the devil herself, or, at least, the wicked witch of the South!

After the big confrontation, I went out, hoping to stay out till she got home and went to bed. I still wasn't ready to just get out of there. But, when I got back to the house, she still wasn't home. She'd been there, though. She'd left a note on the fridge, as she always did, with instructions, a list of honeydos that she wanted me to get done before she got home. Just like I'd never said a thing! Ugh! I thought, this woman never stops! But, to keep the peace, I got the stuff done.

I didn't know why, but I still wasn't ready to just move out. I started sleeping in the guest room, staying out of her way, taking the medication, and, when I thought I couldn't take it, anymore, going to talk to one of the Hendersons.

When she was around, I tried to make as little conversation as possible. We ended up mostly communicating with her notes.

On a particularly bad day, I'd taken a few clothes over to the house with Joshua. He'd cleared out the second bedroom for me. Just in case I had to flee. And with crazy ass Angela, I thought that could happen at any time. I was mad, but I was also hurt, I think, because she knew I wasn't happy, but she just went on about her business as usual, ignoring me. For a while, I thought I could manage with that, but finally I had another anxiety attack, a bad one, right in line at the grocery store, and I knew I couldn't do it. It just wasn't going to work.

Henderson said if it was too much for me, maybe I should go ahead and move out, at least, temporarily. I could tell he wanted me to make the decision. Didn't really want to tell me what to do. But, he did keep saying, that I knew it was unhealthy for me living there. Oh yeah, I knew that much! So, I finally told Angela that I was going away for a few days, said I needed to clear my head, whatever that means, but she didn't care.

"Do what you do, James. I don't have time to babysit you. Somebody gotta work around here."

So off to Josh's I went, back to my old house. How foolish did I feel running back over there like some little wounded teenager! But I needed time to calm my nerves. It'd gotten to where just hearing her come in from work made me anxious. But, I also needed to cool off. I was pissed. And being that angry, I couldn't tell if I had any feelings left for her or not. Yeah, I needed space for sure.

The first night was great. I felt relaxed for the first time in a long time. But, when I'd been there for two days and not one word from Angela, I started going back and forth between missing her, wondering why she didn't miss me, and thanking God we weren't married, yet! I'd think one minute, but I love her, why doesn't she love me? And in the next few minutes, I'd think, "At least, I still have the option to get out!"

When I woke up in my old house on the third day there, I had a missed call from the night before, a voicemail from Angela, after midnight. I played it and she sounded like the old Angela, the one I fell for, SunshineA.

I debated deleting the message unplayed, but, of course, I had to know what she said. I played it. "James, come home, baby. You are taking this too far. You know I love you. I know I can be a bit of bitch, sometimes, but that's just the way I'm made. You can keep going to your counseling sessions. I'll pay for them. That's fine. But, c'mon, ForReal J, you gotta know, I love you! C'mon home now."

I didn't know what to do. Should I stay out or go back? Was I just a pawn in her chest game? She said she loved me, but nothing about working together or changing. Did she want me home to do the chores? Or was I just expecting too much from this relationship? We weren't kids, maybe this was it. The best it was gonna be for me now.

I took the rest of that day reflecting on it. I hadn't been happy in a long, long time. I prayed on it. I slept on it. I took my meds on it. But, I didn't call her back.

Sure, it was partly because I hadn't decided what to say, but I also wanted to see if she'd miss me, too, maybe for more than just her handyman or personal assistant or whatever I was to her. After all, I was a pretty good catch, too, right? I mean, how many men would put up with her shit?

Not too many.

Then, I fell asleep thinking about it all. When I woke up, it was 3:00 a.m. and there was noise in the street outside. I looked around at that dingy room where I used to live and I missed my comfortable bed back home.

I missed my master suite with the blackout curtains, and my bathroom with the heated floors, and our sound machine keeping out any little noise, and our nice neighborhood that had so little noise to keep out. And, in the morning, I'd miss my cappuccino maker and my nice laptop and my stereo… and, I knew the truth was… a whole lot of men would put up with her shit for what I had. A whole lot.

I thought, well, damn! Everybody's right. It wasn't that bad. I couldn't ask for a better place to live, a more attractive, financially stable woman, who, yes, is crazy as hell, sometimes, but still wants to marry my broke ass, no matter what. And, all I got to do for all that is follow her instructions. It's not a bad job, really.

So, I decided, I'd go back. If it got bad, I could always take breaks over here, or, hell, let her pay for me to take a little vacation. I could manage. I'd go to the Hendersons, take meds, she had me on some great health insurance….

So, yeah, I'd go home. We'd have make-up sex, and she'd buy me something new, some extravagant gift to win me over…. Hmmm, what would I like this time…?" Gucci loafers, Bond No.9 cologne, new air fryer, a few more shares of marijuana stock, that new F-150 truck I've been checking out…. Yeah… yeah. She got me… no matter what.

JUDY HIBBLER

When I announced that I was marrying Tyler Malone, everyone kept saying, "Are you sure?" I even heard some girls in the bathroom at church, "He's too perfect, you know he got to be gay?" That hurt my feelings. Just because a guy looks and smells good, has great taste in clothes for men or women, and stays in church doesn't mean he's gay.

I never had a whole lot of experience with men, or anything else. I lived a pretty sheltered life. My Dad, the minister, and my Mom, the missionary, didn't allow me to stray too far away from them or the church. I wasn't allowed to play or listen to the blues or any hip hop stations, or to play any games that involved dice. I was not allowed to wear anything sleeveless, no sleeveless dresses or blouses, unless it had a jacket that had to stay on at all times, and especially red, no red nothing. No red dress, blouse, shoes, lipstick, nail polish, ribbon, bra, nothing.

The only friends I could hang with were mostly from our church. I'm an only child and my Mom and Dad waited till they got old to have me. Ugh they were so outdated, so old fashioned. They were even selective about which girlfriends I hung out with. They thought if there's no mother and father married in the home together, then the kids just weren't good enough for me to hang out with. They considered them low class, and that means trouble. I tried to tell them I knew plenty of kids at school who have good morals and manners in single family homes, but they wouldn't have it. So, I really didn't have many friends at school. Now, if I went skating, it was with the church, to the park, it was with the church, to the movies, that is… the selected ones, with the church, the Delta fair, with the church, and, of course, the only boys I was allowed to talk to were also from the church. Throughout my years of dating, I brought home several different guys, but no one was good enough, nice enough, from a good enough background, had parents good enough to suit my Mom or Dad. And if they didn't approve, then that was the end of it.

They did really like Marlon when I brought him home, that is, at least, they did in the beginning. His father pastored a church, just like my Dad did, and they would allow him to come over for Sunday dinner. We dated for a year.

He came over to the house each and every Sunday for dinner after church service, and sometimes Dad would take us out for dinner, and he was always invited, without question. They felt I was safe with him. But you know what most people say about us - PK's are the worst ones.

Marlon was my first real, real boyfriend. He was the first boy I ever kissed, and he taught me how. I mean, he taught me how to really, really kiss. He taught me a few other things that boys and girls do, too, that made me feel all warm inside. When he came over after church on Sundays, after dinner, Mom would be on the phone talking to sister so and so, and Dad would be resting before evening service, me and Marlon would be in the great room kissing. He had sticky fingers and every chance he got, he kept those fingers in my panties, and it felt good. But we never went all the way. We came close many, many times, but it never went that far. We had fun, and I always looked forward to Sunday. That was the best day of the week for me, until, well, somehow word got back to Mom, and then she told Dad that Marlon had a new baby girl by one of their church members, and that was the end of that. No more Marlon. I was no longer allowed to see him, period, end of story.

I tried to explain to my parents that Marlon was a good guy, and he had never disrespected me. I explained, we always have a nice time, Mom, and he's never tried anything with me. I also tried to explain that the girl he has a baby with was older and tricked him, but they still weren't having it. The answer was no, we forbid you to see him again. He's too old for you, anyway. He is not allowed over here or anywhere near you, anymore, and it's not up for debate, don't ask us again, it's over.

I was so hurt, upset, shocked. I told Marlon that our friendship had to be over. He begged me to let him try and talk to my Dad and Mom, let him try to explain but I said no, no way. He even convinced his Dad to have a talk with mine. But, my Dad wasn't hearing that either. After that, we saw each other a couple of times at different church engagements and that was it. He finally gave up and faded away.

So, I filled my time on the computer and cell phone. I played all the Sims games, I was on Youtube, Twitter, Snapchat. I had a Facebook account for a minute, but they made me deactivate that when they found out that my Facebook had a picture of me in a bathing suit. How they found out was

Justin. That old hater, Justin, always liked me, and was constantly trying to hit on me, and I couldn't stand him. His Mom overheard him talking on the phone with some of his homies and heard them saying Judy's got a hot picture on Facebook man, check her out. She told Mom, Mom told Dad, and I thought my Dad was gonna have a massive…. He went on and on about how I had embarrassed him in front of the church, how I set a bad example before the other young ladies at the church. He said he was trying to save souls and here I was making it hard for him, making him look bad. I thought he was gonna kill me, but, instead, I got grounded for ninety days. No company, no computer, and definitely no cell phone. Ninety days seemed like forever. After my time out was up, I got it. No more Facebook for me. It's nothing but a snitching device. At least until I get grown and outta their house. Which wouldn't be long, I was almost 18, but, boy, I hated my life back then, ugh!

That was, until I met Tyler Malone. I had never paid any attention to him before then. Tyler had never hung out with any of the other girls at church, so I hadn't really noticed him. I later heard that quite a few girls had tried to hit on him, but I never saw him with anyone. When I first noticed him, I was still sulking about ending my friendship with Marlon when the church picnic came along mid-August the summer after I graduated high school. I was so excited. Finally, finally a chance for me to mingle and have some fun. At the summer picnic, everybody always brought a friend from some other church or from their neighborhood. The picnic was always at Okabutaler Lake, and I couldn't wait. They'd have all kinds of food, games, people, and all kind of raffles. There were kids playing with Uno cards, they had Frisbees, hula hoops… they were blowing bubbles, throwing darts. They usually even had a jack and ball contest.

When it finally came, I loved it, and I was all over the place. That year they even had hopscotch, one of Mom's old school games and jacks. Mom said she used to play that when she was a little girl and was pretty good at it, so even Mom was in a good mood. They even had a water slide. Me and my friend, Morgan walked all over the place, and Okabutaler Lake was huge.

My parents didn't like Morgan's name, said she had a boy name, but, Morgan's dad was the lead deacon at church, so, they approved of her, and let us hang out together. We finally found a shady spot, sat down, and spread out our blanket. We both had iPods and iPhones, and you know we had more than just gospel songs downloaded on them. As long as Mom didn't see me dancing, popping my fingers, or playing that music loud, I was safe. And, why not? After all, I was a young adult, for God's sake. I'd graduated in June and, in a few months, I'd turn eighteen. I was nearly an adult in a lot of places, but not to my parents.

But Morgan and I, just then, felt like young women, and we were playing what we wanted and enjoying the day. Then I saw Tyler. He was tossing around a Frisbee. Whenever he tossed it, some girl would run, catch it, and toss it back, that is when the dog didn't. Tyler had the most adorable dog with him, Ruddy, a cute, busy, smart Miniature Schnauzer. This little dog could jump and catch a Frisbee better than most of the people around there.

I could tell Tyler was showing off and noticing me. Whenever the other girl was running after the Frisbee, he'd look my way to see if I was looking. I thought, hmmm, he thinks he's hot. Well he kinda was. Then Morgan said, "Girl, let's mess with him, he can't have all the attention."

So, we hooked up the Bose speakers to my iPod and turned it up loud. We played a Marvin Sapp song, "The Best In Me." We were both wearing our long sun dresses and we started doing our praise dance. Everybody started coming over and gathering around to look, including him. When I looked around, we had a pretty big crowd. The song was finished, and everybody applauded. He came over and said, girl, you're pretty good. I smiled and said thanks. He said, oh, this is my pal, Ruddy. I said, hey, Ruddy. Ruddy was black and silver. He started wagging his tail and trying to get out of Tyler's arms to jump and lick on me. I told him, this is my best friend, Morgan.

"Hi, Morgan."

She smiled showing all her teeth, even the gold one. "Have you eaten, yet?"

"I haven't." He kinda raised his brows at me, questioning.

"Would you like to join me and Morgan? We were headed over to the food area."

"Sure."

We three, no four, if we count Ruddy, headed for the food area. The girl who was catching the Frisbee looked kinda annoyed, but then just went off with some other people. And, that's how it all started with Tyler. I found out quite a bit about him. First of all, he was twenty-four to my nearly eighteen. He had a good job with FedEx in Human Resources. He was attending LeMoyne College for a degree in business. He had his own apartment and car, and the only person he was obligated to take care of was Ruddy. He loved to sing and play piano, and, later I heard him, and he sang really, really well. He got to be one of our choir members and whenever he led Lord, Lord, You've Been Blessing Me, the whole congregation got stirred up. He set the whole church on fire.

At that first picnic, he seemed like such a gentleman, and before the picnic was over, we'd exchanged numbers. I'd explained the rules to him, explained that my Mom and Dad were pretty strict. I had a certain time to be on and off the telephone and computer and my parents monitored things pretty close. Even that first day, I told him, "I can't wait to get away from home. I want to be able to get out on my own, so I can do what I want when I want and how I want."

He said, "Rules are good, Judy, and structure makes good character."

Boy, I thought, my parents are gonna love you!

After that, we started talking and texting every day. He told me part of why he had his own place was because of his Mom's new husband. He said that man, his stepfather, was horrible. That's what he called him, "that man." And. he did not like him. At all.

At first, he just started by saying he just didn't like the way Mr. Shelly treated his mother. Said he was always screaming at her about a whole lot of nothing. "He would yell at us that the house wasn't clean enough, the dog used the bathroom in the wrong part of the yard, the cat was sitting on the outside grill, the food wasn't cooked at the right time, I was staying in the shower, too long, sitting on the couch too much…."

Pretty soon, it was clear that Tyler had a big problem with the way his stepdad treated him, too. He told me one night when we were hanging out, "that man" was always going on about how his momma did a piss poor ass job raising him. "He was always saying I was too soft, calling me a punk. He wanted me to be manly, like him. He said my hands were softer than a girls, and all I liked was books and church. Said I needed some kind of manual labor job where I could come home smelling funky and dirty like him every day. He also didn't like that I didn't care for alcohol, his favorite thing. He drank that scald, as he called it. When I couldn't drink that stuff, he called me a sissy. Said he didn't trust a man who couldn't drink like one."

"That sounds rough." I was actually kinda shocked. I'd never heard talk like that in my house. "Why'd your momma stay with him?"

"I don't know. She loved him, I guess, but was kinda afraid of him, too, I think. He collected guns, and he went out and bought this huge ugly gun case and put it dead in the living room where everyone who came to the house could see it."

"Wow. That sounds awful."

"Yeah, the last time we got into it was about me not taking out the trash and washing dishes as he saw fit. We almost came to blows, and my momma didn't even stand up for me. That's when I knew, it was time for me to go."

"I'm glad you did."

"Yeah, I needed to get out of the way." He shrugged. "So now, Momma doesn't hafta worry about me anymore. She can go ahead and be happy, if she can, with old crazy Shelly."

Tyler had worked as much overtime as he could and saved every dime. He'd found a nice little place just around the corner from the church so he could walk. And he did, each and every Sunday.

"I wanna do what you did. Get a job, save up, be independent."

But Tyler didn't seem to get it. "Girl, why you want to leave home? You have a happy home. Pastor Hibbler and your Mom seem to love you and each other. You guys have a very nice big house, nice cars, and you don't hafta work."

"I know, I know, maybe I'm being a spoiled brat, but I can't help it. I'm trying to grow up, and it's like they don't want me to. I have got to get from under their thumb and find my own way. I'm so tired of being treated like a little baby."

"Girl, you're blessed and don't even know it. You should be grateful!"

Oh, Lord, he sounded like my parents. And as predicted, they loved Tyler! Even though, Tyler'd never known his father, my parents knew he'd been looking out for his Momma with her disability since he was eleven years old, and, I guess, since his Momma was married now, it was ok with them.

My Mom said, that's the kind of young man you could have a nice future with, and I thought, yeah, I probably could. I liked Tyler, he was very good looking young man. And there were so, so many girls that had their eyes on him, but he seemed to only have eyes for me. I was happy my Mom and Dad trusted him, and Tyler was always a good listener, I guess, and a nice guy, but, in those days, I was already thinking he was... kinda dull. He never tried any of that stuff Marlon used to do to me. After three months of spending time together, we finally kissed. Mom and Dad got comfortable enough to let me go over to his place for a few hours on occasions.

But, still, not much happened. I was looking for a walk on the wild side, like some of the stories I'd heard from Morgan. But Tyler was such a gentleman with me, that, basically, I only lived the wild side through Morgan. I listened to her stories about the times she had with different guys and looked forward to my turn.

Morgan even kept me updated with the 411 on Marlon. She told me Marlon hadn't been the same since my parents made us break it off. Rumor was he just couldn't get it right. Kept running from pillar to post, as the old folks say. Guess it would be kinda hard to trust after you find out the girl who claimed she was having your baby was lying, just trying to trap you.

After two years of chaste dating, Tyler had his business degree from LeMoyne College and got a better position at FedEx. I'd been in school, too, just doing odd jobs and stuff at the church, but I'd just been offered a clerical job in a law firm, my first adult job.

Tyler was excited for both of us. "Judy, I want to go out and celebrate my new job and yours. I want us to go somewhere special, sweetheart. Let's go to Ruth Chris."

Dinner was very nice, and he insisted that we get dessert, so I ordered cheesecake. We were waiting for it, when Tyler said, "I have something very important to ask you. Now, I want you to take your time and really, really think about it."

"Sure, what is it?" I was hoping he was gonna ask about going past this dull, kissey, feely stage we'd been stuck in forever. Take our friendship or whatever it was to another level.

Well, another level was exactly what he wanted. He was so nervous his hands were shaking and so was his voice. He struggled to pull a little box out of his pocket. It sad Lasavell Jewelry. He asked me to marry him.

I wasn't even sure what was happening, I was so surprised, but when he opened the box offering me the most beautiful white gold diamond ring! I couldn't think of anything else. "Oh, Tyler, it's so beautiful!" I tried it on, and watched it bling. I never wanted to take it off, but... after just a minute, I did.

I handed it back. "I can't. I mean, I do. I will. I mean, Tyler, I love you, and my Mom and Dad love you, but, in my family, you have to ask my parent's permission for my hand in marriage, first. I mean, I say, yes. Yes, Tyler. But nothing is a go until you get their permission, their blessing."

"I love you so much, Judy. I want you to be my wife for the rest of our lives." He moved to kiss me, and, this time, he really kissed me.

The romantic restaurant, the amazing ring, the kiss. I thought to myself, now this is what I've been waiting for! We agreed to speak with my parents after church the next Sunday. I couldn't wait to get home and call Morgan. I was thinking, she's gonna faint!

As soon as I hit the house, I called her. "Hey Morgan, it's Judy, girl, guess what?" I was jumping in my bed while lying flat on my back with my legs crossed and wagging my feet.

"What?"

"Tyler asked me to marry him tonight."

"What! Girl, you know you don't like him like that. Plus, you ain't even twenty-one, yet."

"Well, I'm old enough, and my parents love him."

"What about finishing school, what about that?"

"I know, I know, I'm still going, I just wanna get out of this damn house, out from under this roof. Wow, I could have my own house."

"But—"

"And I do like Tyler. I just got a decent job, and Tyler said he'd support me whatever I decide to do about school. We'll be just fine."

"What about sex? Do you know if he'll be able to please you? Does he have any experience?"

"I don't know. I think neither one of us has much experience. So, what? We'll just learn together."

"You don't even know for sure where he's been. I think you'd better ask around, check his track record, you know? Maybe even get your Dad to call his friend on the MPD and ask him to run a background check on him."

"Girl, we've been together two years! Stop being so paranoid. Hey! Help me plan my wedding. Wow! I'm gonna have a wedding!" I couldn't stop smiling. "I think I'm gonna have sage and blue and brown, my favorite colors. Of course, Mom would kill me if my dress wasn't white, so white it'll be! After all, I am still a virgin."

"Those heffas at church are gonna be mad, they already J."

"I know, right!"

"Well, I'm gonna get off this phone and go to dreamland and dream of my gorgeous wedding to come."

"Okay, girl, holla later."

Lying there in bed, I thought… and pictured, and thought, and pictured. How we were gonna be. My beautiful wedding, my house, my babies, three of them to be exact, my bridesmaids, my graduation, my mind was gone! There was a committee holding a meeting in my head, and finally, finally, they shut up, and I drifted off to sleep.

Tyler came over the following Sunday after church as planned. We all had dinner together as usual and after dinner he said, "Pastor, I'd like to speak with you and the first lady for a moment."

"Sure, son, give me a minute, I've got to help my sweetie get the kitchen straight. Now you not gonna tell me nothing to make me hafta repent, are ya?"

"Naw, Naw, no sir, no sir!"

"Alright then, give me a minute."

Tyler's voice was trembling, as he began speaking. Same tremble as when he proposed to me. The sound that you get when, as a kid, you'd sit under the fan on high speed and try to talk or sing. "Pastor, I've been spending time with your daughter for two years now. I've graduated from college, and I have a great job that pays me enough to provide Judy with the lifestyle she's accustomed to. I have no interest in distracting her from her own goals, of completing her degree. I respect Judy, as well as you and first lady, and we have no hidden surprises. I love her and would love it if y'all could… could… would… would… would give me permission to marry your daughter. There was a big silence in the room. It was as if the house paused.

Mom spoke first, "Well, I have questions."

In unison, we said, "Like…?"

"Well, are you sure you guys are not keeping any secrets from us, like… an unplanned pregnancy?"

"Mom! Never! I can't believe you'd say that or would even think that of me."

"Well, you just never know these days…."

"Mom, we plan on waiting until I finish school. Then, I'll give you and Dad a grandkid or two." I grabbed Tyler's arm, smiling. "Or three."

Then, abruptly, Dad burst out in prayer. "Let us pray." He grabbed my hand and Mom grabbed Tyler's. We made a small circle, bowed our heads, and he began to pray.

OMG, he went on and on and on. Lord bless this marriage, hallelujah! Let it be a blessing, Lord, hallelujah, bless the children that my come from this bond, Lord, let them be healthy, let them have all of their limbs, teeth, eyes, and toes, Lord. Let my granddaughter or grandson be able to hear, see, feel, smell, walk, talk. Let them have a sound mind, Lord. Let these two people be a blessing to one another, Lord. Lord protect them from the robber, the rapist, the drive-by shooter, Lord, let the mother be able to stay in good health, and bring forth a healthy baby, Lord, teach them how to be kind to one another, Lord, teach them not to cheat on one another, Jesus, as his pitch changed to almost a scream. Lord, bless them financially, bless their going out and their coming in, Jesus. I realized that my Daddy was on a roll, and wasn't thinking about stopping.

When I looked at my Dad he'd worked up a sweat, he had forgotten all about time, he must've prayed a good 30 minutes straight.

Then I blurted out, "Daddy!" He, then, snapped out of it and said amen.

Mom asked, "The wedding? Have you guys set a date? I want you to have the biggest wedding ever, baby! Let me help you with your special day."

"Well, Morgan and I have ideas, but we have a lot more to do. We're thinking February 14th."

"Valentine's!" Mom had tears rolling down her face she was so happy for me, and we hugged tightly. Maybe just a little too tightly. When Dad finally pulled her off me, my left shoulder was soaked!

So the parents were happy and I, finally, finally got my ticket out. I could finally get out of their house and be a grown-up! Finally, feel free, free to do whatever, whenever, and however I wanted to, and not feel like I was gonna burn in hell for it. Finally out from under the thumb of Mom and, especially Dad, Pastor Hibbler!

TYLER MALONE

I felt like the luckiest guy in the world when I married Judy. She was my jewel. We'd dated two years when her parents finally gave us their blessing. I remember Judy and her mom were crazy excited for the wedding, while me and Pastor pretty much just did as we were told. It was mostly, "How much money for flowers? How much for the dinner? How much for the cake? How much for this? How much for that?" And it was a lot.

The wedding was held at the church, of course, with an open invitation to the whole congregation. Never seen so many people come to a wedding. So many, many, people, so much going on. It was crazy and expensive, but beautiful.

When it was finally done and we were just about to head for the limo, Pastor started pecking on the mic. "Attention, please! May I have your attention please? I'd like to make a final toast to the bride and groom. Judy, Tyler, we wish you the very best and now Mom and I have a very special gift for you."

His wife joined him carrying a huge box. "Judy, Tyler, please come up. We want you to open it now." Morgan helped Judy with the train on her dress and then stepped off to the side. When we were both ready, we tore into the wrapping together. Inside was a smaller box with a card, keys, and a remote.

Pastor said, "We wanted to give you guys a head start, so this is our gift to you." The card was a picture of a gorgeous two-story house on a hill and said just 4777 Stonington Drive. Pastor looked at Judy with wet eyes and his voice choked a little, "May you find peace there."

Mom added, "And bring us grandbabies!"

Everyone applauded and we both cried, kissed and gave the both of them big hugs! I felt as if all eyes were on me. But, I'm sure Judy felt the same. Morgan and, of all people, Shelly, "that man," had volunteered to help Pastor take the gifts to our new home, so all we had to do was go off on our honeymoon at the Metropolitan Hotel. We ran through our cheering friends to our waiting limo, pelted with rice the whole way! The best day of my life.

Two days later, we left the hotel, picked up our car with the keys, and headed straight to our new home. There it was, sitting on the corner. We used the remote that Pastor had tucked up in the visor and drove into our new garage.

The door there put us into the kitchen. It was beautiful. All stainless-steel appliances, granite countertops, plantation blinds in the kitchen with a view to the backyard. Later we'd see it was completely landscaped along with solar lights. Half bath off the kitchen along gorgeous pecan floors to a great room with a large fireplace. To the left, a door leading to a huge screen porch with patio furniture. To the right, stairs to the second story where we'd find three bedrooms (the one at the end of the hall would become my man cave) and the master suite. The master had skylights, its own gas fireplace, and a luxurious bath with separate shower and toilet and his and hers sinks. Someone had sprinkled rose petals all over the floor and bed. What a blessing, in that moment, we were both so happy....

I think Judy must have gotten pregnant on our wedding night. It happened that fast. Even though her parents, especially her mom, really wanted grandbabies, Judy'd planned to keep working. She loved her work at Rutledge & Rutledge, loved the legal world she'd discovered there. Of course, when she got pregnant, I wanted her to quit school and work and take it easy, but she wasn't having it. She worked all through her pregnancy. Even after we found out she was having twins, she kept working and even took on an extra online class in the summer to get farther along in her degree.

Our babies were due November 8th, but, I guess, they were in a hurry. They were born on Halloween. Trick or Treat! And they were both, trick and treat. Even though we'd never expected babies so soon, especially twins, they were certainly a joy, our beautiful little son and daughter.

Judy let me know right away that even though she loved the babies, and was a proud momma, she wanted to get back to work as soon as possible. I wished she'd take it slower, not be in such a rush, especially since she was breast feeding, but she was determined. Thank goodness, FedEx was great. I got paternity leave to help out at home. One of my co-workers came by bringing cards from everyone and about a million gifts. They'd thrown a shower at the office and, since the babies came early, I hadn't even known it was planned. The church folks brought even more gifts and food so we didn't have to cook much those first weeks. The gifts were great, but it was still pretty rough taking care of twins. One or the other of us was up every three hours all night long. I was exhausted long before Judy went back to work and school.

It seemed like a full time job taking care of twins even while Judy was still home, but once she went back to classes and her job and I had to go back to work, too… I felt like I had three or four full-time jobs - my babies, my job, my relationship with my wife… and my secret.

When and how would I find time for Josh?

When Judy and I took our vows, I took mine seriously, wholeheartedly. I promised to never, ever leave her side, and I did just that. I went to all the church parties, the funerals, the weddings, the graduations. I went with her to the grocery store, shopping malls, family reunions, everything. I loved my Judy to death, and the thought of her even considering leaving me just made me sick! I couldn't do without her. I claimed her that day we met at the church picnic.

But, I still needed to see Josh.

When Judy was home and we were up every few hours with newborns, Josh understood, but as things settled down, he started to ask when I'd be able to see him like before. When we could spend real time together. I didn't know what to tell him. We were even having trouble finding a place to meet. I wasn't bringing him near our house or the twins.

We had been meeting at his place, but after a while, his cousin was in and out of there, taking breaks from his old lady, it sounded like. I just couldn't work it all out, and I kept putting Josh off. I knew he was losing patience.

He finally got pissed one late night when I was supposed to see him, and all I could manage was a quick call. "Tyler, you just all talk and no action. How long do you think I'm gonna wait?"

"Please, baby, I promise, I'll figure it out. Just let us get the babies weaned so we can get sitters, and—"

"Action, Tyler, I need to see some action."

I knew if I wanted to make time for Josh, I had to take care of Judy first.

And, I tried. I always made the runs to the store. I stayed home to give her time out to go and get her hair and nails done. As the babies got a little older and Judy's schedule filled up with class and work, I started to push to take Grandma and Grandpa up on all their offers to babysit. The grandparents were just dying for their time to keep the babies. So were my mom and "that man" if you can believe it. So, with a little gentle urging on my part, we set up a schedule. Her Mom and Dad would give us time out one day a week and my Mom and Shelly would give us one day a week. I told myself it was the best thing for Judy, too. I encouraged her to take one of the days to have some girl time out, and she did just that.

And, that was my time to kick it with Josh.

Judy always trusted me, never questioned me about where I went or who I was with. The first time, I got the nerve to finally meet Josh again after the babies were born, Judy was out getting a massage and having a girl's day out. It helped the guilt a little to know she was, at least, having a good time.

That time, I'd planned to meet Josh at the Hyatt over off Hacks Cross Road. I had him secure the room and told him what time I would be there. I watched my every turn going there. I texted Judy to see how her day was going to make sure she was where she said she'd be. She didn't respond. Hopefully, that meant she was in the middle of her massage.

"Room 356," Josh texted.

I was nervous as hell. I got there and gently knocked, and there he was. We made eye contact, and were instantly like two wild animals. But, afterwards… Josh was purring like a cat, but I felt so ashamed, so dirty… the guilt hit me. I wanted to tell him how I love my wife and my babies. How fucked up this was. But I couldn't.

When we parted, I'd promised to spend his birthday with him. And, I did.

We kept meeting, sometimes at the hotel, once or twice at his place. I was always careful to make sure no one was following me. Always watching for familiar cars or people I knew. I always planned to be home before Judy. I thought I had everything under control.

Then, one night, Josh and I fell asleep. It was much later than usual when I finally got home. As soon as I walked in, I heard the babies crying. Then, I saw Judy's face. She was crying, too.

My stomach dropped. For a moment, I thought she knew everything.

But, she flew into my arms, started crying that the babies had been screaming for nearly an hour, first one, then the other, and she was just so tired....

I wrapped her in a hug with the kind of little kisses that always comforted her. I was sure she could smell that I'd been drinking. "I'm so sorry, baby, I got caught up with a few of the fellas from work—"

"I'm just so glad you're here!" She seemed so relieved I was home that she never asked one question about where I was.

But, I felt horrible.

I told myself I would never put her through this, again. "Next time, just call me, baby. I don't ever want you to be crying and overwhelmed like this." I tilted her face up and wiped at her tears. That's why you got me, right?"

She smiled a little, but she looked exhausted.

"Here, I'll take care of the little monsters now, you go fix yourself a glass of wine. I'll put them to bed and then set you up with my special relaxing bath."

I picked up baby Tyler and quieted her down and, by then, baby Hibbler was just about sleep. I put them in the crib together, and they both went quickly to sleep. I guess they'd about cried it out with poor Judy.

When Judy came into the bathroom with her wine, I had everything set up for her. Sage and citrus candles lit, eucalyptus spearmint bath gel, soft gospel jazz music playing. There was a full moon shining through the skylight and the candles reflecting on the water and chrome and Tulsa grey stones.

I'd taken a quick shower and brushed my teeth, too. I didn't want her to smell anything on me. She slid into the tub, and I got down on my knees and washed her back, her hair, her feet, her toes… even though, she'd just given birth just months ago to twins, her body still looked good. I started with soft gentle kisses around her neck and then lower…. She relaxed against me as I got in with her and started massaging her back.

Next thing I knew, we were making love. Later, in bed, as she curled up into my arms. I thought, this is how it's supposed to be. I love my sweet, innocent Judy, always will. After giving me the twins, I love her more than ever.

I was her first and she belonged to me only. Sometimes I just wanted to kick myself for being the way I was. I didn't deserve her! My Judy was so innocent, so naive, God knows I never wanted to hurt her! What if she found out that I'd been with Josh just hours before being with her? Oh God! I just knew I could never let her find out! My stomach felt sick. I pulled her a little tighter against my chest.

But, what about Josh? I had been meeting Josh long before I met Judy. Hell, I was his first, too!

I loved Judy so much. I wished with all my heart that it were enough.

But, I loved Josh, too.

I loved them both. I hated me! Why? Why was I like that? Ever since I was a kid, I'd prayed asking God to change me. I wanted to end this whole mess I was in. But I didn't know how. I felt so guilty, but I couldn't stop. Sometimes, I tried, for a day, or a week. But, I could never forget Josh. I'd have my mind made up, to stop for good, but then he'd call. Or I would. I'd hear his voice, that voice… and I just couldn't say no, I couldn't resist. I'd tell myself, just one more time. Then I'd fall right back in… in love, lust, like, call it whatever. But, I was in. And, I couldn't get out.

But, damnit, I was married. A father! Then, I thought, oh my God, what if I lost my children? That's when I knew, I had to get some help! The secret was killing me!

The morning after that sleepless night, I made an appointment with Henderson & Henderson. I didn't know what they could do, I just knew I had to get some help before I lost everything.

When I finally made it to their office, I finally got to express it all. Mr. Henderson was a great listener. He let me get it all out! I told him that, for once, I felt I could openly tell someone just how I felt. How guilty. How much I hated the secrecy and lies.

"What do you think would happen if you stopped keeping the secret?"

"I... I don't know... I could lose everything! I...."

"What makes you think that?"

"I think... well, I've had a lot of bad experiences. Like, this girl, Natasha, when I was a kid, calling me out in front of everyone saying I was gay, before I even knew myself. Or, all the rumors, people who think they're whispering at my office. The church is the worst. I heard some women in the choir talking shit about me and my wife, like, 'poe Judy, she don't have a clue she ain't got a real man.' And, 'yeah, you'd think she'd know the difference but Pastor kept her so locked up she probably only been with him.' Damn those hefers! They need to mind their own business." I felt some of my anger drain when I thought of Judy, though. "But, they're right. Judy's so innocent. It's not fair to her."

"Do you think Judy has the right to know who she's married?"

"Yeah, she does, but what if she leaves me... I can't... She could never love me... like this."

"Like what?"

"Disgusting." The word just burst out of me. I don't think I knew I felt that before that moment. Not really.

He looked at me very gently and spoke quietly. "You say you're in love with Josh. Is Josh disgusting?"

"No!"

He just nodded and let that sink in. Then he settled back in his chair and changed the subject. "What was your childhood like?"

"Rough." I told him about never knowing who my Dad was and how I had to watch my momma being controlled, treated like she was stupid by that mean ass man, Shelly…ugh!

"Is that a still a problem for you? Do you still have to deal with that man?"

"No, thank God… I mean, I know it sounds bad, and I'm sorry to say but that man wasn't good for my mom or me. He passed away recently. I don't wish bad on any one. Lord knows I don't, but… I'm glad my momma's finally free of him now."

"And, you, too."

"Yeah, but he… The way he treated me! Shamed me. Over and over again." My fists were clenched and he was looking at me, letting me get it out. I was starting to realize where all my shame and fear came from.

"Tyler, do you have any gay friends who are out, open with friends and family?"

"Josh, and… before I was married, I knew a few."

"And how do you feel about them?"

"I'm happy for them."

He nodded. "So, being gay and being shamed and keeping secrets… those are separate things."

"Yeah, they are."

We were out of time, I was exhausted and my head hurt. Mr. Henderson said it might take a while to work through my feelings, but I knew in the first session that what was killing me most was lying to Judy. I had to find a way to tell her, and I prayed she'd still love me, anyway. I was terrified she'd leave me, but I knew it should be her choice.

I wasn't ready, yet, though, maybe a few more sessions…. But, when I got home, Judy said, "Honey we need to talk," and I knew I was out of time.

I tried to act casual, in case I was wrong, "What is it, pumpkin?"

"Look, Tyler, you're a good husband. You never let me cry. If I'm sad, you've always dried my tears, you've always made my life easier. You're supportive. You're a wonderful, loving father. You make a good living and bring it home to us. But I've known for a long time that something's wrong."

"I love you and the babies so much, Judy!"

"I know you do. But… it's partly my fault. People tried to tell me. Morgan was always telling me you're prettier than most of girls I know, always dressed, perfect shirt, tie, shoes, always smell good, teeth bleached, eyebrows arched, nails manicured…. I told her that don't mean nothing. So what if you have great taste and you keep house better than most women? You're a Godfearing man who loves the Lord, attends church and Bible study, sings in the choir…. that was enough for me."

"Judy—"

"But I'm not enough for you, am I?"

"Judy, I'm so, so, sorry, baby, I've been trying to figure out a way to tell you—"

"You wanna know who really hipped me to you? My momma. She said, she's had to look the other way, herself, a few times. Said she knows the signs. I knew what she meant, and I did not want to hear that. Not about my daddy. Not about the Pastor." Judy stopped and shook her head. "That's just too much, but, she was right about you, wasn't she?"

I didn't know how to respond. Tears filled my eyes.

But, she just shook her head and went on talking. "Once I started paying attention, it was obvious. How you act so different when you get home from your… adventures. So happy and energetic you are after…. Tyler, I may be inexperienced in a lot of things, but I can tell when my husband's been with somebody else."

"I wanted to tell you. I did. baby…" I was near breaking down, but I thought, no, I didn't have no right to break down. She deserved to say her piece and to hear from me, too. "I just couldn't, Judy. I didn't know how. And… and… Lord knows, I never wanted to ever hurt you! I've been praying and asking God to give me the courage to tell you the truth. I've… I've been going to a counselor… trying to—"

"Are you in love with him?"

"What?"

"You heard me."

"You know… who it is?"

"I know. Once I knew, thought I knew, I had to find out… I followed you, and I saw you with him. From there, it wasn't hard to see, the emails, texts, the way you schedule time for me out, then you come home… different. This has been going on a long time, hasn't it? Is it just him? Do you love him?"

"Yes, yes, and… yes. I'm so sorry."

"Do you love me?"

"Oh, God, yes! Judy! So much! I love you and the twins so much! That's why I was so afraid to tell you." I was shaking, so scared she'd leave me. I wanted to beg, plead, cry… She stood there so calm. I was afraid to breathe.

She looked at me for what seemed like forever. "We have a beautiful home, good jobs, nice cars, we look good together. Mom and Dad love you. We have two beautiful, healthy babies who need their Daddy. I need you. And, in spite of all this, I love you. When I took my vows I said together forever, so… forever, it is! I was shocked at first, though I probably shouldn't have been, but now that it's out in the open… I'll live with it. And, I expect you to do the same."

"You won't leave me?"

"No, and you won't leave me. But no more lies."

"No. Yes. No more lies."

"Good." Judy went on to say Grandma and Grandpa were coming up for the weekend to babysit, and she and I were gonna spend time together. "Tyler, we need to air out some things. Now, if you want to slip off to go see Josh, well, then damnit, this time, he'll be seeing both of us. I'm not gonna let some young punk ass boy steal you from me. You're stuck like a truck."

"Oh Judy…." I stood there with my mouth open, face flushed. I started sweating, my hands were shaking, my heart was palpitating at what seemed like a hundred miles per hour. Felt like I was going to pass out!

Judy walked over and gave me a gentle kiss on my forehead and a very tight embrace. "So this is how it's going to be, baby. As long as you stay with one person and don't get wild with it, I'll deal. Don't bring home any drama, and, for God's sake, stop going to that hotel near the church, before somebody sees you like I did. If necessary, I'll even agree to you bringing him to the house, sometimes. Hell, you two hang out here and babysit, and I'll go out with my girlfriends and have some fun of my own. We stay together, but you stay discreet. We don't embarrass my parents."

"Ok, and—"

"And, when I finish my BA, I'm going to law school."

That was new. "Law school?"

"That's right. As long as you continue to take care of me and the kids, and I have my career the way I want, I'll deal with you having what you need. Maybe the good Lord will change you, cause I know only he can, so I'm not going to try. I'm glad you're getting the counseling. If you want, I'd like to go with you. We're going to have stuff to work out. Either way, we're a family and we're gonna stay a family."

"A family." I tucked her against my chest. I was exhausted. It was so much to take in. To feel. To be grateful for.

"Oh, and by the way…" She pulled away and looked up at me. "Remember that night in the tub?" She smiled. "I'm pregnant again."

All I could do was grab her, kiss her, and wipe away her tears and mine… "I love you, Judy, and always will."

We turned out all the lights in our dining room and headed upstairs hand in hand. We checked on our adorable twin babies and quietly went to bed. Before I nodded off to sleep, I whispered in Judy's ear, "Hopefully just one baby coming this time."

She laughed. "Hopefully, but you never know."

I hugged her tight. "I love you."

Life is good, things have been going great! Everything has fallen into place with my wife, the babies, and Josh. He was a little unsure at first, but we've all made it work. We have a good life together so far. I have the perfect wife, house, cars, church, babies, job, even the perfect dog. I couldn't ask for better in-laws, and Pastor and I plan on keeping it that way. Judy's parents still consider me the perfect husband, and Judy likes the picture we paint of the perfect couple, the perfect family. I love Judy, we're making a nice life for ourselves, and I plan on keeping it that way, no matter what!

BROOKE BOATWRIGHT

I've been in love, or so I thought, three damn times now and each time I thought, for sure, "He's the one!" Like... Javier, I was so in love with him, and he's such a fine specimen of a man! They need to make more like him. I loved the way he talked, walked, the car he drove, the way he danced, even the way he chewed, and everyone knew I was in love with him, that is, everyone except him.

I made it a point to show up at every function he attended. He always had a girlfriend, but I didn't care. I just keep thinking, one day, he's gonna notice and realize it's me he should be spending all of his time with. Then, he'll leave that THOT alone. He knew I liked him and was always around, but he never gave me any play at all. Oh, I tried all kinds of ways to catch him. I made friends with his sister, learned how to cook Mexican food, and listened to all the Mariachi and R&B music that he liked.

When I found out he was going on the class trip to Denver, I booked myself a flight there as well. I never spent much time with classmates but when Angela told me he was going, so was I. I bought all kind of cannabis at this dispensary called The Denver Stress Free Cove. And guess who I so happen to run into? None other than Mr. Jazzy Javier himself. He was coming out of the store next door called Herbals 4 Me. I saw him before he saw me. Guess we had the same idea.

When he looked up, I had my purchases and they were all bagged up and ready to go. It looked as if I was leaving. He said, "Hey, you there, what you doing here? Don't tell me you here for the all-white ball, too, girl!"

"Yes sir! I wouldn't have missed this one for the world."

"Girl, we coulda come together. I know this town like the back of my hand. You know I spent some time here when I was in the military. I still have one piece of rental property left here though I keep threating to sell it. And I've a whole lot of friends. It always gives me an excuse to come and let my hair down, de-stress. Where are you staying?"

"Over at the Mariott."

"You came all this way by yourself?"

"Yes, I sure did, I'm a big girl." I smiled, thinking wonder if he brought that thang with him? I don't know why he can't put two and two together and see it's me longing for him.

That night the party went off with a blast. It was great, got hit at a few times, but no one of any interest to me. So alone I went, one more time to my room, disgusted wondering why, why, doesn't he see me, really see me? I did get to hang out a bit with his sister, Angela, but that was about as close as I could get to him.

On my departure home, my head was talking, give it up girl, he don't want you. He's got a girl. Then I'd erase all of those thoughts and say one day I'm gonna get him... just wait... he'll come around one day.

I got home, unpacked, called his sister, and told her it was great seeing her and her brother and to keep me up to date next time something else good comes along.

She said, "Girl you know I will. Javier asked about you. He's just starting to put two and two together and notice that you seem to pop up a lot at some of the same places he does. He asked for your number—"

"No! Girl, no, you kidding?" I was smiling as big as a rainbow in the sky. "Girl, give it to him, call him back, and give it to him right now. You think he—"

"Girl, I don't know what he wants, but he asked for your number."

"Okay, sure, oh boy! This is the best news I've had in a while. I can't wait to talk to his fine ass. Ooh! I'm so excited, I can't wait." That evening I waited, and waited and waited, no call from Javier.

The very next morning, he called.

"Brooke?"

"Yes, this is Brooke speaking."

"Hey this is Javier, my sister gave me your number. She said it was okay to call you. How you doing?"

"I'm great! It's so great to talk to you—"

"Look Brooke, I just wanted to holla at you for a minute. You seem like a nice girl and all, and it seems as if you think we might hook up or something, and... just so you don't get it twisted, and I certainly don't want to mislead you. I have a woman and I'm happy with her. You seem cool and all but you and me, could never be. I don't want to sound so cold, but I don't want any misunderstanding, that's why I'm calling. I'm in love with my woman, she's my wife, and I ain't looking for no side piece. I just wanted to clear the air. I saw you've sent me several Facebook friend requests. I don't want to be connected with you, okay? You're cool people and I know you and my sis hang out but, baby, I just don't like you like that!"

Tears were rolling down my face as he spoke. It was as if someone had it blasting on a loud speaker. What a letdown! I was so embarrassed. I felt so rejected! So fucking stupid, then I thought, who told him, anyway? I felt like a stalker, and in a way, I guess I kinda was.

"Thanks for calling Javier, I got ya." I hung up.

So, I backed off, but continued to watch him from a distance for the next two years. I watched everything, what he posted on Facebook, followed him on Instagram, and Twitter, each and every tweet that I could. I never said another word or showed my face anywhere near him. No more, incidentally or coincidentally, meeting at the same functions.

But I did remain friends with his sister, Angela. I found out from her that his wife's name was Aja, and that she was crazy as hell, and the family hated her! Angela gave me all the juice, said he had to go get her from crazy ass places all times of the night, says she started fights, and he had to come to her rescue over and over again. They'd been bugging him to leave her ass for ages.

Ugh, it felt like such a waste! He was supposed to be with me! My feelings were hurt. It hurt all the way down to my bones that he should've been with me, and for a long time, I still believed that one day he would. I just couldn't give up hope! I just knew one day he'd be mine. For nearly three years, I just lived with the memories, I celebrated his birthday every year on August 28th, making myself his favorite cake and going through all the pictures I had of him everywhere, in my house, my car, my cell phone, my screen saver, my cell phone cover, a tee shirt, my mouse pad. Ok, maybe that was a little crazy, but, I just kept hoping one day he'd come around, and I was determined that when he did, I'd be ready and waiting.

But three years and still no Javier. I had a couple other men coming around in that time like there was James, who hit on me, not a love connection at all, with his honorary broke ass! He thought he was the shit, and that I should've been happy to be with him, but he was no Javier. No one was. I mean, I'd been in love once in the past. I'd even tried my hand at marriage, with Chad, but he was crazy and I was way too young. Most of the time I forget I was ever married. Other guys came around, but I was just too hung up on Javier to really notice.

Except for one. I have, all this time, kept up this one relationship, a kinda sorta relationship/friendship with Marlon, because, honestly, Marlon has chased me for just about as long as I'd been chasing Javier. So, sometimes when I just couldn't take my yearning for Javier any longer, sometimes I'd settle and spend time with Marlon, but he just ain't Javier, and most of the time I was with him, I was just fantasizing that he was.

Still, really, we do have fun. Marlon and I have done all kind of things together, skydiving in Atlanta, snorkeling in Mexico, he's my stand-in date for family and work functions, holiday parties, weddings I can't get out of.

I'll never forget that crazy ass wedding we went to for poor Vincent and Camille. No, poor Camille. Seems Vincent had a side piece who showed up at the damn wedding uninvited. That was some fucked up shit, brought this girl with her that acted a plum fool! I remember we said… man… that what happens when you think you got a secret.

Sometimes, I do feel a little bad… poor Marlon, I know he truly loves me, worships the ground I walk on, even. He's stable, got good credit, has a nice savings, has his own home, he's justa good old guy. What more can a girl ask for? I know Marlon was living with some girl for a while but he always kept hitting at me. Always seemed to find time to do something with or for me, every chance he got or every chance I'd give him.

Now finally, finally, I realize I ain't getting any younger, so a girl gotta do what a girl gotta do. I'm gonna give up wishing and waiting for Javier. I've been through one stupid marriage and three long years, waiting on Javier and still didn't get him. Marlon has left the girl he was with and wants to settle down with me, marry me. He has no idea who I really am. He just thinks he does. But, dammit, I'll go ahead and marry Marlon, after all he's been my fall guy forever.

MARLON BENSON

Brooke finally agreed to marry me. I been chasing that girl off and on for years and when she finally agreed back in May, I wanted to do it right then, run off to the courthouse and lock it down, but she insisted we wait till August 28th. No idea why that was some special day for her, but I woulda done anything she wanted at that point.

Despite the wait, we agreed we didn't want a big wedding and all, so we headed to Las Vegas and got married. No guest, no family, just the two of us at the Little White Wedding Chapel. There were pictures on the walls of some of the famous people that got married there. It was pretty cool to get married in the same place as Michael Jordan, R. Kelly and Anita Baker. Our wedding was straight to the point, cheap, short and sweet, and afterwards we partied non-stop for the next five days.

We got the Aria honeymoon package. It gave us the royal treatment for two at Spa Aria. Oh, what a beautiful place. The entire time we were there, I had Jack all day and Brooke had champagne day and night. We stayed fucked up! We slept it off a little during the day, woke up and drank more and gambled all night never stopping before dawn. We'd have breakfast then head back to our suite for bed. We made love just as often and as wild as we drank. In the bed, in the bathtub, on the bathroom counter, on the wet bar, on the sofa, in the sitting area, up against the windows, on the elevator, even in the casino bathroom, wow, what a wild pair we were.

We got a little tired of gambling near the end, so I offered to take Brooke shopping and she grabbed a few souvenirs for girlfriends. We rode the rollercoaster at New York, New York and bungee jumped at MGM Grand, tried an oxygen bar, and went to see comedian Eddie Griffin. Brooke even insisted we go to a strip club. I admit I was a little embarrassed sitting there with my wife, but when I saw how relaxed she was, I relaxed to and it was off the chain.

And we talked, more than we had when we were just friends. I told her about being a church boy for a while, and falling madly in love with Judy, the

Pastor's kid, whose parents never approved of me especially after some girl lied and said I got her pregnant.

She was genuinely surprised. "I can't believe you never told me that before."

"You never really asked much about me." I realized, and I think Brooke did, too, that we'd never really talked that much. Honestly, she never seemed that interested.

"Well, I'm asking now. You still go to church?"

"Nah, my Dad wanted me to be a Pastor like him, but I don't even go much, anymore. Been to church enough for everybody."

So, we talked. We didn't see eye to eye on church or politics. We didn't seem to like the same foods or entertainment, but sex, shopping, gambling and money, we were on the same page. I think Brooke had kinda taken me for granted before, but in Vegas she seemed genuinely happy to be with me.

When we finally came down off our honeymoon high, we had to settle down, come back to earth, get focused, and go back to work. I was a salesmen then at Nissan and Brooke was a Sales Associate Manager for Macy's. We both worked Monday – Friday and had to work one weekend a month at each of our jobs. We were both extra busy around the holidays because everybody buys cars and gifts at the end of the year.

I wasn't sure at first if Brooke married me because she really loved me and wanted to spend the rest of her life with me or if she was settling cause she couldn't get that guy she really wanted, but, the honeymoon was great and the first six months of our marriage was great!

Brooke seemed happy, at first, but then, I noticed she started having a problem with me asking where she was going and or what time she'd be back. It wasn't a problem in the beginning. I'd just ask an innocent question, like "Hey, baby, where you going?" And her response would be, "I'm grown, and you don't ask grown folks where they're going, boy!"

It irritated her, but I kept asking, I couldn't help it. I worry. But I worry because I love her. I don't want her to come up missing. It took me way, way, too long to win her over, and I want to keep her. Plus, one heartbreak is enough for a lifetime. Judy was supposed to be my wife, but her Dad wasn't having it, and I never got a fair chance. Things are so crazy these days, you just can't be too careful.

I tried to tell her. "Just the other day, the news reported the body of a woman found by some farmers. Turned out that woman came up missing cause she didn't want to tell her old man that she was going to the casino. C'mon, baby, I worry. That woman was dead with several bullet wounds to her head, buck naked!"

"Ugh! Stop with that! You're either smothering me or scaring me. All at the same time!"

Brooke thinks I'm becoming a control freak, that I'm just paranoid. I'm not, I am just genuinely concerned about her well-being. The more she goes out without me, the more I'm gonna pay attention to her whereabouts. I don't think she's cheating on me, but I feel like something is going on, and I'm gonna find out what. When we were friends and for the first six months together, we were always able to talk to each other and, when we weren't working, we went just about everywhere together. So why is she so secretive now? I don't get it.

I do know that I love Brooke more than she will ever love me, and I accept that, I knew it from the start. I knew all about this long hard crush for some guy named Javier, that just wasn't that into her, but I never met the dude. I know I was her fall guy, and if she had her way she would've married him but he was married to someone else. I heard it was a bad move on his part, that the girl had some serious mental issues. Oh well, better for me, his loss… I got who I wanted.

And I'm gonna keep her. She's getting ready to go out this evening, and I'm gonna follow her. I'm gonna find out just what the hell is going on. While she was still getting dressed, I told her I would be leaving soon, too, to go by my Mom and Dad's house to check in on them. They're getting on up in age and I hafta check on them at least once or twice a week.

Brooke gave me a quick smack on the lips and headed out. "Ok, see ya later, baby." She got into her car and was backing out of the driveway before I could get my shoes on. I just made it to my car before she got all the way to the corner. This time, I'm gonna find out just where she's disappearing to.

She was about two cars ahead and weaving in and out of lanes, down Poplar then left on 2nd street, heading south. I thought this woman drives so damn fast, where is she going? To Tunica, Southland? Where. She turned left. So she's not headed across the bridge. Maybe Beale street? Main street? Where? I still had no idea. But I kept following slowly behind. She took 2nd street all the way until it ended and from there she headed to Crump Blvd, made a left and continued down to GE Patterson Boulevard straight to where the old projects used to be, which is where she grew up. Now who, what the fuck was she doing or who did she still associate with that lived over here? I knew she graduated from Booker T. Washington, but she never mentioned that she still kept in touch with anyone from high school. Maybe she was going to see that guy. Javier. But, surely she's over him by now? Surely, that can't be it. My mind was racing, but who else, what, why, I just couldn't figure it out. She made a U-turn and parked, right on the side of what used to be Claybourne Homes Apartments.

She got out with her purse on her shoulder, Bluetooth head phones in her ear, cell phone in hand. She walked as if this was a regular place for her. I thought who, what or why is she here. She's got some explaining to do. I'm gonna sit here and see just how long she stays up in there and who the fuck comes out of there with her.

That car of hers sticks out like a sore thumb. I like to call her car "the guy magnet." Because, it's definitely a head turner. I remember when she bought that car from me. Actually, that's how we met, seems as if it was only yesterday. I was flirting with her and trying to make a sale at the same time. I don't know what attracted me to her most… those dimples, her big sexy eyes or that plump, round butt. But I was instantly attracted, in love, in lust… all of the above. She was very demanding and knew exactly what she wanted.

When she saw the 370Z, she stopped and pointed. "I want this car with all the bells and whistles because I'm not buying another one for a long while."

She said she had a budget that she exceeded, but I was smiling so hard and trying to hit on her that I gave her everything and more, at her price. Brand spanking new 370Z mahogany with a cognac convertible top, navigation system, XM radio, heated seats, rear view monitor, Bose audio system, keyless entry, iPod, Bluetooth, lighted floor boards, the works. I gave it all to her, and she looked so damn good in it.

Now, here she was seeing someone else in it and I'm getting tired of waiting for her to come out! It's been a little over an hour now. I'm giving her another 30 minutes and if she's not out by then, I'm leaving. But I didn't. 9:00 pm. 9:30, and she still hadn't come out. I waited till 9:45, then left. I was furious, my head was pounding, I was puzzled, confused, my mind racing. What the hell is she doing here? Who the hell did she go in there to see? Another man, a woman, what? She's hiding something from me, and I want to know just what the hell it is.

As I drove away I thought, I'll give her a chance to tell the truth about what's going on first. If she doesn't give me a straight answer, then I'll tell her that I followed her, and she needs to explain. I need a damn drink. I made a quick stop at the Liquor Bank.

BROOKE BENSON

"The last time I borrowed $1600, and I've paid you half that back already. Come on Mr. Spencer. I just need $800 more. I promise that'll be it for a while.

Spencer shook his head. "Girl, you are getting yourself in too deep. That would put you right back at $1600, plus interest. I know your momma would be rolling over in her grave if she knew you were down here borrowing this kinda money. Hell, she'd be rolling over in her grave if she knew I was even letting you borrow half that much money. Don't you have a husband now?"

"Yes, I do."

He squinted at me, disapproving. "Well, girl, I can't tell! Ain't he got a job?"

"Of course, he does. I just don't want to tell him about my money problems. We haven't been married that long."

"Why not, little lady? If he's with you, he's with you. Maybe, if he knew he'd try and help you straightened things out."

"I don't think so…." I really didn't want to tell him, but he'd known me since I was a kid. He'd lent my Momma money many times. I sighed. "The thing is, I've messed up a lot of his money, too."

"Damn girl…." He sat there shaking his head at me, again. I felt like a kid who'd messed up and was about to get into big trouble. He looked at me sternly. "Look, the way I see it, you have no choice but to tell him. If he loves you, like you say he does, he'll forgive you and help out."

"Just help me out, now, Mr. Spencer, please!" I tried not to sound whiney. I took a breath and tried to explain more calmly. "I've been to eight different payday loan places now. I've run out of things to pawn, and soon Marlon is gonna notice that some of the jewelry he gave me is missing. It's a bitch paying back. I should've learned my lesson by now, stupid me. I think that's the shit that sent my Momma to an early grave. But I had the money, Mr.

Spencer, I had it. If I'd just cashed out when I hit $8000 last month at The Hollywood, I'd be okay now."

"Aww, Girl, that's bad, you can't be chasing that casino jackpot! I see it all the time. Gambling is as bad as crack! I say, who needs drugs; when there's gambling?"

"I know, but I can't seem to shake that secret man of mine, Mr. NeedMore. Whenever he and I are alone, he smooth talks me right out of my money. He has a way of convincing me that everything is gonna be alright, keep playing, that jackpot is coming in the next few spins, then I'm tricked again and all of my money is gone. Our relationship is quite dysfunctional, but I keep hanging with him… ugh!"

"I'm telling ya, you better talk to that husband of yours."

"Marlon is a great guy, I love him… no, let me put it this way, I love that Marlon loves me. It's not his fault he's not who I really wanted. I know Marlon is a good guy and has my best interest at heart. And, sooner or later, Marlon is gonna catch on to me and I could lose him."

"And you don't want that?"

"Lord knows, I don't want that! But I can't tell him. I… Marlon's check is deposited into our bank account with mine. He never checks the balance. We also each have separate accounts and he never asks about mine. He just has no idea how far behind I am on everything."

"So you've been taking his money?"

"I have access to his, no… *our*… bank account that we use to pay bills. He trusts that I pay what's due and so far, he's never checked. He knows I gamble, just not gamble-holicly. We've even gone together to the casino a few times, for dinner, and in Las Vegas, we gambled hard, but he has no idea that I gamble all the time… on everything."

"So, he has no clue of the money problems he has now because of you. What about credit?"

"Maxed out and even a few new cards he doesn't know about. Listen, I know what a mess I've made. I gamble when he's not around. I buy $20 and $10 scratch off tickets, lottery tickets, I play the numbers almost every day, I bet on the horses, too. The Kentucky Derby, The Bellmont, The Preakness every year. I borrow from check cashing places, and you."

He just looked at me. He had such a sad face. "Your Momma did the same."

"I know! And it killed her. And I'm doing the same shit, but worse! I've run through Momma's insurance policy as well, $100k ran out so fast."

"You've been gambling that much! After seeing what it did to your mother?"

"No, worse. I spent most of the damn money chasing and trying to impress a man that never wanted me. Plane tickets, clothes, hair salons, then I started making anonymous donations to Javier's organization called Brothers in Sync. They get help for troubled youth. I started doing it because he always sends a personal thank you card and I get invitations to all their special events which, of course, I don't dare show up for.

"Good Lord, woman! You need more than financial help. You need to talk to a shrink or something."

"I know, it's pathetic, but I love that man, always have and always will. For the life of me, I can't stop wishing he were mine."

"Gambling makes that feeling go away for a while."

"Yes, but I have a husband now, who, for some reason lately, has become noisy and clingy as hell. I promise once we get our tax refund this year, I'll get things back on track. If you could just help me now... I know Marlon's gonna find me out, soon, but I gotta hide it as long as I possibly can, so I can fix it."

"He must love and trust you a lot not to have questioned anything by now."

"He does. But I've also got all the bills that I pay electronically linked straight to my email, and the few paper bills left go straight to my P.O. Box. All the check cashing places, loan, or pawn shops have my cell number. Just a little longer, please. Please, I'm begging you.

Spencer pulled out his special grey box, opened it, counted out $800 and handed the money to me. "I don't like doing this, girl. I hate to see you mess up your marriage, hell, you just getting started. Marlons don't come along every day, you know.

"I know. I don't like it either. Marlon's a good guy, I know he doesn't deserve this. He deserves someone better than me, and I know it."

MARLON BENSON

When Brooke got home, I was waiting for her on the sofa in the dim living room. "Hello, Brooke."

She looked nervous the minute she saw me. "Hey, babe, how was your night?"

"It was okay, how about yours?"

"It was fine, See there, I came back home without a scratch! No one shot, kidnapped or hurt me! You worry too much. I'm going to bed—"

"Babe, hold up! Sit down. I got you a cold Yuengling."

"I'm really tired—"

I grabbed her hand. "Babe. Sit. Have a drink with me."

Her eyes flicked to the hallway like she wanted to run, but she sat on the edge of my big reclining leather chair next to me and took a sip from the bottle. Her palms were damp, just as if she'd just washed her hands and didn't completely dry them.

I relaxed back on the recliner. "Let me tell you how my evening went. When I got home after… after checking on Mom and Dad… I got to thinking about our anniversary. I was thinking we're both doing well at work, we can afford a nice trip. So I was looking online to get some ideas… There's all kinds of all-inclusive trips. Cuba, Punta Cana, Bahamas, Puerto Rico, Italy, Paris, Dubai. I was thinking Punta Cana. Would you like that?"

"Umm, sure…."

"It sounded like someplace you'd like. So, I found this site with great deals. If you join, you get discounts on any trip and all sorts of perks, so I thought sure, why not, so I joined."

"Great."

"Yeah, great. Only when I tried to join, my damn card was declined."

Even in the dim light, she looked pale. "Well, that happens online sometimes."

"Yeah, so I tried another card, and another, then I tried the ATM card, direct from the bank."

She took a long drag from the bottle.

"Have you looked at our checking account lately? It says it's overdrawn." In fact, it was minus $2000, combined with the credit cards at their limit.... I slammed down my beer on the table and turned to her. "When I saw it, I thought, surely there must be a fucking mistake." I looked her in the eyes and made sure she was looking back. "Is there something you ain't telling me, Brooke?"

BROOKE BENSON

"Like what, Marlon, what… you questioning me? I have no idea what's going on at that bank of yours. I can't stand Suntrust, anyway. Must be some weird mistake, but… you know… weird shit happens with banks all the time, hump. Damn technology… I couldn't explain it all away, so, I went for distraction.

I said, "Let's go to bed, baby, it's been a long day. You can deal with this shit in the morning! You wouldn't let me go to sleep, so now you've gotta pay for it! I get turned on when you fuss over me and money." I started touching him, everywhere, did everything he liked. We fondled and fucked from the sofa, to the hallway, to the bedroom… till he finally passed out asleep.

I lay there on my side afraid to move for a long time, thinking, seemed like maybe all night. When Marlon's alarm went off, I wasn't sure I'd slept at all, but I kept my eyes closed and my breathing even. I felt him standing over me for a minute, but I stayed still a stone. As if I was really asleep. It seemed like forever. I heard the outside door close, and I lay in bed for a minute longer, afraid it was some kind of trick, but then I thought, no, Brooke, Marlon's not the one playing games here.

I threw off the covers and started throwing things in a bag. I knew Marlon. He wasn't going to rest until he figured this shit out. He had an early meeting at work, then he'd start trying to sort out whatever the fuck was going on with his money. I had to get gone before his ass got back, woe is me!

MARLON BENSON

The meeting seemed to drag on. I thought about Brooke. Brooke's mouth. Brooke's hands. Brooke's... she loved me. She wouldn't do no shit like this on purpose. Right? So, she went somewhere last night, so what? I suddenly realized with all the worrying about the money I'd forgotten to ask her where she'd gone, and she damn sure didn't mention it! As soon as the damn meeting ended, I went to my desk and called the bank. I had to get this shit straightened out. I do not like people fucking with my damn hard-earned money!

I was on hold for 11 minutes, according to their stupid ass recording, before I said fuck this and hung up. I'm going down there and talk to a live person and get to the bottom of this shit.

At Suntrust, I immediately asked for the manager, saying my accounts had been compromised. Ms. Natashia was very professional. While she pulled up my account, she spoke to me in a soothing banker voice, saying they take security breaches very seriously, and she'll be happy to help me.

There was a barely detectable shift to her voice when she saw the screen for my accounts, "Are all of your accounts shared accounts, Mr. Benson."

"Um... yeah... I think so. No. ... there's an old savings account that's still in just my name...and, maybe... I'm... not sure."

"Well, you're right, your checking is overdrawn and your cards through this bank are at or close to their credit limits."

"Damn. Something is seriously wrong here."

"Your Money Market account is also depleted."

The blood drained out of my head. I thought I was going to faint, then I felt a wave of nausea. "What?"

"You have a Money Market account with us, ending in 6407. A minimum balance is required on that account to avoid fees, but I see a fee will be charged with the next statement."

"That account had 95,000 dollars in it."

"Um... she went back to her screen. As of May of last year it did, yes, I see that."

"And now?"

She turned the screen around to face me.

"Oh, my God." I was shaking. My fucking retirement savings. Gone. "But... I'm not liable for... identity theft... or whatever this shit is called, right?"

"Sir, those withdrawals were made here in this branch, in person, with a written check. The person making them would have to show us ID and her bank card."

"Her bank card."

"Yes, Sir. I have scans of the checks here. Signed by your wife. A legal owner of the account." She clicked a key on her keyboard and the screen switched to a lot of low resolution pics of checks. She scrolled through for me. They seemed to be all in the last five or six months.

Hollywood Casino - $500

Horseshoe Casino - $750

Title Loan - $1250

Kwik Cash, Greyhound Park, Money to Loan, Ace Check Cashing...$950, $1000, $2000, $5,000

"$5,000. Who is that?"

"It looks like Amos Spencer – CPA."

My brain felt like mush, my stomach was churning, heart beating fast, palms sweaty. "That's... he does our taxes... maybe...." For a brief second, I thought maybe that was legit..." I scrolled down and there were a few checks all to one payee...Brothers in Sync... what the hell is that? Sounds like... what... a band? A Club ... what the hell? And she's been paying these motherfuckers that amount every month for a while.

Then I saw it and it fucked me up! The first check of all the checks. To Brother's In Sync. Written on our wedding day! I saw that date, that date. Written in Brooke's handwriting. That was the lick that killed dick!

I asked Ms. Natashia to give me a minute. At that point, I was so fucking pissed. I was hotter than fish grease! I wanted to hit a wall or the granite desktop where Ms. Natashia sat. She could see I was coming undone! My stomach convulsed! If I didn't get out of that bank I was gonna vomit all over Ms. Natashia's very professional desk.

BROOKE BENSON

My head was racing. Where could I go? I thought about Angela. But she and James were going through some shit… I wasn't even sure if he was still living there or not. What could I tell Angela if I went over there? Hey girl, I just fucked up my good thang, let's fuck up together.

No, not Angela. I should go to Peggy's. Peggy would be better. Angela would pry, but I can give Peggy half the truth, and she'll wait and let me talk it out when I'm ready.

I hit 55 South, headed downtown. Just have to call Peggy and tell her to let security know so they'll let me in. I'll just tell her that Marlon and I had our first big fight.

The call went to voicemail, but Peggy called right back. "Hey girl, you called?"

"Yes! Hey can you stand a little company for a minute? I just had a big fight with Marlon and I need to get away for a few days. You… got anybody there?"

"Oh no, girl, come on. It'll be good to see you.

"Great, I'm actually almost to you. Can you call downstairs to let them know I'm coming?"

"Sure thing, I was just sitting here, not doing a damn thang."

Now that I had a place to go, the city seemed friendlier. Beautiful, really, with all the lights. I hoped I wouldn't be asking too much, hoped Peggy was ok now. Lately, she'd been more low key than usual. She claimed she stopped messing with her plunder, and I hope so, she needed to take it from me, stop that wishing and settling for somebody else's shit. It was pretty clear to me what kind of guy he was when I saw him at the wedding. I mean, Vincent's wedding was beautiful and all, but after that scene Peggy's sister pulled, he was still standing there like he was the perfect guy, all innocent! Hump, I know better.

I stopped at the liquor store on the way to Peggy's. As I stood in line at the cashier, I thought, better focus on my own shit, Marlon still didn't know I'd lost my job. The first time my department drawer was short $500, I got a verbal warning. I just kind of made it look like it could've been an employee error, since I had 6 employees under me. The second time, it was $850, and it brought more attention to my area and the employees under me, but nothing happened. I thought I had it all covered. Then, the last time, I was sure I could run across the bridge, get that money, and replace it before they even noticed. But that's not what happened. Just after closing, the GM showed up and told me that they were letting me go. Informed me that they'd been watching and that they could bring criminal charges, but instead, were just terminating me. He said the shortages would be deducted from my last pay check. I was lucky I had enough to pay for the booze, honestly. I don't know what Marlon will do when he finds out the whole truth.

By the time I got to Peggy's, I was just praying, please God help me figure out how to keep my man. I was sitting there praying like that when the phone rang.

It was just Peggy. "Girl, where you at?"

"I'm out front, coming in now." I got out grabbing my bag and locked up, juggling my phone to hear her.

"I have a little wine here, do we need to go get more?"

"No, girl, I'm way past wine, I need some old school shit! You won't believe this, but I got me some MD 20/20. Wine won't get it! I need to go to oblivion."

"Girl, do what you do."

"Okay, coming up, now."

Turned out, I didn't get near as deep into that bottle as I planned. I was so tired from not sleeping the night before, I crashed pretty early. I woke to an empty house. My head was pounding, I woke thinking about the last time I saw Marlon, that disgusted look on his face. What the hell have I done? I just lay there, staring at the walls, and listening to the waterfall trickling from

Peggy's guest bathroom. Then, my tears started rolling. I never meant to mess up his money, no, our money. I just thought for sure I could put it back before he'd notice. I have gotta get some help before I lose my mind. Oh Lord, please help me. I took some of the Valium Peggy left on the night stand and rolled over in bed. All I could do was rock and cry… and hope these pills kick in sooner rather than later.…

I guess I slept really hard because when I woke up it was early morning, the place was still dark, Peggy must still be sleeping. Out the windows, no sign of the sun yet. I got up and headed for the bathroom, then the living room. The house was so quiet, I could hear the clock ticking the seconds from her kitchen. I went close to it and startled a little seeing my own face reflected. The face was a mirror. The hands showed 6:30. Wow, I'd slept hard! That pill really knocked me out. I was starved. Guess I'd better find something in here to eat. I flipped the TV on low, so I wouldn't wake Peggy and checked her freezer. She had all kinds of frozen entrees. I found something from PFChangs, shrimp fried rice. So, I nuked it, ate, cleaned up after myself and headed back to bed. I thought I'd try to at least read something. Here I am at someone else's house, in someone else's bed, and I have a nice place and bed of my own, with someone in it. I thought about calling him, picked up my phone… still no messages or missed calls, nothing from Marlon all night. Then I did a double take, and damn it was 6:34pm, not am! Boy, was I ever sleeping hard! Then, I heard Peggy's key in the front door. She must just be getting home from work.

"Hey, Brooke, You in there? You up?"

"Yeah, yeah, come on in. Just woke up. That valium knocked me out."

"I guess so, you didn't budge when I left this morning." She sat on the bed beside me. "Okay girl, you've had a rest, now tell me. What's going on? What did you and Marlon fight about that made you have to come stay with me?"

A lump come up in my throat. "Girl, I did a terrible thing. I've got a problem and I've had it for a while, but I've been afraid to tell anyone about it, I've been so embarrassed."

"Brooke, you know we go way back, you can talk to me about anything."

"No, it's really, really bad. Marlon was trying to surprise me and take me on a trip for our anniversary and found out that I've been misusing our money. Girl I've got a...." I couldn't get out nothing more... I just started crying and crying, and my words came out all babbled.

"Calm down, Brooke, it can't be that bad."

"Yes, it is. It's that bad. I'm so ashamed. I think it might even cost me my marriage. I don't know how to fix it."

"You don't want to tell me what it is?"

"I just... I..." I just couldn't get the words out and I felt so scared. My hands were shaking. "Peggy, I... I feel like I'm going crazy. I... I think I need professional help."

Peggy looked scared and that didn't help me feel any calmer. Then, she started looking around for something. "Wait a second... I've got something... a card.... I thought it was in here...."

She hopped up and ran off to the living room and was back in a second with a business card. "Here, I haven't called these people, but I hear they are good."

The card was for Henderson and Henderson Psychological Services.

"Why do you have this?"

"Oh, girl, I got that card from sorry ass Vincent. He thought I should've called them because of how down I got when he got married. But, I didn't need them, I just rocked myself through it, and--" She looked up at me and her tone changed. "But, I probably should have called. Really. And, I hear they're pretty good. It's a husband and wife business. I mean, that's good, right... then know couples but they do lots of stuff...."

"Yeah, maybe... in the morning. Right now, I just want to go to back to sleep and forget about it all."

Peggy reached for the bedside table. "You want another Valium?"

"No, I… man, that stuff is strong, I think I still got some in my system. Anyway, I'm still tired."

She shook the bottle, gave me a look, and took it with her, closing the door behind her.

For a few minutes, I heard the TV playing low and her messing around in the kitchen. I couldn't believe I felt like sleeping more, but I was already drifting off, thinking I've gotta get to those therapists, get in a group or something.… and I've gotta figure out how to save my marriage. I don't want to be alone, I need Marlon. And, finally, just before I fell asleep, I turned back to prayer. Please God, I'm begging you! Help me.

I finally woke up the next morning feeling normal again. I'd been at Peggy's for three days and not one word from Marlon. He hadn't called at all. I'd tried a couple times to call, but his phone went straight to voice mail. I thought again about calling those therapists and getting an appointment right away, but… well… first coffee.

I headed to the kitchen and, awe, so sweet, Peggy had already made a pot.

She'd also left a note, no, more like a letter:

Dear Brooke,

I know you are going through a lot, and I'm here to talk whenever you're ready. I know you're a grown ass woman and I can't give you much advice on marriage, never been married, myself. But for what it's worth, here's my two cents. Girl, try, try as hard as you can, to make it work with Marlon. Beg, if necessary, for his forgiveness. A good man is so hard to find. I don't know what you did, but it must've been something terrible to land you over here with me. But I hope you work it out. I would love to have someone to call my own. I spent a lot of years playing around with somebody else's man. Now, he chose to marry her, and I hafta start all over, and it ain't easy, finding someone to trust and spend time with when you've been alone for so long. Stay as long as you like, but for God's sake, fix it, girl! You got a man that, from what I can tell, loves you to death. So, you better learn how to treat him right or you know what… SOMEONE ELSE WILL. I'll see you later tonight. After work, I'm running by to check on my sister. She's been having marriage problems, too. Boy, you two! How am I supposed to keep the faith that I'll get a good mate when I see y'all tripping? Ugh! Give a girl some hope, will ya? Anyway, I'll be back soon, and you know the drill, kick back, relax, and make yourself at home, mi casa es su casa.

As I read her note, the tears started flowing down my face again. Just like rain running down the side of a window pane. I hated myself right now. How could I have been so stupid? Looking for a jackpot when my jackpot had always been with me. Marlon. I sipped on my coffee, went out on the patio, and sat there with my phone in my hand. I stared out at the view of the mighty Mississippi river and bridge, the red and blue lights. I thought how, did you get so fucked up? Get honest with yourself, you're sick, you need help. You can't do this alone. I sipped more of my coffee, looked at that card again from Henderson and Henderson. I should call. Get an appointment right away, but... I didn't have anything decent to wear, right? I couldn't call, yet. I'd hafta go by the house to get a few more clothes. Marlon was usually gone by 9-9:30 in the morning, so if I got there around 10, he'd be gone.

When I pulled up into the garage, I could tell it hadn't been too long since he'd left. The garage was still warm. I entered the house right into our kitchen. The kitchen was clean, the bar area, clean, the den clean, the house looked so still. Looked just as I left it... my shoes were still sitting right by the chaise lounge. I checked the refrigerator and there was beer inside, he had some to go stuff, looked like he'd been eating out since I left. I headed to our room to grab some clothes out of my closet, and that's when I saw them. Marlon had still purchased tickets for two, to the Dominican Republic, Punta Cana. Oh my God, this man still loves me!

I stood there, stock still, feeling... I didn't even know what... happy, relieved, scared... but in the next second, I decided, no matter what, I'm not saying one word. I know him. He needs space right now. I'll give him all the space he needs. I know he'll call me soon. I'm just gonna stay out of his way and let him do that.

I knew I needed professional help with the gambling, the money stuff, maybe lots of other stuff, too. I also knew I was scared to call anyone, I'd left the card for the Henderson's back at Peggy's, but when I saw the tickets...

knowing Marlon still loved me gave me strength. I decided to call as soon as I got back to Peggy's.

When I called Henderson and Henderson Psychological Services the next morning I didn't get an answer. I got the voice mail recording that said, "Thank you for calling Henderson and Henderson Psychological Services, licensed marriage and family therapists, where we specialize in you. If this is an emergency, please hang up and call 911. If you've reached us during our normal business hours, please leave a message." I immediately hung up, I thought what kind of place is this? It's a weekday afternoon and no one's answering the phone? I can't do this.

Then I remembered those tickets to DR. All right, Brooke, put on your big girl pants. They said leave a message. Leave a fucking message!

"Hello, my name is Brooke Boat...Benson. I would like to schedule an appointment as soon as possible. Please call me back at this number." I left the number clearly and slowly and hung up. I'll give them till the end of the day and hopefully someone will call me back by then. I've gotta have something of substance setup toward correcting my problem when Marlon calls. I just know he'll call. That is, I think he'll call. What if Marlon won't even talk to me, let alone stay married to me? Ok, stop thinking like that. Once I get myself an appointment, if Marlon hasn't called, I'll call him and ask if he'll talk. Hopefully, he'll hear me out and give me a chance to make things right. I felt a little better with a plan.

I thought I'd write it all down, and went looking in my bag for pen and paper. Somehow, I'd packed my journal. Just tossed it in with the underwear. I hadn't journaled in months, maybe longer. I used to do it all the time, back in the day. I flipped to the front and saw Javier's name over and over, page after page, then a page with dollar amounts in the margin.... I had been so stupid for so long. It was time to face facts. I was messed up and I needed help. Maybe, just maybe, I could figure out where I went wrong and hopefully someone could help me. Lord knows I needed help! The kitchen clock with my own face looking back at me said 5pm. Already? And, still no response from the therapists. I don't know why I think nobody else has problems as important as mine. But they should just pick up the phone and call me, don't they know how much trouble I'm in? I'm praying, Lord, please. let me get some help and please let my husband have mercy on me. Lord, let him love me enough to say he understands and will help me get better. Ugh! I want another valium. Peggy took those but I still have the MD20/20. I started sucking it down… I most have fallen asleep on the sofa, I woke and there was a blanket over me. The place was quiet and dark, very little traffic noise outside. What time is it? I felt around for my phone.

A missed call from Marlon. And a few texts. My heart was pounding. I dialed the voice mail first. A long pause, then his deep, dry voice, "Call me." I could hear the hurt. I wanted to hit redial right then, but stopped. It was almost 2 in the morning. I hit the text messages, instead. "I miss you, I still love you, and we are still going on our first anniversary trip - no matter what." About 17 minutes later, another one. It killed me to know he'd probably been waiting for a response. "Maybe there we can talk and figure out what next. Guess you should try to come home to pack sometime next week. We leave two weeks from today." Much later. Probably just before he gave up and went to sleep. "Call me, love u."

I couldn't call him in the middle of the night, and I was glad. I wanted to call him after I had an appointment scheduled for some kind of help. I just felt I had to get an appointment set before I could face him. This time, I set an alarm on my phone to wake me at 9. No more sleeping all day. I had to get this shit done now.

*

I was up before it went off. I grabbed some coffee from the pot Peggy had left and my phone. Lord, I need you to help me now. Please let these people answer the phone. I'm sorry and I don't want to lose my husband. I've lost me and I know only you and the help of some kind of professionals can get me back on track. Lord, please let these people answer the phone.

I stood in the kitchen, listening to the phone ring, watching my own face in the mirrored clock. I looked rough, not like me at all. It kept ringing. What if they didn't—"

"Henderson and Henderson. This is Loretta. How can I help you?"

"Oh my God, a real person finally! My name is Brooke Benson, and I need an appointment to see one of your counselors right away, as soon as possible, today, if possible, please."

"Ok, Ms. Benson, Brooke, um… are you in danger of harming yourself or others?"

"Um… what? No, no. I just…" The face in the clock looked scared. I turned away. "Please, I just need an appointment."

"Ok, Ms. Benson. I can help you with that. Are you a patient here?"

"No, I've… I've never had any kind of… no."

"I'm afraid we have no private appointments for new patients until next month. The therapists are only seeing current patients till after vacation. I would be happy to schedule an appointment for you next month, or I can refer you to a few other therapists in the area. Do you want to schedule for our first available? Or would you prefer a referral?"

"Oh my God, not until next month?" I made the mistake of looking in the mirror again, and it looked right back at me with huge eyes. I fled to the living room.

"I'm sorry, all of our therapists are unavailable until then. What would you like to do?"

I sat on the sofa, my back to the kitchen and just tried to breathe. It had been so hard for me to make this call. I knew I wouldn't call another therapist.

"Ms. Benson?"

I just didn't have it in me to shop around right now. "Okay, no, no, I don't want to go anywhere else. What's the first day you have available next month?"

She scheduled it. I wrote it down, calmly thanked her, hung up. And promptly burst into tears! Loud, ugly tears.

And that's what poor Peggy walked in on. "Oh, girl, I had a feeling I better come check on you before I went to Aja's." She wrapped her arms around me, and I blubbered all over her about Marlon calling and no appointments and the mirror in the clock and how it was 6pm not am and how the journal had Javier's name and not Marlon's and--

"Ok, enough of this. First of all, have you eaten? God knows you've slept. Imma get you one drink to calm down, then I'm pourin the rest down the drain, cuz you been self-medicating since you got here, and this stops now. Is that what all this is about? You got a drug problem?" She poured me a short drink and then tucked the bottle under her arm. She meant business.

I just shook my head, gulping the drink down. "It's not drugs. It's—"

"Yeah, you're telling me now, girl."

I told Peggy all about it and she stopped me about halfway through me losing my job on top of all the money in the casinos, so she could call Henderson and Henderson again. She said, ok, maybe they don't have an appointment for private therapy, but, they'd sure as hell have a group or know of one, a Gamblers Anonymous meeting or something.

And, they did, of course. A meeting every night. She said she'd even go with me to the first one if I wanted, and, when the Henderson's got back from their vacation, she'd take me to my first therapy session, too.

I was so relieved to just have something to get me started, something positive I could tell Marlon, because, she also said, I needed to call him.

"And now, Girl! He's calling you and texting you, saying he still loves you. Buying you damn plan tickets. You don't make him wait on that! You gotta let him know you're still in!"

Once I was calm, she kind of tucked me up on the sofa with my phone and went off to make me something to put in my stomach besides booze and Valium while I called my husband.

ANA HENDERSON

The plane was packed. So many different people, old, young, single, same sex couples, heterosexual couples, everything was on this plane. I try not to take work with me when I'm on vacation, but it's hard. I caught myself assessing everyone's mood. Everyone on this plane looked pretty happy. What's not to be happy about going on a tropical vacation?

Well, everyone except the couple sitting directly behind us. Their seats were so close, I felt like he was whispering in my ear. "Maybe this was a bad idea. I don't think this will ever work, I don't even know you. I don't know who the fuck I married!"

The only response I heard from her a choked I'm so sorry.

I looked at George and he looked at me. Then he leaned over and whispered, "Tell me you didn't hear what I just heard."

I put a finger up to my mouth to shush him. Then, gave him a kiss on the lips and at the same time we both said, "We've been working too much."

He settled back. "Right, right, yes, let's just enjoy our vacation."

I tried to settle into my O, and he opened his Esquire.

I think I had dozed off a little when a sudden jolt of turbulence woke me. The couple was still at it. The man said, "You think I'm letting you in the casinos, you really are crazy."

"I can win, Marlon. I win a lot!"

"Of course you win, that's how they get you! But you can't ever win when you really need to."

"Okay, okay, you gonna beat me down the entire trip? I thought this trip was to try and relax and decide what we can do to fix our little problem—"

His voice rose. "Little?" Then dropped to what sounded like a snarl. "It's a hell of a lot more than a little problem."

"Ok, go ahead, beat me up, say what you want. I can take it."

I'd already heard TMI, too much information. I put my head phones on, tried to relax and just listen to my jazz. We'd be landing soon. But, oh! That bothered me! Yeah, yeah, I knew I should just let it go, George was over there sleepin like a log, mouth wide open. I tried to turn my brain off, tell myself I'm on vacation. but hearing that stuff just bugged me to death.

I was relieved when I felt the plane finally start to descend, and everyone started shifting and bundling their things, getting ready to land. George opened his eyes, still a bit bleary, then smiled and perked up with excitement. "Here we go!"

I breathed deep and smiled back. "Let's do this!"

Once on the ground, all our focus was on getting through the chaos of gathering our bags, passing through customs, getting to the hotel - the sights, the sounds - the colors, the lilt of Spanish all around us… We'd have seven days to just relax. Not to think about what's going on in other people's lives. No thinking about other people's problems, worries, or our own, no business, not even worrying about our dogs safely with our favorite caretakers. We were way past due, this was a trip well-earned and well-deserved.

As soon as we got into our hotel room, we both headed for the balcony overlooking the water. The weather was just perfect or should I say… perfecto! I was already having fun using my Spanish. George was looking forward to getting his golfing on. For a couple days, all I wanted was beach, food, beach, food, beach, food, spa, beach…. We'd each do our own thing for a couple days. One of the things I love about being married to George is we are one, yet, we are always two very different individuals. We know we each have needs that we can only meet for ourselves as well as needs that can only be met by helping and caring for each other. But we had plenty of plans for couple stuff, too. We'd hit the casino, shopping, dancing, a bike ride, some natural pools, the sauna, some lazy private time… and oh! the beach! Yes, indeed, the beach!

I thought I'd head right out on the sand, but, to be honest, I felt a bit kinked up from the long flight and, probably, from the tension of hearing that poor couple on the plane, so I decided to hit the spa first. Anyway, I wanted to be super relaxed and looking great for the evening, because George and I had a plan. We'd spend a little time on our own, then we'd meet in the hotel bar.... as strangers! Just a fun little game we play sometimes when we're away from home, but it'd been a long time, too long! I headed off for the spa, really looking forward to meeting my handsome stranger later that night!

The spa package was a sort of group excursion. I counted fourteen other women. We were given a number, then taken out to a boat, where we showered then waited for our number to be called for a massage. My massage and full body scrub was just heavenly! They scrubbed everywhere. The best way I can explain is, it was like the bath, the scrub down that your Momma gave you as a kid, aww, it was fantastic. Never had a massage quite like it!

But the next part was really wild. We all met in this room with a large aquarium-like bowl full of little fish, Garra rufa fish, the "Doctor" fish. You put your feet in and they eat the dead skin off. That definitely struck me as weird, I noticed I wasn't the only one that seemed to feel that way. A lot of the women had skeptical looks, but we all did it. It felt weird, too, and we all started laughing about it and relaxed. That's when I noticed the woman from the plane sitting across from me. I was glad to see her getting a chance to relax.

After the pedicure, they led us out to the end of the boat where we could get on floating rafts. We could just bobbed there on the big beautiful sparkling blue ocean, sun shining on it like sparkling champagne. They'd even bring out some sweet tropical rum drink to sip. I was there! I noticed, though, that there didn't seem to be that many floats... well, I was getting mine. I had my shades, my sunblock, my straw hat... I was first in line! Then I realized about half the women weren't even looking, they were just heading back in toward the bar. I shrugged and climbed onto my float. I was lying there, basking, the sun warm on my eyelids, a cold piña colada in my hand, just chillin, when something nudged my raft.

"Oh sorry, let me give you a little space."

I didn't even open my eyes. "No problem."

I could feel her struggling a little, then realized we'd have to both push off, if we wanted to move apart. I sat up a little. It was the woman from the plane. We kinda chuckled the way strangers do when they have to balance their cocktails while shoving apart two awkward rubber rafts.

Once we settled back down, she said, "God, this is great! I can't believe these women are so chicken, who would want to miss this?"

"I was just thinking the same thing!"

We just floated for a second, then she said, "I think I saw you on the plane we came in on."

"Oh?"

"I think my husband and I were behind you?"

"Oh, yeah, maybe so." I didn't want her to feel uncomfortable thinking I'd heard their private conversation.

"Yeah."

We floated for a minute in silence.

"Yeah, I'm just trying to relax as much as possible and not do anything to ruffle my husband's feathers." She sighed. "I'm really lucky he brought me on this trip at all. After what I just put him through. It's our anniversary."

I certainly recognized someone who needed to talk. I hoped I could keep the conversation light. "Oh. Nice. How long have you been married?"

"It's our first year anniversary. We've been friends for years, though. Marlon waited for me for ages. So now that we're finally married, it's a really big deal. This was supposed to be a big celebration for us."

I couldn't not ask. "Supposed to be?"

"Yeah, I did some very, very, excuse my expression, very... fucked up shit, and I don't know if we'll make it after this."

"Well, marriage takes a lot of work, but I've seen people make it through some very hard times."

"Really?"

"Absolutely."

"I just… I don't know… how could he possibly forgive…"

If I didn't say something comforting, she'd be sobbing right out there in middle of this beautiful day. "Listen, sounds like your husband loves you a lot. Waiting for you and bringing you here… You know being friends first is a huge advantage."

"Really?"

"Sure. And, you know… once we find a mate that truly loves us, we can make it through anything." I knew I was going out on a limb, but my instincts kicked in and I went for it. "You know, I've found that, often, when one person loves harder than the other, that actually works really well."

"Wow, you sound like have experience with this kind of thing—"

"Yeah, I get that all the time." I lay back on my raft and closed my eyes. "But, right now, I'm a relaxed woman, on vacation, enjoying the fabulous weather. Blue ocean, white sand, great massage, nice rum…."

"Right. We're here to relax." She settled back on her float. "Let's do that. Relax. But, hey, thank you for the encouraging words, really. And if we run into each other again, I promise to not bore you with my problems."

BROOKE BENSON

When I got back to our hotel room, Marlon was sitting out on the patio. The room was perfect for us. It was very private, on the back side of the hotel. Our view of the gorgeous patio was nothing but sand and palm trees. And there he sat, looking so handsome and cool. He was sipping something on ice and listening to some jazz he liked. He had no shirt on, just drawstring khaki shorts and flip flops. He looked really good. He always looks good, still no fat on his stomach, just the right amount of hair on his chest, perfect teeth, nice hands and feet. Some woman would be glad to take my man… and I thought to myself.. and you about to give him away… you stupid!

He looked so relaxed, like he didn't have an angry bone in his body. But I knew he was boiling inside over my stupid actions. I thought about what that lady said to me while out on the ocean. If someone really, really loves you, then you'll get through it. That's Marlon, I know it. I know this man loves me. I also know that what I did wouldn't go away overnight or with one tropical vacation. I love Marlon and I love him more for how he's loved me so unconditionally, that is… until now. I pray he still does. So, right now, I'm just praying, hoping, trying to believe that somehow, someway, we're gonna get through this. That's all I've got to hold on to for now.

I walked out on the patio, gave him a kiss. On the cheek because he didn't turn his face to me. "The spa was great, what did you do?"

"Not a lot, just went down to the beach, relaxed, laid out, had a few drinks. Thinking, mostly." He looked at me. "Just trying to think it all through, baby." He looked… sad, maybe? Not so angry. I thought maybe we should talk, but he said, "Right now, I don't want to talk about nothing."

I nodded. He seemed a little inebriated. "Have you had lunch, yet?"

"No, not quite ready, yet."

"So…" I thought I'd try not talking, then. "So… how about me, then? For lunch. How about me for lunch, Marlon?" I started kissing him, pushed my body against his….

Whatever else he was feeling, he responded. Just like he always did, with enthusiasm, excitement. I don't know if it was all the frustration built up from him being upset with me, or us just missing our normal passionate love making because we were used to giving it to each other any time any day. But, from our first kiss, we went at it, just like old times. We went from the patio to the room, to our king size bed. What little clothes we had on went flying! From slow, passionate, intense, to rough, fast, hot, sweaty, it was as if all of our anger, frustrations, and feelings went into our lovemaking. I cried, and I kept repeating to Marlon, I'm sorry, I'm sorry, lo siento, my husband, lo siento, mi esposo! And, each time I spoke in Spanish, he plunged into me harder. Finally, he put his hand over my mouth, to tone down my whimpers, to tone down my moans. He kissed my face over and over, not saying one word, and just kept hitting all the places that he knew I loved best.

When we finished, we lay there listening to the sound of the ceiling fan. Bump, bump, bump. Marlon got up and grabbed a cigar out of a gift shop bag he must have gotten earlier and headed out to the patio in just his underwear. The last time I'd seen him smoke a cigar was in Vegas when we got married.

He took a couple of long hard pulls, then called to me. "Brooke, can you come out here, baby?"

I grabbed my short silk yellow robe and flip-flops and joined him.

He looked at me, but I couldn't read his expression. "I know, that you know, how much I love you. God knows I was persistent getting you." He took a few more hits off the cigar. My heart raced. Did he regret getting me now? Was our lovemaking just breakup sex? He sighed. "I was in a relationship with a woman that loved me, but I just walked away." My heart sank. Was he thinking about her?

But, in a moment, he sighed and then looked right in my eyes. "I only wanted you."

I leaped to speak, "Honey, I'm so so—"

He waved me off. "What you just did. Our finances. Most men would walk away, or better yet, hurt your ass. I'm not gonna lie, I sure as hell wanted to hurt you. But, how can I hurt something that is so special to me. We've been so happy together, but honest to God, baby, you've thrown me for a loop. I said I didn't ever want to be without you, you know until death do us part. But now. You've made me take a look at my choices."

It broke my heart to hear him so hurt. Suddenly all my apologies sounded so weak. Tears filled my eyes, but I didn't even feel like I had a right to cry when it was Marlon who had been so hurt, not me.

"Brooke, help me understand, how we can possibly get past this shit? I've lost my trust in you. All this makes me wonder what else have you been hiding from me? I don't know what to believe anymore. And you've fucked up our financial situation, royally! Just that… I don't even know what to do with that."

Marlon looking so defeated probably hurt more than anything else he could have said. "I know Marlon, I know, and I do love you. So much. I'm so ashamed. I never thought I could get this wrapped up, this consumed in…in…gambling…. But I did. I tried to fix it, but every time I tried, it just got worse."

"And, yet, on the plane, you were still trying to say I should let you gamble! Are you fucking kiddin me?"

"I know, I know. I—but, maybe I could win it back--" He shot me such a look! "No, no, I know… I can't. I am trying, baby. I called some therapists, back home, before we left, and they told me about a group, this Gamblers Anonymous. I went a few times already."

"You did?"

"I did."

"And that's gonna fix it?"

"Maybe. I don't know… no, I… not just that, maybe, probably… but, I made an appointment for some therapy, too. I even got the card with me. To show you. I thought you might want to look em up. See what you think."

I went and dug the card out of my suitcase and brought it back out to Marlon.

He took it, read it, and nodded. "Yeah, I've heard of them. Chad used them for a while."

"Chad did?"

"Yeah, he doesn't tell everybody his business, but he did tell me about it in confidence. Some…" He looked at me like he was deciding if his wife could be trusted enough to tell something private. That hurt. "He had some… pretty deep issues… some PTSD and stuff. So… yeah… I've heard of them and I think they're pretty good, but you gotta be honest with yourself and be ready to make a change."

"I don't want to lose you!"

"No, not just for me. For you. I know enough about AA and addicts and stuff. They gotta change for themselves or it ain't gonna work."

"I'm ready, baby! I promise you, I'm ready. I wanna be right, for me, too, but Marlon, baby, I don't want to lose you. I… I love you. I love you so much. And I want our life together. I don't know how to make this right, but I want to. I really do."

I couldn't hold back, anymore. I started crying. In a minute, he put his arms around me and it felt so good, so right, to be comforted by my husband, then I realized he was crying, too.

I stopped crying myself and just tried to comfort him. "Oh, baby, I'm so sorry. I love you so much."

"Brooke, why did you marry me? You didn't love me. You wanted someone else. You settled for me, that's not love. I thought that was ok, before, but now--"

"No! Babe, I do love you. I did. I always have. I was… I don't know… I was obsessed with… him. I think it was like the gambling. That wasn't love. But you… you were my friend. I loved you. I just didn't know how to… how to do it right. I'm messed up, Marlon. I am. But, I do love you."

"Yeah? Would you still want me if I treated you the way you've been treating me?"

"I'd... try to forgive you." I wanted to be forgiven. I was pretty sure I didn't deserve it and pretty sure I wouldn't be able to do it if the situation were different.

"What do you expect me to do with the financial mess you've made? No, it's not even that, it's... I thought we trusted each other, had each other's backs. I thought... well, we were friends as well as partners." He pulled away from me. "Sure don't look like it now, though."

"Babe, please, just give me a chance to earn your trust back, please. I know it's bad. But, I'll get help, and I'll do everything I can to pay it back. I'll work, I mean—" I stopped. I hadn't told Marlon that I'd lost my job. I really didn't want to pile something else on. But... "Ok, I guess I better start earning that trust right now."

"What do you mean?"

"I hate to...I... I'm just gonna tell you the truth. I lost my job."

"You're shitting me."

"I just... I'm sorry, no, I can't just keep saying I'm sorry, can I? Babe, I got in trouble at work, moving money around where I shouldn't, they fired me a few weeks ago."

"Are you gonna be in trouble with the police? On top of all this!"

"No! No... I was lucky. They didn't report nothing. They just let me go."

"Thank God for that."

"Yeah, so I can still get another job."

"You'll have to."

"I will. I'll get two. I'll get three... four?" I finally made him smile. Just a little.

He smiled at me a little more.

"I love you."

He shook his head, looking a little more relaxed, but utterly spent. "I love you, too. I sure don't like you much right now."

I smiled at him and hugged him. "Baby, I don't blame you! Right now, I don't like me, either! What you say we use this sunshine for something besides crying?"

"Abso-fucking-lutely. Let's enjoy it. Go have some fun. We've always been good at that!"

"Party boat?"

"Let's do it."

*

For about three days, Marlon and I just had fun. We shoved our situation deep down somewhere and just partied just as hard as we could. It felt a little forced a few times, but fun had always been easy for us, so, for the most part, we just enjoyed the sunshine, the ocean, and each other, like old times. We walked the beach at night, took a safari tour, went to a few clubs. The last night, we danced almost all night and had a lazy room service breakfast in bed kind of morning. By afternoon, we were still in bed when Marlon said he wanted to play some golf.

"Ok." I felt a little tension, but it wasn't unusual for us to do stuff on our own on vacation after a few days together. "Sure, I guess I'll...."

"What? What are you going to do if I'm not with you?"

"I... I don't know, yet, I saw that woman from the spa thing for a minute yesterday. She said she'd be out shopping. Maybe I'll find her. I don't know. I'll find something."

He pushed out of bed. "Yeah, I just bet you will."

"What?" He turned away from me. "Marlon, what's going on? What happened?"

"Nothing." He started pulling on his clothes.

"Marlon? Everything was fine last night... this morning... right?"

He looked pissed, but he sat back on the bed. "Yeah. It was. But... I woke up thinking."

"Ok, tell me, we're gonna be honest with each other, right? Make this work?"

"You're not gonna like it."

My chest got tight. Was this it? Was he done? "I... it's ok, baby, just tell me."

"I woke up thinking. I love you. I do. But I can't ignore this. I don't trust you with money. Simple as that."

I breathed with relief. "Well, babe, I don't trust me with money either." I tried to laugh, but he didn't crack a smile. "Ok, what do you want to do?"

"I've given our situation a lot of thought. We're gonna continue to enjoy this trip, and, when we get back, I'll give you time to go see those therapists people, give them time to help you. I know it's not gonna be overnight."

"And, I'll do my best. I'm so grateful. I—"

"Yeah, but, in the meantime, we're gonna make some changes."

"Ok."

"No more joint bank accounts. I've taken your name off all our joint accounts and credit cards. I had to. While I still had decent credit to protect."

That stung a little, but it was understandable. "Fair enough."

"I'm not gonna try and police you and count every dime you spend, but you're not gonna get a chance to mishandle, fuck up, our money like that again! So this is how it's gonna be. If you need money or need to use a credit card, you tell me, and I'll pay. Until you get another job, which you will do, right?"

"Of course."

"Ok, you use your unemployment checks for your stuff. Maybe you can clean up what you owe and start a savings of your own. Maybe if you work hard for it, you'll build it back up and appreciate it."

I knew it wasn't really about that, the gambling, but I got what he was saying.

"Thank God I stashed money in another account that you couldn't get to, or you would've fucked that up, too! baby I'm not gonna lie to you it still hurts, hurts like hell! What you did with our money, I'm not gonna forget that. But, I'm not, I can't, watch you every day, your every move. You're a grown ass woman and I do love you, even if, right now, I kinda hate you for taking advantage of me, my money, my trust…. I just… that's it. That's how it's gonna be."

"Ok, it's ok. I understand."

"All right. I'm gonna go out for a while. Play a little golf. Blow off some steam." He slipped on his shoes and headed for the door. "You… You have a good day, Brooke."

"You, too, Marlon." I felt like the honeymoon was over, then, but maybe we were on the road to really fixing this thing.

I felt a little let down, a little sad, probably still a little hung over, but by the time I stepped out of the shower, I was starting to feel pretty good. My husband was amazing. I could see he was struggling but I no longer felt he was gonna kick me to the curb any minute. Hell, with most men, I'd probably be wearing a black eye or have some broken limbs by now, and, for sure I'd have been served divorce papers. But instead, Marlon's been patient, talked it out with me. So, the ball is in my court, and I'm praying, please, Lord, help me get it together for both of us.

I was about to head out to do something fun when I realized I wouldn't be able to use my credit cards… what could I do? I had a complementary ticket already to a tour of a local market. Well, better than nothing. I checked the time and it was leaving in a few minutes. I grabbed my peach straw hat, grabbed my Dolce Gabbana sunglasses and out the door I went. I got downstairs to the lobby and headed straight out the door to the bus pick up. There should have been a crowd waiting, but there was no one there. Damn.

I'd missed it. I headed back inside to ask the concierge about the next bus. I showed him my ticket.

"Lo siento, señorita, no hay más viajes hoy." He looked up at my blank face. "I guess you don't speak Spanish."

"Not really." I blushed a little remembering I spoke just enough to turn my husband on.

"No problem, miss. There are no more of these tours today, but there is a free air conditioned bus every fifteen minutes to Hard Rock Casino, very nice there, free drinks, free wifi, you will have a lot of fun there!" He handed me a free drink ticket smiling.

I took it, but I knew I didn't have any business going to a casino. I wandered outside and skirted the crowd already gathered at the bus stop. I was just bending down to see the souvenirs being offered by a little boy in the street when the bus pulled up. Suddenly, I thought, well, why not? I don't have anything to lose, anyway. I don't even have any money to play. I'll ride over there, get my free drink, and take it out by the water or something.

There were all kind of people on the bus, it was quite full, and as I headed toward the middle to find a seat, who did I run into, but Ana from the spa. "Hey, girl."

She looked up and smiled. "Hey! Lemme move some of my loot here so you can sit down." She shuffled some shopping bags onto the floor and her lap.

I squeezed in. "Looks like you had fun."

"For sure! What you up to? You been shopping?"

"I... I got a late start today. We slept in."

She grinned. "That sounds good. Things are going well, then?"

I reminded myself the woman was on vacation and probably didn't want to hear my life story while she was doing it. "Yeah... yeah, pretty good. We've enjoyed our time here. You?"

"Oh yeah. I'm not much into the casinos, but I've got some free chips, so thought why not? You play?"

"Um… yeah… sometimes."

"Great! You can show me how. I don't know much. Tell you what, I'll give you a couple of my chips. For the lessons."

She dropped a chip into my hand. Was that $100? "No, I couldn't--" I tried to hand it back.

She waved me off. "No, no, really, it's fine. They were given to us at the hotel, you know, and seriously, I don't even really know how to play. It'll be more fun with someone who knows."

I knew I shouldn't accept it. I felt it in my bones. I suddenly realized I shouldn't even be on this bus. My head was screaming don't. You are doing good and Marlon has said he's with you. But you gonna mess that shit up before you even get home. I wanted to stop that crowded bus right there on the road. I looked around at all the laughing people. Not a care in the world. They could go to the casino and just have fun. But not me. Half of them were probably like Ana, didn't even know how to play. I started thinking, go on, Brooke, you can win a nice jackpot. Show Marlon you can get back his money. Maybe enough to clean up that whole mess. Ana was smiling. I smiled back, but my palms were sweating, my heart racing fast. Ana was looking out the window chattering about the beautiful views along the way, the flowers, the palm trees, the ocean, white sand, the people walking, riding bikes, everything was so beautiful. What if I could get back Marlon's money. With free money! Just one good break and all this mess would be gone.

It took about 30 minutes to get to the casino. The place was huge. The bus driver announced to everyone where he would pick up from and reminded us that the last bus was at midnight.

Ana laughed. "No way I'm gonna be here that long."

"No, me either. Let's get a drink first."

We got drinks and wandered around a little. I told her some strategies to use with the different slots. She was all ears and in no hurry, but I heard the sounds of the slots rolling and ringing and that chip was burning a hole in my pocket. Ana still hadn't settled on anything. We passed by some 5$ slots and heard the winning bells going off. A woman shouting. Laughing. The coins rolling out—

I had to play. "C'mon, let's play." I chose a machine that felt right and fed in Ana's chip. First spin... and damn! I won $200! That woke me up, and I thought... here I go. Ana was cheering and laughing, saying something about shopping, but I didn't even take a breath. I stepped to a $100 slot. Lost. Stepped to a $20. Lost. Another. Up $60. Now we're talking. I stuck with that machine. This was the winner. Next thing I knew, I was down to $20 dollars. My heart skipped a beat, but I played it, and it paid me $60. Again, another $40. Down $30. Up a $100. Now we're talking. I looked up to show Ana, but she'd moved off to play on her own. For some reason, seeing her at a little distance already, I wanted to move farther from her, wanted to play where she couldn't see me so clearly, so I just slipped to the other side of the row.

I had a little winnings. I said, okay Brooke. Twenty more dollars and then back to get Ana and leave. I started playing again, hit a good pot, then down, then back up, then way up. I couldn't believe it. I had a good $5k, I was in the zone! I pulled the handle again, then someone next to me said something about needing to go, for the last bus. What? I looked at my watch and it was 11pm! I glanced around for Ana just as my last pull hit. The bells ringing. Lights flashing. Coins spilled into my cup. I still have an hour. It's all good. Ring. I could do this! Ring. My big win! Ring. I could do it. Ring. I bet big, knowing I had it. Silence. No ringing. No flashing. The thunk of the arm and nothing. I stood there like I'd just woke up. The place was much emptier than it had been. I looked at my watch. 11:57. Oh my God!

I started running for the door. I couldn't miss that bus! I'd forgotten everything - Ana, my promise to Marlon, to myself. I ran for the shuttle pick up stop. I was in a panic! I couldn't miss this. I had no money left even for a taxi. I'd have to call Marlon to come get me. No, God, please. I had to get that bus! I was frantic, out of breath, probably looking like a wild animal or a crack head, no... just like the addict I was. Just I reached the stop, the bus pulled up. I stopped at the edge of the group breathing hard just as people started to board. The crowd thinned and there was Ana.

I was a little surprised she was still here and a little embarrassed I'd lost her. She had all kinds of shopping bags, her hair was wild. She had a big frozen drink in a Hard Rock cup. She looked exhausted, but pretty damn happy. "Well, you look like you had a ball! What'd you do?"

She juggled her stuff and we boarded and flopped down. "Well, I lost you in the crowd, I guess. I looked for you for about an hour, but then I met some guys at the bar and they showed me how to play video poker and we had a drink, then another, then another, just playing and drinking. Then, guess what? I got a royal flush. $1200. A jackpot! Me!"

"Wow." I tried to look happy for her, but I felt like a fool. Why did I come here? Even though I hadn't really lost any money. I hadn't had any to lose, I felt so guilty. This is the cause of all my problems. How did I think it'd be different this time? This must be just how a drug addict or alcoholic feels, disgusted, demoralized, ashamed… and maybe worst of all, right now I just wish it was me with that $1200 so I could go back and play it some more…. "Did you keep playing?"

"Oh, hell, no. I went shopping. I had the biggest lobster in the place and then just took a lot of pictures all around this beautiful place to remember it by. What about you? Sorry I lost you."

"No, no problem."

"You have fun?"

"Honestly, no. I was dumb, did my usual stupid routine, played all of my money, didn't eat, shop, drink, meet anyone, didn't talk to anyone but that sorry ass slot machine and now I'm broke and disgusted."

Ana's voice turned serious. "Oh, hey, Girl, you're sobering me up! What's wrong? Don't beat yourself up, it's called vacation. We're supposed to be doing dumb stuff, right?"

I finally just couldn't put on a smile anymore. "Yeah, for you it's just a vacation, but for me? This trip will make or break my marriage, and I'm not helping by coming, of all places, to a casino." I tried to hold it together, but tears started burning my eyes and would soon be rolling down my face. I hoped the darkness hid the worst of it. "I'm sorry."

"No, no, don't apologize. It's ok, really." All her teasing and laughter was gone. "Brooke, are you saying you got a problem with gambling?"

"A big problem."

"Oh, Girl! I'm so sorry!"

"What? No, why are you sorry?"

"Oh, Brooke, I had no idea. I never would have encouraged you to… I'm so sorry."

"It's my own damn fault and now I feel like I've ruined everything and Marlon—" I was crying for real now and I know people must have been looking.

Ana leaned close and talked to me low and gentle. "Listen, now, it's all right. When we get back to your hotel, we can check on our husbands, and then find a nice quiet place out on the beach to talk. Just me and you, ok?"

"No, no, you're on vacation. I'm not going to cry all over you. Again."

"Brooke, please, let me help. I feel responsible, and I can help. I mean… it's what I do. I'm a counselor back in Memphis."

"What? For real?"

"Yeah, for real. My husband and I are Henderson and Henderson. Please let me help. I would just feel horrible if I couldn't help now."

As soon as we got off the bus, we checked in with the men, then took some beer out on the beach and sat just the two of us, and I had my first therapy session.

At first, I kept trying to apologize for wasting her time, but she insisted she was happy to do it. "In fact," she said, "Maybe this is meant to be, you know? I mean… I first noticed you on the plane, then we kept running into each other, and then… maybe even me giving you that chip happened the way it was supposed to, so I could help you now."

"You think?"

"Maybe. Maybe, it's fate. Or God. Either way, seems like there's someone looking out for you, you know? Don't know if you're a religious person or not, but, I think, God always looks out and loves us in spite of ourselves. I didn't plan on working this vacation, but now I'm happy I can."

We talked for quite a while. She said I'd done great starting out with Gamblers Anonymous and told me that, even at Hard Rock, there were some resources available. In Santa Domingo, there was even a group, so if we went on a tour there, I could catch a meeting, too. She said my money problems weren't the worst she'd ever heard, but still a problem, of course. She'd give me some resources for financial counseling when we got back. Meanwhile, she suggested I start by writing everything I don't like about myself and what I'd like to change. "But, then," she said. "Be sure to write down everything you do like." She said to do the same about Marlon. And start right away. "Find yourself a nice palm tree out on the beach somewhere in the morning. No alcohol, just your pen and paper. You must be totally honest with yourself. This is just for you. No one is going to judge."

"This sounds great, I'm so grateful. You've given me hope. Just by giving me some things to do, you know? To get started. Some practical things. I'm so anxious to get started now!"

"That's great. But don't feel you have to get everything done on vacation. Take time to enjoy your time with your husband. Just be sure to get it done by our first appointment, ok?"

"One thing."

"Yes?"

"I guess this means we won't be friends, though, right?"

"That's right. We need to protect the therapeutic relationship. But I think this is the best thing right now, right?"

"Right. Again, thank you so much!"

"You're most welcome. Shall we go find those husbands now?"

We shook the sand off of ourselves and said goodnight. When I got to our room, Marlon was sound asleep. I grabbed my pen and journal and quietly went into the bathroom. Sitting there on the floor, leaning against the tub, I began writing.

I wrote how amazed I was at what had happened. I still can't believe I met my therapist all the way over here, all the way in DR! I can't wait to tell Marlon. I hope he'll be happy for me and give me a chance to prove myself. Thank you, Lord, for the miracle.

I started in on my assignment. Time enough for thinking about what I don't like later. Right now, I was so happy and full of hope, I started with what I so like about myself. Well, I like that I believe in prayer and believe that God works miracles every day, and I know that I am a miracle. And Marlon, I like, no, I love, that he's loved me no matter what. That is so far! And, I like that I seem to be a no-matter-what kind of girl. If I wanna do something, no matter what, I'm gonna do it.

Marlon tapped at the door and it opened. "Hey, baby, I was sound asleep. I didn't hear you come in. What are you doing in the bathroom?"

"Well, I am following instructions from my therapist! I am writing!"

"What? What therapist?"

"Baby, you're not gonna believe this. I think... I honestly think it's a miracle! That woman I met at the spa? The one I told you about? She and her husband are from Memphis. They're Henderson and Henderson."

"Who?"

"The therapists I booked an appointment with. She's one of them."

"You're kidding me, right?"

"No, I'm serious, I'm still a bit in shock about the whole thing, myself, but, Marlon, baby, I really think it's a miracle. A sign for us."

Marlon's face went soft and he leaned down and gathered me up off the floor into his arms. He snuggled me into his chest. "Well, baby, God knows we could use a miracle."

"Marlon, I love you so much."

"I love you, baby. Let's make this marriage work. Let's do the damn thang."

"Oh, yes, baby. I want to. More than anything."

"Then, here's what we're gonna do. From this day forward, we start over. So, right now, I'm giving you my all, babe, and I just want the same from you."

"You have me. I'm yours."

"No more secrets, Brooke, ok? We're open with each other. From now on—"

"I went to a casino." I just blurted it out as fast as I could.

"What?" He pulled his head back to look at me, but his arms still held me tight.

"I just want to be honest. I went to a casino with Dr. Henderson, Ana, before I knew she was Dr. Henderson, and I gambled. I lost... well, not exactly, I didn't really have anything to lose—"

"I know you didn't. But you went?"

"Yeah."

He sighed, and tucked me up close to him again. "Oh, babe, I know, it's not gonna go away overnight, but with time it'll get better. The money? Yeah, that's gonna be hard, but, you know, life is short and no one is promised tomorrow. And, you know, nobody gets to take none of that money with them. I love you."

"I love you."

"Then, we just start all over again."

TO THE READER

Okay, so now that you've read my story, guess what? If we didn't have no-matter-whats, we'd probably have a lot fewer stories, CEOs, lawyers, judges, teachers, preachers, therapists, self-help books and classes, massages, medications, mind-altering substances, and new babies being born. Now, some of those things we could do without, but some of them we'd sure miss, so, keep on living, learning, loving, taking chances, and experiencing life. No Matter What!.

The End

Made in the USA
Columbia, SC
06 September 2020